Shaun Prescott is a writer based in the Blue Mountains in New South Wales. He has self-released several small books of fiction, including *Erica from Sales* and *The End of Trolleys*, and has been the editor of *Crawlspace Magazine*. His writing has appeared in *The Lifted Brow*, the *Guardian* and *Meanjin*, among other places, and *The Town* is his debut novel.

Further praise for *The Town*:

'This novel signals its author as someone who understands what literature is for. It is one of the strongest and strangest contemporary Australian novels I've seen, an uncompromising look at regional Australia and small-town life.' *The Age*

'A deep dive into weirdness that reads like a blend of Donald Horne and García Márquez . . . A gentle, if gnawing, safari of the existential dread on which Australia is built.' *Saturday Paper*

'This is one of those rare books that bothers your thinking by making you feel uncomfortable without necessarily knowing why or how. The aftermath is a kind of free-fall. It's a remarkable achievement.' *The Australian*

'We read this brilliantly weird debut from Shaun Prescott on our holidays a few weeks back and have since bored almost everyone we know by continuously droning on about it.' *i-D*

'*The Town* is perhaps an allegorical mirror reflecting the evils of ignorance and xenophobia that lurk in all humans, everywhere, and the fragility of existence.' Benjamin Myers, *Spectator*

'Conjures a remote, inward-facing landscape that carries disaffection, loneliness and darker forces beneath.' Arifa Akbar, *Observer*

'A bizarre novel – a séance for Kafka, Walser, and Calvino – that tackles the ever-disappearing boundaries between youth and aging, music and silence, the past and the present. In a spry and lonely voice, Prescott has written an ominous work of absurdity.' Catherine Lacey

'*The Town* moves with a gentle command amid the obvious reference points of Calvino, Kafka, and Abe, but it also invokes less-celebrated English-language predecessors, like the novels of Steve Erickson, and Rex Warner's *The Aerodrome*. In the manner of Erickson and Warner, Prescott seeks the universal in a meticulous paraphrase of the here and now, and finds the dislocation hiding in locality, to show us just how lost we really may be.' Jonathan Lethem

'*The Town* is about meaninglessness and disconnection, about the forlorn and the futile, the faded and failed attempts at small-town life.' *Times Literary Supplement*

'*The Town* offers an experience of profound estrangement, not only from place and landscape, identity and community, but from reading a book, and perhaps even from meaning itself.' *Sydney Review of Books*

'It's hard to convey how fascinating and readable a book can be when it deals almost entirely with disappointment, boredom and emptiness. But there is quiet wit and charm here even as the novel conveys the opposite, and it's certainly far from boring. It's an extremely thought-provoking novel, and an impressive achievement for Shaun Prescott, whose debut it is.' *Shiny New Books*

Shaun Prescott
THE TOWN

FABER & FABER

First published in the UK in 2018 by
by Faber & Faber Limited
Bloomsbury House, 74–77 Great Russell Street
London WC1B 3DA

This paperback edition first published in 2019

First published in Australia in 2017 by
Brow Books, from TLB Society Inc.
(trading as Lifted Brow) www.theliftedbrow.com

Printed and bound by CPI Group (UK) Ltd, Croydon, CR0 4YY

A CIP record for this book
is available from the British Library

ISBN 978-0-571-34562-5

1
THE TOWN

It was only possible to see the full extent of the town if you spent many years there. Only then could you see the barriers shimmer at its edges, and know what the edges meant.

It was only possible after many years in the town to notice the strangeness of certain aspects of familiar visions. Only then could you stand at the foot of a quiet street and at a certain time of day, and from a very specific angle, pretend that you were somewhere else. It was possible to stand at the foot of the old gasworks, and to stare upwards, and to believe that briefly you had gained access to one of those speculative worlds outside of the town.

When inside certain towns, the rest of the world disappears. So it only makes sense that to the rest of the world, certain towns are forever disappearing—or else they appear as a figment, or as a ghost town, or as a spot on a map purely decorative. A spot carefully placed by a cartographer anxious to fill a lonely space.

—

When I arrived in the town I needed to find a café in which to regularly sit, and which would serve as headquarters for friends once I had made them. Searching a shopping plaza, I chose a Michel's Patisserie in view of the Big W. At the head of the escalators a man sold Australian flag fridge magnets and tea towels. I sat inside the café and thought: well, this is a start. I now have a location to meet people once I have met them and it is civilised.

The plaza was typical of plazas in towns of the Central West, and belonged to one of two major corporations competing for dominance in the area. I drank my first coffee and thought about my journey there, as a means to reward my past self with acknowledgement of how, back then, only hours ago, I had suspected in the back of my mind that I would not arrive anywhere at all.

Later on I wandered the plaza. I looked at the Sanity and thought about the CDs I would buy once I had found a job. Then I browsed the Angus & Robertson and made mental notes of the books I would purchase, and read, and discuss with the people I would meet in the café opposite the Big W, once I had met them. Then I bought a cheese-and-bacon pull-apart from the Bakers Delight and sat in the food court eating.

The main street of the town ran five blocks, each block bordered by minor thoroughfares that were also lined with shops. I had dreamed about this town before. In my dream there was a second storey flat on one cross-street. The flat overlooked a petrol station, and I sat on the balcony with a woman. We smoked cigarettes there, and sipped from schooner glasses of beer. I suppose this dream was born of the journeys I had made through this town in the past, along the main street, travelling from one town to some other, never stopping on the way, not even for refreshments.

This dream was not a catalyst for my arrival in the town, but when I arrived on that day I tricked myself into believing it was. It was an important dream, I recall thinking, hoping to lend gravity to the occasion, though I knew at the time that I was lying to myself. It was a harmless thing to lie to oneself about.

———

I moved in with a person named Rob. He sublet me a room in a townhouse near the school, advertised in the local daily paper. Though I was eager to meet people I was not eager to know more about Rob, as he was very enthusiastic about sport. He asked what team I barracked for and I said Australia. Occasionally Rob and his friends would watch sport in the lounge room while drinking. They exchanged earnest appraisals of each sportsman, and spoke of these sportsmen in a manner that suggested they had mingled with them in real life.

I paid rent directly to Rob, who delivered it to his landlord parents. Every week I left a sealed envelope in the kitchen drawer marked 'RENT'. At times when it was impossible to avoid coming into direct contact with Rob we would talk about our plans for the weekend, even if it was Tuesday. Once I told Rob that I was writing a book about the disappearing towns in the Central West region of New South Wales. He told me that he was going to have a beer.

Rob showed no interest in me until one night after some grand final, when arriving home late he found me cooking my dinner in the kitchen. He told me he was surprised how rarely I left the house, and that a grand final offers the perfect occasion to "get among it". I lied that this day was the anniversary of my father's death, and that besides, I was working on my book about the disappearing towns. This time he seemed to admire that I was attempting to write a book, and asked whether he would ever be allowed to read it. I told him he was welcome to read it whenever he liked, finished or not, because this book was falling from my mind to page in what I believed at the time to be a fully formed state. I doubted I would even need to edit it, let alone write a second draft, because this book was a very easy one to write. It would be no masterpiece, but it certainly would be a book. Rob said he would like to read some of my book right that very second, so I lead him into my bedroom, sat him in front of my computer and flicked to a passage I believed to be especially interesting.

The passage was about the town Meranburn. I had written it in a daze. Days previously I had written it feeling as if I were sitting cross-legged in the dirt by the derelict station at Meranburn. Rob read it, and wanted to know where Meranburn was, so I told him that it was necessary to speak of Meranburn in the past tense, since it no longer existed. He suggested that it was a ghost town, to which I replied that it was not a ghost town, not as he understood what a ghost town was. Meranburn had not deteriorated economically, its residents had not flocked to the closest regional towns in search of work, the buildings had not been dismantled. Meranburn had simply disappeared. Hence the name of the book, Rob said, *The Disappearing Towns of the Central West*. He did not go on to say whether he enjoyed or disliked the passage, only that he was now curious about the town of Meranburn. And, he said, that actually, it's not really disappearing, is it. It's disappeared.

—

I got a job stacking shelves at the Woolworths. I bought a personal recorder so that I could record myself reading at home, in order to listen as I carefully placed items. As a shelf-stacker I was not much called upon to communicate with people, though customers would often ask for help finding this or that item, to which I would always reply that I did not know where it was.

Sometimes I would become disaffected with my book while listening to my dictations at the supermarket. I wanted there to be a section, or a chapter, or even just a passage, which would truly horrify people. I wanted there to be something embedded in my writing that filled a reader with dread. I wanted there to be a single passage which would reflect my vague notion that the disappearing towns of the Central West of New South Wales needed to be as important to the reader and the world as they were to me. During these fits of disaffection, a certain image would appear in my mind: a crisp green grass plain, and standing in it naked people being flayed by a cloaked figure. I supposed, during my evenings packing the shelves, that it might be interesting to have that scene conclude my book, that it could be the culmination of all my isolated chapters about each separate town. Maybe each citizen of each town had been abducted and flayed in some remote field towards Dubbo. The location of this plain was always the same: in the region just before the green slopes and plains give way to the browner flatness which prevails much farther into the rest of the country. The book would contain eight chapters of flat journalistic prose describing what may have occurred in the disappeared towns of the Central West. None of these eight speculations would be particularly violent or even interesting, but then this final ninth chapter about the naked people being flayed by the cloaked figure would close the book, and in doing so it would manage to create the effect that this scene was somehow factually related to everything in the book that preceded it. It would never be explained, but it would be true. The reader would believe that the chapter was intrinsically related to the stories about the disappearing towns of the Central West of New South Wales.

———

I visited the library after a couple of days in the town. I was looking for books about the town, but I was also hopeful that I might find books about towns that had disappeared.

After a thorough search through the shelves and stacks I inquired at the desk about the local history section. The man behind the counter wanted to know why I sought the local history section, so I told him I was writing a book about the disappearing towns of the Central West of New South Wales. I wanted to borrow as many books about the town as possible.

The librarian wondered if I thought his town had disappeared. I speculated aloud that it was possible but unlikely, because towns don't disappear in the modern age unless they cease to serve a purpose, and surely this town had a purpose. I wanted the local history section because I wanted to know the purpose of the town. Surely it was built for a reason. If not for a reason, then why exactly here?

There are no books about this town, the librarian told me. What we need is someone like you to write one, but then, it wouldn't exactly be a bestseller. Nothing of note has ever happened in this town, and by the time it does, there will no longer be any point in remembering it.

The librarian explained that many comparable towns have stories about how they were founded, stories about how they once served some wider purpose in history. Some towns even had fictional stories set in their streets. This town is just here, though. No one remembers how it got here, or why the presumed founders built it, except maybe the really old people, who are too addled by old age to speak in complete sentences. The town has no books of its own because there's no reason to know about it, so far as anyone can tell. Books are generally about phenomena, he said, and there is nothing phenomenal about this town.

He admitted that he himself had tried and failed to write a book about the town. He'd always disliked the town, ever since he was a kid. He'd always intended to leave for the city or abroad, but it was impossible, so there he was, working in the library.

Lacking any of the life experience one needs to write a book about any other topic, he'd decided that he would write a book about the town, because it was where he had spent all of his life. It would be simple, he had thought, because all of the source material was right under his nose, and there were plenty of old people to interview. Most importantly, no one had written a book about the town before. Maybe his town would seem strange to those living in other areas, those areas more commonly depicted in books.

He did not know at first how his book would take shape—whether it would be a straightforward history or something resembling a memoir—but he thought that writing this book would offer him the opportunity to address some of the issues that had affected him personally throughout the years — for example being uninteresting, and therefore lonely. He would write the book in a manner that would communicate to the reader that he was lonely. It would ostensibly be a history or memoir about the town, but it would truthfully be a book about his loneliness. It would not be explicit, but it would be the theme that critics and exceptional readers would seize upon, and he hoped that one day a commentator in the city, or perhaps abroad, maybe in a newspaper or magazine, would label his book an authoritative account of loneliness.

Even before he started writing the book he thought too long and hard about it, and so lost hope of being read by anyone of consequence. But he thought he might at least attract the interest of people in the town. He spent many months researching the town before he wrote a single sentence. He discovered many facts, but none of them were interesting. He learned about the local MP who had died from lung collapse, and the various shops that were on the main street back in the olden days. In the council chambers he read about the opening of schools and banks. He found images of quaintly dressed men and women standing in the main street, gawping at the camera, as some or other politician snipped a ribbon. He read about disputes pertaining to the layout of roads and the development of shopping centres. He found anecdotes about certain prosperous farming families, stories that could only be of interest to people in the relevant families.

He soon discovered there was no way for him to use a history of the town to elicit the type of emotion in readers that he wanted to elicit. People would not be able to get past the first page of his book without knowing how dull it would be throughout. He could not open the book with "the town was founded in so and so year by so and so explorer or colonist", because no such facts were anywhere to be found. He could not even give a rough estimate to any of it.

He insisted that in order to write a history he would need to have these simple facts. And he could not open his story with the earliest known fact he had, because it was an especially boring one: that there was a drought in 1932 and Joe McGee lost all his cattle. As far as he understood, the way you start a book is meant to signal what the book will be about, whether quietly or otherwise. Dead cattle did not belong in the book he wanted to write.

He then resorted to the memoir angle, but encountered similar problems, chiefly that he was not an interesting person. He had been born, he went to primary school, then high school, and then he started working at the library as a shelver before being promoted to the front desk. His life had been trying, draining, without intense pleasure, but also without the variety of struggle that readers delight in reading about.

It's true that he had felt many sensations and seen plenty of sights, some of which had left a deep impression. For a while he tricked himself into thinking he could present these feelings and visions in a way that would affect other people. There were many details in his life that appeared dreamlike to him, piquant and modestly resonant, like passages in song that seemed rooted to the essence of everything. Maybe if the people in this town were more artistically minded he would have written a book about these small details alone, but they were not. Things would need to happen in his book. Interesting things.

But he soon discovered that he was unable to make up good stories. One failed story involved a political conspiracy involving many of the shops on the main street, and he deluded himself into thinking that he would scandalise the town while simultaneously writing about his loneliness. He would please his tiny audience, he supposed, simply by depicting them in some fashion or another. They would be intrigued enough by these depictions that they would reach the final page, at which point the topic of his loneliness would be impossible to ignore. But he didn't understand how politics worked, nor did he have the ability to write dialogue or shape compelling narratives. Ultimately he decided that he was probably not a writer.

The problem then, he said, was that he still had nowhere to deposit his loneliness. It was just inside of him being wasted. He could not relish being lonely because he could not use it, and nor could he share in it with an empathetic reader. Talking to me about it wasn't enough—and I remember him then pointing at me, rather too firmly—for he needed to turn it into something important. But the time when a person such as him could write a book like this had long passed. It was no longer sensible to write books at all, he said, unless they were capable of reflecting the misery of towns and cities far away, places where the weight of the world collapsing is felt as a prolonged, agonising decline. Unlike in his town, where such trauma will likely not be felt at all, unless as a suspected fiction, or as a series of cold charts and numbers.

Another customer came into the library and caught the librarian's eye. I was finished with the library anyway, seeing as there was not a local history section. There were many books about the big city on the coast, full of black-and-white images of men and women laying on the sand, lifesavers lined up in front of their surf clubs, and stern women serving fish and chips across beachfront counters.

———

In the early afternoons I would sit in the pub at the end of my street and drink a beer. It was typical of all the pubs in the town, with sticky floral carpet, a TAB corner, and plastic bistro décor.

The bistro in this pub, however, did not operate. The bar was run by a woman named Jenny, and it was through Jenny that I learned much of what there was to know about the town.

I would sit at the bar within earshot of where Jenny typically stood. On my first visit she asked where I was from and I lied that I was from another state. She asked what I was doing in the town and I told her I was working on a book about the disappearing towns of the Central West of New South Wales.

Jenny did not care about my book, and she did not pretend to be interested in the town Meranburn when I talked about it. I listed the few things that I had learned about her town since arriving – chiefly, that there was nothing to learn. She agreed that this was true.

Jenny busied herself for extended periods in the basement, tending to the underbelly of beer taps. Other times she would remove dust from linen in the rooms for rent upstairs. Jenny's pub did not attract customers. There was no one ever there to enjoy the local radio aired softly through lost speakers, or the poker machines' ditties, or the races on the televisions. A Keno screen flashed cryptic numbers in one high corner, permitting the illusion that the stakes were high for punters no longer there.

Conversations I had with Jenny were tinged with her hostility. I asked questions about the town, and gleaned answers based on what she said she didn't know. Everything I said to Jenny seemed to demonstrate whatever point she was trying to get at, even if I suggested the contrary, and even if I thought she wasn't trying to make a point at all. She was not interested in why I was interested in the town.

I asked Jenny how the town was founded, but she said it hadn't been. Thinking of being founded was the height of arrogance. People just ended up living there.

I suggested there might have once been some geographical benefit for settling there—for instance the creek, which ran shallow behind the KFC and several petrol stations. She conceded that I might be correct, that back in the olden days people may have wanted to be close to it. Perhaps they drank straight out of it.

For long periods there would be silence. Jenny would polish the bar and glasses, or else check the poker machine cash trays, while I drank from a schooner glass of beer. Then I would ask a question and it would be like a fight.

She didn't know how old the pub was. She supposed her dad had bought it from someone, and that was it, and there she was. Anyway, why would I want to know something like that?

I said it was because I wanted to know how old the town was.

She made a gesture that suggested I had just made her point. You ask one question, she railed, expecting the answer for a whole other question. And you say you're writing a non-fiction book!

Some days we would not speak at all, except to transact the beer. Though her pub was empty, Jenny did not appear worried about her livelihood, nor did she treat me with any gratitude. She went about her duties as if quiet were the natural condition for the pub, and when she poured my beer, she did so as if there were other customers waiting. At some point in the past, Jenny must have practised her publican's demeanour on many drinkers at once, and would have been exposed to the type of gossip and hearsay that came with her profession. No conversational stupidity was a surprise to her – she had heard it all, and she seemed to have cultivated an understanding of the various leniencies beer could afford. But rarely did my conversation qualify among these.

One day, in a rare fit of expansiveness, Jenny said that the town was shrinking and yet expanding at the same time. She clarified: the town was expanding outwards while the number of people living in it was dropping. I was curious about this statement, but she didn't have any statistics, and she slammed the till shut.

A few days later Jenny felt compelled to elaborate. She observed that as time went by, the town felt emptier. She didn't know where people were going. They might have been staying at home more. They might have moved away. And then she lit a cigarette, which meant she wanted to say something.

There was a time, she told me, when elderly men and women would sit at the bar and talk her ear off for hours at a time, about the football, about local controversies, and sometimes even about the state of the world. Such talk made the days and evenings go quicker, and while she couldn't get a word in edgewise—even if she had wanted to—she thought it mildly interesting to hear what elderly people had to say about the big issues of the day.

But then, seemingly within the space of a week, these people started to die. First Ron Fenton died of a stroke. Then Rhonda Gardner tripped, fell, and died. Then various cancers were diagnosed, and heart conditions needed around-the-clock supervision at home, and nursing homes were booked, and the only men and women left at the pub were too scared to speak as freely and aloofly about the troubles of the day. They shuttered themselves, fell into brooding silences, their faces grew sour and frightened, and then finally they would just stay home. Life became too ugly for them. It had proven itself ambivalent to their well-being.

Jenny speculated that people in the town had tended to believe that the natural order worked in their favour, and that nothing bad was ever likely to happen to them specifically. But the old generation was dying, often without dignity, in either solitude or following protracted intolerable illness, and none of them had ever expected this to happen. Yet it did, and so the terrible things they saw on the television and read about in the newspapers seemed suddenly in closer proximity. These people primarily lived during a time when nothing bad ever happened, not in the town, not in the country. Bad things only happened to other people far away. Old age and looming death had changed that, as she supposed it did for all old people, with the added bonus that indeed, the world was becoming more hostile. But not here. She waved towards the races. Not just yet.

I did not drink many beers during any session at Jenny's pub. I did not know how to get drunk. Always after three beers the alcohol would go to my head and then I'd walk home and have a rest, or else transcribe from memory my conversations with Jenny at the pub, before going to the Woolworths to work. Everything Jenny said seemed untrue once I'd written it on paper.

I told Jenny one day that I never had more than three beers because I did not know how to get drunk.

You're obviously from another state, she said.

———

The town was quiet and lonely on a Sunday morning. Few shops opened, and those that did attracted no customers. Only the petrol stations and fast-food chains lining the highway West to East had any people in them.

The highway was the real main street of the town. Cars crowded the drive-through lanes and parking lots of the KFC and McDonald's, while the petrol stations were alive with bowser boys pumping petrol and scrubbing windscreens caked with the entrails of locusts. Visitors passed through the town ambivalently. Few turned left or right into the town centre proper, but a barely perceptible sadness awaited those who did. On a Sunday morning the town seemed lost to the countryside and highways surrounding, and the people there pitiable in their inconsequence. During a lengthy drive from the country to the city, passing through the town could make the world seem larger and more unfathomable, because how did these people get here, and why did they stay?

The four-lane highway led all the way to the city, and in the opposite direction, all the way to the centre of the continent. The town was lucky to be situated here, lucky to be connected to somewhere else. Yet few people in the town believed the busy highway represented a proper route out of, and away from, the town. Instead, it was the direction from which others arrived.

Rob worked as a car washer at one of the half-dozen petrol stations lining the highway. He could tell if people were from the city or the country just by the look of them. If they came from the country their headlights and windscreen were caked with locusts. If they came from the city it was city grime. You could run your fingers deep through that grime, he said. Fumes and pollution.

All visitors were vague threats, distant and unchallenged. Those who arrived from the city were not to be trusted, while those who arrived from further inland were suspected of possessing a more authentic claim to country life than anyone in the town. The city was always the city, while the country—the far western country—was hopeless and remote. The city was built-up suburbs and then even bigger buildings, while the west was just a vision of flat brown paddocks and dirt roads. The town was somewhere in between. There was nothing wrong with it.

Arabs, Asians and wogs all come from the city, Rob advised.

Normal white people, farmers, business-owners, and dole-bludgers all come from the country, and he pointed west. Especially dole-bludgers.

On two consecutive Sundays I decided to follow the highway on foot in both its westerly and easterly directions. Travelling west, the town petered out with a final destitute car yard, its faded coloured flaps wilting in the heat. Facing out in this direction the shimmer appeared, a foreboding haziness on the horizon, shrouding some impenetrable frontier. Travelling east, road signs enticed with three digit numbers indicating the distance in kilometres to the coastal city, but the signs also featured other place names, all unrecognisable. Had anyone verified they were there?

They're towns, Jenny told me. Of course they're there.

On a Sunday morning in the town it was impossible to know what to do with yourself. It was possible to lose hours of the day staring out of windows. Maybe some people had barbeque lunches in their backyards, while others watched the football. I could do nothing but drink beer and browse the town's local newspaper, searching for evidence of its origins but also, hopefully, of its future.

Jenny said she didn't know the town's population, nor how old it was, nor what its name meant, nor how many houses it had, nor what its people thought, nor what its favourite colour was. It's just a bloody town, she yelled at me, and then turned the races up before leaving the room.

During the evening hours when I felt most free to wander, I monitored the streets of the town for evidence that I could belong. At times, certain angles on settings seemed to suggest that it might be a place I could in some fashion adapt to. The greening wall of a two-storey townhouse, exposed to the footpath, where the traces of a certain determined moisture lingered, especially at night, seemed to belong to a place where I might find my roots. It required a great amount of concentration to detect the threads, apparitional as they were. The appearances of such threads occurred most frequently when gazing at the tiled roofs of the oldest buildings, set against the starry rural nights. At all times, these appearances occurred at the very edge of some form of structure, and taking in the whole of a setting would usually undermine the strange, alluring sensation of having been there before. I had long suspected that willpower was not enough to transform a setting full of apprehension into a welcoming one, but the occasional small breakthrough, fleeting and unsatisfying, compelled me to keep trying.

My efforts to trap these sensations, to apply them thinly across the town's expanse, always failed. I held some small hope that if these small glimpses existed, these illuminating angles, then maybe they were pitching their own quiet battle against the cold, ambivalent spread. Maybe inside the town there was another, parallel town, itself scarcely populated with the wandering lost, occupied by their own search for a hidden angle which could permit their access home.

———

Ciara was Rob's girlfriend and she was a local of the town. Rob made a point of mentioning that she was a local. He lived in the townhouse because his parents happened to own it, and aside from working at one of the highway petrol stations he also went to TAFE.

Rob told me that he and Ciara were an unusual coupling. This was because, according to Rob, it was undesirable for TAFE students to have close relationships with the local townspeople. It was fine to be in relationships with women from other towns and vice versa, but it was most prestigious to be in relationships with women from the city, though Rob admitted he had never met anyone from the city.

She's a bit of a local but I don't care, Rob would sometimes say.

Ciara spent a lot of time at our house and we got along well. She always seemed interested in whatever I was doing at any particular time. If I was cooking my dinner in the kitchen she would say something like, cooking your dinner there are you, before launching into a discussion about the best things to have for dinner. Light conversations like this would inevitably branch off into more interesting discussions. Ciara asked so many questions that I began to suspect she was trying to understand me.

One day she arrived at the house as I was walking from my bedroom into the living room. She asked what I had been up to that day, to which I replied that I had been writing my book about the disappearing towns of the Central West of New South Wales. This elicited a response I will never forget: she was more impressed about my writing a book than anyone else I had ever encountered. She asked when she would be able to read my book, and I told her that she was welcome to read it whenever she wanted, even now, should she wish. She said that if I made her a copy she would read it later.

Rob sometimes asked whether I was annoyed that Ciara was always over. It's true that she spent most days at the townhouse, but that did not bother me. As long as she didn't interrupt work on my book, I told him, she could do as she wished. Rob would watch less television when she was around, and he even shaved on days she was to arrive. Based on these habits, I gathered that he was in love with her.

In Rob's townhouse the smell of vinegar was rivalled only by the smell of mould. Fly corpses littered the windowsills behind greasy venetians, and dusty cobwebs hung from the ceiling, left swinging further and further towards the carpet for days at a time. Neither of them seemed to care. This filth was transitional, almost an obligation. Rob, and presumably Ciara, did not want to clean up after anyone, least of all themselves. There wasn't the time right now, and as the days and weeks wore on, the right time seemed more remote and less inevitable. The shape into which one is expected to grow had long lost its form. In someone older it would be a depression, but in Rob and Ciara it seemed an act of defiance. Ciara would even sometimes laugh at the filth. One evening, as I carried my bowl to the kitchen in order to fill it with bread, I caught her smiling at the mushed penne latched to the edges of the drain.

This is chaos, she said. You can have everything in order, a roof and several walls, functioning electricity, endless gas, running water, a cupboard full of quick meals, a fridge full of luxurious sparkling soft drinks, a telephone for emergencies, but the gunk in your sink will undermine it all. She turned the tap on high, and pushed the pasta down the drain with her index finger.

She found filth funny because it undermined everything. She appreciated its villainy. She explained that in the city they have cockroaches so numerous that whole rooms can appear to be breathing, like a blackened lung, as the pests scatter with the flick of a light switch. In cities it's important to have filth, she told me. It's what makes a city a city. And yet, cities are meant to be civilised, they're meant to boast the type of facilities people such as us could only admire from afar. This sink—she turned the tap off and wiped her hands on her jeans—wishes badly that it was a city sink. If only the window—and she waved at the window above—looked out on buildings much higher than the ones around here, where the density of homes is so great that statistically, chaos is within a stone's throw. The town's chaos, where it exists at all, is in sinks, in the corners of ceilings, in the muck beneath refrigerators, among the lost socks beneath lounge suites, in old sheds barricaded by useless old appliances and furniture. The chaos is pathetic, but you can't feel sorry for it, so you can only laugh at it.

After a couple of weeks I could no longer just respond to Ciara's questions, could no longer simply listen to her expound upon vague worldly topics as a means to bridge a gap. In order to not appear cold, I would need to ask her some questions too.

I asked whether she thought her town was mysterious. She did not. I asked whether she had ever read any books about her town. She had never read a non-fiction book. She only read the newspaper, because she believed it was the objective of the newspaper to find the strangest and most violent happenings in the town. And yet, apart from the odd act of violence or robbery, always fuelled by alcohol, there were never any secrets in the town the likes of which you can read about in bigger newspapers. She brandished a week-old edition of the *Sydney Morning Herald*.

One day Ciara arrived at the house and knocked on my bed-room door. She told me she had read the printed extracts from my book about the disappearing towns. She needed to sit down in order to offer all her thoughts about the extracts, so I invited her to sit in my desk chair. I was not nervous about her feedback because she was not a writer of books.

Her feedback was not favourable. She couldn't tell whether the book was fiction or fact. She thought it was written well, but also felt as if I were trying hard to draw a singular message from the disappearing towns, and ultimately side-skirting the message because I did not know what it was. So really I would be inviting other people to find something important about the disappearing towns for themselves, and she suspected I might just waste their time.

Ciara asked what was so important about the disappearing towns. I told her that there was nothing important about the disappearing towns. That the disappearing towns were the opposite of important, since nobody knew they existed, and, even when they did exist, no one cared to write about them. There were no facts about the disappearing towns except for minor references in books written about larger towns that hadn't disappeared, and the existence of train stations that had fallen into disrepair along the routes leading to the centre of the country. Occasionally there was an old water tank, or a lone colonial building absorbed by Paterson's Curse, or a well shaft boarded up, or a clearing with foundations showing evidence of a narrow main road. There were no memories, but there were town names that had lingered on maps.

Imagine if this town disappeared in one hundred years, I said. Everything it stood for, or represented, would turn to dust. Everything noble about it would be forgotten. You cannot imagine it, I told Ciara. You might also hope it couldn't be true.

This did not adequately explain all my feelings about the disappearing towns, but Ciara nodded, albeit dubiously. I hoped she would feel unqualified to fathom my book, but she insisted.

She suggested that it couldn't be a non-fiction book, since everything in it was made up.

It was true that I had speculated on a large variety of issues, but this did not make the book strictly fictional. What cannot be verified is not necessarily fiction, I said.

I waited for her to ask more questions about my book, but she appeared to believe that she already understood. She pretended to be chastened, and then asked me what else I had done that day.

———

At first I rarely strayed from the central district of the town. Arranged in long symmetrical grids, it was where the elderly and wealthy people lived, on roads wide and empty save for the parked sedans. Townhouses, petrol stations and open-air asphalt car parks lined the blocks at the fringes, as did more modern single-storey homes.

Outside of the central district the town was disorganised. Roads wound through estates of modern brick mansions and undeveloped land, trailing off into dirt fields littered with discarded whitegoods and felled gums. There was no way out of these winding streets except back the way you came. The sun found no resistance, just scorched everything grey and brown and every other dull colour in between.

I asked Rob whether he had ever explored the tentacle roads, but he didn't even know they existed. His family owned a stately colonial home in the imported leafy outskirts of the central district, and had done so since he was born.

I asked Jenny why the tentacle roads were laid out so strangely, but she said it was only natural.

What's so interesting about roads, she said.

Only one bus operated for those in the town who did not drive. It left the central district at 8:30am and spent an hour stopping at key landmarks on the southern side of town. Then it travelled each of the tentacle roads, lumbered through the north, and then returned to the terminal in time for a late afternoon tea.

From there it would start again along the same route.

The bus driver was a man named Tom. He drove, opened the doors at stops, waited ten seconds, and then commenced driving again.

One day I waited at one of these stops. Tom asked where I was going, and I said I wasn't going anywhere. I only wanted to see the town from the vantage point of a bus.

Well, this is the best way to see the whole town, he said. The bus goes everywhere. It's an exhaustive bus route, but unfortunately an impractical one. From the end of any of the roads it takes two hours to walk to the centre of town, whereas from any given point in the route it takes two and a half hours to travel a similar distance by bus. It would be practical to have another bus and two routes, Tom said. It would be more practical to have two more buses and a total of three routes. But since no one ever rides even this route, the council won't buy more buses or employ extra drivers.

The tentacle roads did not appear to belong to the town proper. Many homes on these roads were for display purposes only, and unlike in the central district trees were rare, save the occasional preened shrub or stunted trunk.

Tom performed a U-turn at the end of a tentacle road. No one in the town ever rode his bus. They all had cars: usually two, sometimes three. It was impossible to walk to the shops in any timely fashion, so people would drive to one of the shopping plazas for everything. The only time the bus might have been useful was of an evening on the weekend, when everyone was too drunk to legally drive home, but the bus didn't operate during that time. The bus terminated at the centre of town at seven in the evening, and that was when, according to Tom, most people started drinking.

He had mentioned this to his bosses at the council but they

weren't interested in adapting the timetable to suit the town's needs. All they'd told him was that the town must have a bus, so it had a bus, and that was all he needed to worry about. So Tom drove in circles every day for the benefit of no one.

The bus turned out of one tentacle road and into another. Immaculate cars baked in white cement driveways, and sprinkler systems doused the brown lawns with bore water. Curtains were drawn, and no one wandered the pathless nature strips. It was possible to see where one lawn ended and another began by the different shades of brown and dull green, or by the bumpiness of the turf, or by the dirt strips left between houses, marking contractual borders respected to the nearest centimetre.

Tom lived on the bus; he never left it, save to eat at the McDonald's and shower at the football oval. I was the first passenger he'd had for several years.

Tom told me a story about one of his most recent passengers. This man had boarded at the central terminal some years ago and hadn't wanted to go anywhere in particular—he'd boarded to speak to Tom. He did so because, for many years, Tom had sang in a local rock group. This local rock group were the most popular local rock group in the town, and they went by the name The Stern Gentlemen.

Tom told me he was proud that a young man, though odd, would board a bus just to speak to him. Being the most popular local rock group for a period of time did not attract the level of ongoing respect I might imagine, he said. If it did, he supposed the bus would have attracted more passengers.

After a few formalities and polite exchanges, the young man, Raymond, said he fronted his own local rock band in the town. According to Raymond, the music in the town was not what it used to be. Tom had agreed for the sake of politeness, but in truth he couldn't have cared less about the music in the town at that current point in time, because he attended a concert many years before that had ended his music career. It was a concert which had revealed all of his efforts to be useless.

Raymond was unhappy because he believed the people in the town no longer cared about rock music, and he wanted Tom's help to revitalise the town's interest in it. He made a proposition: if The Stern Gentlemen played a show with Raymond's band as support group, the former would receive all of the takings. Raymond believed this would be a good opportunity for his own band to gain exposure. After their chat, Raymond alighted at the edge of town, where the highway led to the first of the modern estates.

Tom pondered the opportunity for several days, and brought the topic up with his former bassist. He was excited at the prospect but no one else in the band was, least of all the drummer, who had gone on to manage Clint's Crazy Bargains.

Tom and the bassist decided they would play a two-piece acoustic set in support of Raymond's band. The concert would take place in town, Raymond would handle promotion, and The Stern Gentlemen would receive all earnings at the end of the night. Tom thought about declining the generous offer of full payment, but driving an empty bus did not entitle him to a high salary.

Tom and the bassist practiced in Tom's living room for many weeks, and it was exhilarating to revisit the songs that he thought he'd never hear again. The sound of their songs, even without the keyboard and percussion elements, served to demonstrate how much the town had changed over the years. The songs were capable of conjuring the way the town had felt back then, even though the band had never designed them that way. It was especially powerful because Tom, and the bass player, and presumably everyone else in the town, had never noticed any drastic change occur in the town at all. When they rehearsed the songs together it was apparent that much had changed, and not necessarily for the better. Tom was excited for the opportunity to illustrate this change, even though he couldn't articulate exactly what the change was. This sense of dimension had arguably been what his music had always lacked, during the years when he was still naïve enough to write it. He even fooled himself into believing they had been underappreciated. These songs, presented in this new light, might lead to a renaissance for The Stern Gentlemen.

But things were not right as soon as they arrived at the venue to load in. For starters, Raymond's band had not arrived. Secondly, there was no stage. Thirdly, the barperson did not know of any gig happening that night, and couldn't even remember the last time the venue had hosted one.

Tom turned onto the highway and towards the terminal. He should have called it a night right then, he told me. He should have taken his gear home and admitted to himself that he had been conned. But he had worked himself up to that night for many weeks, and had established a strong urge to express himself one last time. So with the encouragement of the bassist, who had long wanted the band to reform due to an unrealistic opinion of the band's significance, Tom suggested to the barperson that they play an impromptu performance in the bistro. It was an acoustic set after all, and since few diners were seated in the bistro it would not inconvenience anyone. "If people in the bar are interested, they will come in and listen," was how Tom tried to convince the barperson. But this barperson was too young to be swayed by a mention of The Stern Gentlemen, and besides, the barperson said, live rock music was banned from pubs and venues.

Tom was shocked. He discovered that live rock music had been banned in the town for nearly fifteen years — as many years as The Stern Gentlemen had been out of action. It was now illegal to have a guitar in a pub. Illegal to sing in a pub. There were signs throughout the bar warning patrons not to sing along to television commercials or poker machine ditties, as it would put them at risk of being kicked off the premises.

There was no way to play a gig that night, so he went home. He didn't even say goodbye to his bass player, who was busy trying to pick a fight with the barperson.

At the time Tom was living in a townhouse near the bus terminal, and the next day he cancelled his lease and moved onto the bus. He sold his guitar and all of his furniture. He sent his dog to the pound. He wanted to divorce himself entirely from the town and what it had become, but it was necessary to work—and he tapped on the bus's steering wheel—in order to survive.

Tom had quietly believed that he would play music again one day. And yet, after the events of that night he could no longer bear to live in the town, much less perform in it. But there was no possible way out, so he had to make do with living around the town instead — more preferable to living in a static location within it.

At this point he didn't speak to anyone for months, not even his superiors at the council. He stopped contacting them about anything, and he soon realised that they'd never been the ones to contact him — it had always been he who had initiated any communication. He suspected they'd quickly forgotten about the bus route. He also stopped reading the newspaper and he barely even looked at the town as he passed by it all throughout the day. He fixed his attention on the roads and the bus stops, and became lost in his own thoughts. Who was this Raymond fellow, and why had he played such a cruel trick on him? Did Raymond hate The Stern Gentlemen? Did all young people ridicule the memory of his band? Or was Raymond an out-of-towner?

Tom directed my attention to the bus stop shelter opposite the Woolworths parking lot. A year or so after the night of the thwarted gig, on a miserable Monday afternoon with torrential rain and no one in the streets, Tom had driven past this same location. During rainy weather he sometimes felt like he should never have had his tantrum, should never have moved onto the bus and removed himself entirely from the town. Rain made him feel like it was all a mistake, that he'd be better off sitting in a warm house watching the television.

That day there had been someone waiting in the shelter. She'd waved him down as though she wanted to catch the bus, and Tom had braked towards her. He'd been frightened. Nothing good had ever come of someone boarding his bus, but if word got out that he'd left a young teenage girl alone at the bus stop, he might lose his home. So he stopped.

Tom pointed to exactly where the girl had been standing. She must have been fourteen, maybe a bit younger. He'd asked her where she wanted to go. She didn't want to go anywhere – no one ever wanted to go anywhere on his bus.

Instead, she'd wanted him to advertise a gig in the window of the bus. She'd said: just stick the poster up in one of the passenger windows, or maybe in the rear window, so drivers behind you can see. Tom warned her that no gigs ever happened in the town anymore. They'd been banned.

The girl had said she knew that, but wanted to advertise the gig anyway. The bands don't actually exist, she'd said, and the venues don't exist. But the music exists. She set the posters on the dash.

Tom had told her that she couldn't just go around advertising imaginary concerts for bands that didn't exist. She'd replied that as a matter of fact she could, and she had, and what harm would it do anyway, since no one in the town was interested in music.

She was only very young. Tom used the opportunity to tell her all about his time playing music in the town, and how the music community was back in the olden days. She wouldn't have a bar of it. He'd warned her that he was a living example of what could go wrong when people advertised phantom gigs for non-existent bands, but she wasn't interested. She'd seemed quite hostile, Tom said, as if it were all his fault that concerts could no longer be held in the town, save the special town day at the central park every year.

She'd gotten off the bus at the stop near the central park. Rather than feel angry, Tom had felt sad for her — and Raymond too. It all just reminded him of his predicament: there he was, driving a bus. The bus was there, it operated, it had a driver, it had a timetable, but it was only ninety per cent a bus. The raw components of a bus route were in place, but the town forbade it reaching one hundred per cent. Meanwhile, the life he had lived as a young man was nothing but a memory.

Once Tom had realised this he was less bitter about the Raymond boy. He understood the boy's plight, because nothing in the town was one hundred per cent. There was always a missing fraction, he said. It functioned, but that's all it did, and how it continued to do so was a mystery to him.

—

One day as I was cooking my pasta, Rob revealed that a man in the town wanted to bash me.

Steve Sanders has it in for you, he told me. Some men at the pub have warned that you should watch your back.

I was shocked. I had barely been in the town six months and had not wronged anyone as far as I could tell. I had made a conscious effort to avoid men while in the town, and I had made extra efforts to appear meek and harmless around people of the town who might be offended or curious about my presence.

I told Rob that he must be joking. Or else there was a misunderstanding, that Steve Sanders had mistaken me for someone else.

He definitely means you, Rob said. Steve Sanders wants to bash you, probably because you're writing a book about the town.

I explained again to Rob that my book was not about this town, but other towns – most of which did not verifiably exist.

He shrugged and took a can of beer from the fridge. You don't come to a new town expecting not to be bashed, he said.

I barely slept that week. I skipped two shifts at the Woolworths out of fear. I studied the phonebook for address details about this Steve Sanders, but there were at least three dozen S. Sanderses listed as living in the town: a startling statistic under any other circumstance, but one I simply observed with dread at the time. I grew so desperate for information that I considered posting a note on the message board that stood in the central park, imploring Steve Sanders to call me so we could discuss his problem. But if Steve Sanders had decided he wanted to bash me with no wrongdoing on my part, I resolved that he must hold some irrational hatred towards me. Steve Sanders was a monster that could not be reasoned with.

Jenny at the pub was not surprised when I told her Steve Sanders wanted to bash me, because she already knew.

You get that, she said ambivalently. Men want to bash men. Who else are they going to bash?

I told her that there were definitely situations where a man could justifiably want to bash another. But this was not one of them. It wasn't a situation at all. I had never met or even seen Steve Sanders before.

Just get bashed, Jenny suggested. Get it over with. He'll bash you then it'll be done. Have you never been bashed before? I told her I hadn't. Then it's about time you did, she said.

As the weeks passed I became less worried about being bashed and more anxious about what could have caused Steve Sanders to hate me. Having recalled and analysed every rare occasion I had mingled in public, and having failed, after exhaustive self-critique, to pinpoint a reason for his disdain, I started to imagine what it would be like to have a conversation with Steve Sanders. I imagined striding up to him at some or other pub, ordering us both a schooner of beer, and me initiating a dignified defence of myself. I would admit to him that yes, I do look like someone deserving of being bashed, and for that I have only myself to blame. I have lived with being a prime candidate for bashings all my life, but in spite of all my efforts to reverse this truth, I am sadly still who I am. I would tell Steve Sanders that the reality is that I am actually a sad and depressed man. That I have little to nothing going for me. I would do my best to paint myself as an already-harried and pathetic individual, in order for Steve Sanders to see that I was not worth bashing. Maybe, after I had poured my heart out to Steve Sanders, he would even have sympathy and become my friend. Or else he would become a man in the town eager to come to my defence in the seemingly inevitable event that someone else would want to bash me. He's not worth it, Steve Sanders would warn them.

After rehearsing this imagined meeting out in my head dozens of times, I started to become vaguely fond of Steve Sanders. He might've had a good reason to bash me, even if he never deigned to spell it out. Maybe he didn't want to spell it out because he'd realised after making the decision that he was wrong, but had too much pride to admit it. Steve Sanders was probably not an unreasonable man at all. Maybe he was beaten as a child, or had fallen on hard times. Maybe he was upset that I had a job and he didn't. Maybe he was annoyed that I, a stranger, was living a satisfactory life in the town while he was not.

But in the light of day, I was so worried that I did not feel ashamed to press Rob for more details about Steve Sanders.

Rob was surprised I didn't already know him. Everyone in the town knew who Steve Sanders was. He drank at the Railway Hotel, and was a born-and-bred local of the town.

Rob had not been bashed before. He seemed pained on my behalf, but impatient about my quest for any reasons behind Steve's motives. As time passed, I began to sympathise with his lassitude. Did Steve Sanders really need a reason to bash someone? Maybe he did not. And why should I know why? More important questions remained unanswered in the world, and logic was a precious commodity, especially in the town.

No amount of roleplaying on my part could place me in the mind of Steve Sanders. I looked at men in the Woolworths and tried to imagine wanting to bash them. It was easy to generate a dislike for them, but it was a flimsy and dispassionate dislike. Maybe Steve Sanders was so pure of heart that he could not look at another person without wanting to enact the strongest manifestation of his emotions pertaining to them. Maybe, when Steve Sanders bashed me, I would notice a trick in his eyes that revealed the reasons, and then it would all make sense.

After a while I came to see things as Jenny did: I would need to get the bashing over with. It would be a surrender. I would face him and extend an invitation to beat me, believing that under those circumstances it would be foolish for him to do so.

I visited the Railway Hotel one Friday night after three rapidly-drunk beers. The pub was on a quiet strip of the town and attracted mainly old people. It felt like someone's smoky lounge room, with the Channel Seven news playing from a television in the corner, and the smell of roast and gravy permeating the bistro. It did not seem like the kind of place someone enthusiastic about random bashings would visit regularly.

Apart from some elderly men watching sport in the pokies room, there were only three families eating dinner in the pub. I sat at the bar and ordered a drink, browsing some of the pub's photos for evidence of anything Steve Sanders-related. The photos depicted red-faced men and women waving their glasses towards the camera, having a deserved drink. The publican poured me a headless schooner of his cheapest beer, and I asked him whether he knew a Steve Sanders.

The publican pointed into the bistro at a family eating dinner. Steve Sanders, with his family.

I could only see the back of Steve Sanders's head, but his two young daughters and wife were in full view. They were all neatly dressed and beautiful, with stern faces turned towards the nightly news. It looked as if they were having a routine Friday night pub dinner, the kind of tradition common among normal families in towns. The woman could not have been older than forty, while the girls, with their satisfied, focused faces, both appeared aged between eight and twelve.

As for Steve Sanders himself, I could only see the back of a balding head, and the upturned collar of a football jumper. He wore neat faded blue jeans and working boots, and from my vantage point did not seem tense or aggressive. He was a regular, heavyset man of apparently below-average height. He had a domestic life, and enough money to take his family out at night.

What do you want Sando for, the publican asked me.

I sipped my beer. That's not the Steve Sanders I'm looking for, I told the publican. Little wonder it isn't, since there are so many of them in the town.

The publican grunted in a manner which confirmed that indeed there were many of them in town. He made no move to go about his business, though obviously bored of me.

After that we sat silently for a while. When the quiet between us became intensely awkward, I lied that many years ago I had attended high school with a Steve Sanders in a nearby town, hence my search. I had heard that he'd moved here and often visited this very pub. We had made no arrangements to meet, but I thought I'd try my luck surprising him.

When the publican looked at me I saw doubt on his face. You're that bloke writing the book, aren't you, he said.

I nodded, in a manner I hoped looked begrudging. I'm writing a book about some old towns in the region, I said. I'm certainly not writing about this town, as rumour would have it, and besides, the book will probably not be a very good one. It'd probably be among the worst ever written, and I will likely need to stop writing it one day and focus on something else, such as opening a shop of some sort, or working with the council.

The publican listened. When I had finished my speech he fixed his eyes on a nearby Keno screen and remained silent. I did the same, and wondered how I could escape the pub without appearing guilty. The Channel Seven news theme aired dramatically from the television watched by the Sanders family, so I pretended to watch it also. They appeared to be in conversation now, or at least, the woman and two girls looked as if they were listening to Steve Sanders hold forth about some or other topic.

After a longer period of silence, the publican asked whether I was sure the dining Steve Sanders wasn't the one I was after. He had noticed I was watching them. He said he'd call him over.

I told him to stop, almost yelling. I assured him I was on such intimate terms with my Steve Sanders that I would know, just by looking at the back of his neck, whether he was the correct one. My Steve Sanders has no children, I said. Nor a wife. And anyway, I said, isn't it interesting what is happening on the news right now.

We'll be swamped with them soon, the publican agreed.

Later I told Jenny at the pub what I had done, and she seemed amused. She was honoured that I had taken her advice to get the confrontation over with, even if I had failed because my strategy was too transparent.

She said that I should walk the streets at night, or even by day when the football's not on. Make it seem spontaneous. Act like they do in sport; expect it when you least expect it—she threw my small change into the till—but try to look like you're least expecting it.

———

The town had a train station, but it was now only a museum. It was a historical landmark in the eyes of the townspeople, yet Jenny didn't know when it was built or when it had closed.

I asked Jenny about the train station one day at the pub. I wanted to know whether one could get a train to the city, should one wish to do so. I was careful to add that I did not want to take a train to the city. I was only curious about the town's infrastructure.

She said the town didn't have "infrastructure", and that no one knew when the train station was built, nor when it closed. Old people probably knew both dates, but no one would think to ask them about it, because it was simply a historical train station.

The train station museum didn't have any plaques or signage indicating the train station's age, she said. It was the train station museum only by name, because truthfully, it was mainly a showcase for local arts and craft. Pottery, porcelain dolls, plates, placemats, collectible spoons and teacups were all available to purchase, and all were decorated with images of the train station. It wasn't even a museum: it was a shop.

A freight train raced through the platform at 5pm every weekday, and during that time the train station museum staff ushered all visitors—if there were any at the museum at all—onto the platform so they could imagine what it would be like to board or disembark a train in the town.

One day a man ran and leapt onto the high speed freight train as it passed through the station. It was a talking point for many weeks afterwards, but not because the man had possibly wished to kill himself. Instead, the news reports focused on where the man could be. Where could the train have taken him?

Many people in the town, including Jenny, had never thought about the freight train properly before. It had not occurred to them that the train station museum had once been a fully operational train station. The freight train had been assumed to be a performance put on by the train station museum in order to attract customers, and Jenny admitted this was not a clever assumption. But since no one ever had cause to scrutinise the freight train, no one had done so. It was just part of the train station museum's daily attractions. So no, you cannot get a train to the city from here, she told me. The train line doesn't go anywhere. She busied herself at the register.

I told Jenny that it was impossible for the train line to go nowhere, and that it would not be hard to find its final or even next destination on a map. She insisted that it didn't go anywhere because trains didn't run along it, except for the one freight train.

People in the town talked spiritedly about this for more than a fortnight. The destination of the freight train was of great interest, because everyone wanted to know where the leaping man went.

The fuss culminated when a group of men and women took it upon themselves to walk along the train line, starting from the train station museum and heading west. People gathered to watch them depart. Jenny told me that these people who'd decided to wander along the track, though they had good intentions, were the stupidest people in the town. If someone had asked her beforehand who would take part in an adventure like that, she would have listed the top ten stupidest people in the town, and she would have been correct, because it was these people who went. But if there's one thing the people in this town love to do, Jenny said, it's to watch stupid people do stupid things, and to encourage them.

I asked her what happened. Did the police stop them? Did they walk, or were they on pushbikes, riding next to the tracks? Did they take a packed lunch?

She asked if I knew what was on the other side of this town, though she didn't wait for a response — waving her arms westerly, she told me that there was countryside, of course. And then, on the other side of that countryside, there was more countryside. Then there might be a town somewhere, but no one can walk there. You can walk for as long as it takes to get to the next town, but you won't get there, because you just have to drive. It's simply impossible to walk. You need a car, and you need your car to have a full tank of petrol, and an emergency can in the boot.

Jenny didn't know what had happened to the stupidest people in the town, nor did she have any theories. Best case scenario they camped out and then came home, she said. Where they should have stayed in the first place. At home.

———

There was a customer famous among the shelf packers at the Woolworths. His name was Rick McDonald and he would visit the supermarket every day. At about 1pm he would arrive, retrieve a trolley, and then gradually wander each of the aisles, grabbing only one or two items along the whole way. He would spend many hours doing this, and on some days he would still be in the shop when it closed at 10pm. He was a laughing stock, a local fool, but my fellow packers were fond of him in the way you can be fond of idiotic men. Management never bothered him because no matter how long it took, he always purchased at least one or two items.

Rick was a middle-aged man who reportedly lived alone in the poor area near the old gasworks, where everyone strange in the town was said to live. Myths circulated about Rick – chief among them was that he was an undercover agent for the competing Coles, situated in the competing plaza, sent to assess the price of every item on a daily basis, even on weekends. Yet he was clearly an eccentric, even if most of the myths that had formed around him were rational. All assumed some business-like purpose to his daily visits, as if it were impossible for the town to host a genuine stranger.

One evening as I was packing tinned tuna, he turned into my aisle and bumped his trolley into mine, sending several dozen tins of tuna rolling to the laminate. Upset, he parked his trolley and started bundling cans into his arms – except he kept dropping them, causing an even bigger ruckus. I told him to proceed with his shopping, that I could fix the problem, but he insisted, in a friendly if frantic manner, that he stop and help me shelve for a while.

Rick kept apologising as we shelved tuna in chilli oil together, one tin at a time. He said he often watched us packers, and wondered how we coped with such gruelling workloads. He was obviously eager to compensate me for what he believed was a grievous waste of my time.

I told Rick that I did not care whether I finished packing the shelves or not, since working at the supermarket as a packer was not my life calling. Nor was it gruelling, because I was able to listen to dictations of my writing as I worked. You see, I'm writing a book about disappeared towns, I told Rick, and I'm nearing completion, so it won't be long before I'll never have to step foot inside a Woolworths supermarket again.

He told me that this was too bad, that he thought my situation ideal. The job was as simple as putting products in shelves, and surely that can't be so dreadful, since there are people in the town who do much more difficult things on a daily basis.

I agreed that he was correct. It wasn't the strenuous nature of the job I objected to, I simply thought it was mindless, annoying, and far below my capabilities. Rick conceded that it probably was, but maintained that my job was ideal nonetheless.

He told me that the supermarket was the only thing that made him happy. He loved it because it was a hive of activity. There was always music. It had a nice variety of smells and colours. He'd always wanted to work in a supermarket like this, only he wasn't good enough.

I told Rick that any old idiot can work in a supermarket, and that it wouldn't be difficult to apply for a job and get one.

That's easy enough for you to say, he said, because things are easy for you. For many years he'd never quite believed he'd reach adulthood, because as a teenager he could not stop anticipating it. He'd spent all of his teenage years painstakingly planning how he would use the freedom adulthood would grant him.

When he'd finally made it, Rick had discovered that his adulthood was a substandard and boring way of life. But he couldn't imagine me feeling the same way, since I was working in a supermarket. You may believe there's nothing interesting about your work, he told me, but at some early stage in your life it would have seemed very strange and interesting indeed.

As for Rick, adulthood for him had been just waking in the morning, alone in his bed, only no parent forced him to get out of it anymore. Apart from that there was no difference from being a teenager. The view hadn't changed. He'd always thought colours might be different, but they weren't.

It was beautiful being a teenager, Rick said, pushing my trolley to the next shelf. He'd spent those years wondering about the mysterious times ahead of him. It wasn't that he had great ambitions, nor did he have any specific notion of how he would spend his adulthood, but the promise of events and milestones was intoxicating. The world would change and he would see it change, until eventually he might be in a position to be an authority on change, an expert on transitions.

Between teenagehood and adulthood he had expected a big moment that would bridge the two. Suddenly he would be an adult, and teenagehood would be remote, far behind him. It would be a distant memory, even if it was only moments before. The world itself would change. He'd imagined adulthood as a transformative threshold, and he'd expected every vantage point in the town to become unfamiliar overnight. But nothing like any of this happened.

Shortly after becoming an adult he'd married a woman and they had a child. Neither of them worked, but it was enough to simply live in a house, albeit in the poor area of town, and be adults with a kid.

Life had been all about his wife Ruth and daughter Giselle. He'd enjoyed saying the words "wife" and "daughter". He would say to people he knew, "my wife and my daughter," all of the time. He would sit in the lounge room as they watched TV together, and feel amazed that finally he had crossed the transformative threshold. Yet he hadn't changed at all. He could still remember vividly how it felt to be a teenager. He'd been doing adult things, yes, but he still had not felt dramatically different to how he had felt a mere year earlier, when he'd been seventeen and wondering about the future.

When his wife Ruth was pregnant he had not expected that she would ever actually give birth. As her belly swelled over the course of eight months, he'd assumed that the foetus would either die or that it would prove to be a strange tumour. Then, as Ruth was giving birth to Giselle at the town hospital, he'd expected the nurses to take him aside and advise that it was impossible for this infant to be reared by the likes of them. It would need to go to a carer, and he and Ruth would need to continue being a barren married non-adult couple.

Then, after the midwives had laid Giselle on his wife's breast, he'd believed it was impossible for the child to ever grow. They would always be in the birthing clinic, and Giselle would always be an infant, and his wife would always be incapacitated on the bed. It was impossible to imagine what would come next.

But everything had proceeded as it usually does for anyone else in the same situation. In a matter of days all three of them were together in their house, and life continued. Having a child was difficult, but it was meant to be difficult, because being an adult is difficult. Life becoming more difficult is what adulthood is about, Rick supposed, and adulthood is about meaning and purpose and noble struggle.

They didn't have much money, so during the day they would sit in the town's central park and let Giselle roll around in the grass. They would monitor Giselle's facial expressions and relish all evidences of emotion. Even watching Giselle cry was fascinating, Rick had thought, in the way that she would transform from placid to discontented in less than a second. The baby had not been afraid to express exactly what she felt as soon as she felt it. It was also pleasant to witness her determination to learn more. When Giselle first rolled from her back onto her belly it was an incredible milestone, and for Ruth and Rick, in the moment it was enough. Their baby had learned this one thing, so now she could relax for a while. But for Giselle it had been important to immediately explore all of the possibilities that came with rolling onto one's belly, like crawling. Her inability to immediately do anything else new made her cry.

And so life for Giselle was a deluge of obstacles. Nothing was satisfactory for very long: one development only served to make the next more urgent. Transformative thresholds were crossed weekly, sometimes even daily, but each and all were never enough.

As they'd watched Giselle grow over the course of six months, the fact of Rick not having a job became more and more prominent. He lacked the patience to spend whole days and nights with Giselle, so he would wander the streets with CV in hand applying for jobs, and that became his proxy job. Ruth stayed at home, rocking the baby to sleep, keeping the baby asleep, and tending to whatever needed tending to around the house.

Rick's job hunting had not been successful. For some reason people did not want to give him a job. He knew that he would be a good worker, and he believed that he'd presented himself better than many of the teenagers who worked at the shops in the town. But for some reason managers and owners disliked him, and always would. These types of people were a whole category of mankind unfavourably disposed towards Rick, and this was abundantly obvious after only a fortnight, as by then he had applied at every single shop in the town.

He had not wanted to stay at home all day and listen to Giselle cry while also feeling gloomy about not having a job, so he'd left the house each morning under the pretence that he was still searching. And occasionally, lost for any jobs to apply for, he would stop into the pub for a quick beer just to while away the time. He was an adult in the eyes of the law, after all, even though he didn't feel like one, and legal adults are allowed to drink beer whenever they wish.

He'd mistakenly believed that he had crossed the transformative threshold to adulthood one day when Ruth's father, Don, caught him drinking a beer at the Grosvenor pub. The old man walked in at lunchtime with his coworkers from the council. He'd pretended not to notice Rick.

Many things went through Rick's head that day. He'd immediately formulated a scene where he would reveal all to Don, and

Don would understand that Rick was under immense pressure. He hoped that Don would not tell Ruth, nor would he ever mention the situation during family get-togethers. Surely he would not make Rick's wretched life worse by introducing this new complication. Surely adults did not act reflexively: surely they thought things through and assessed what actions would lead to the best possible outcome.

But of course Don did tell Ruth. He didn't recall her being too upset. She simply said that it was little wonder he had not found a job if he always smelled like beer, to which Rick replied that he only had a beer when he felt especially depressed about not having a job. This strategy worked. He had seen that Ruth felt sympathy towards him because he was trying his very best and failing nonetheless. Adulthood was proving difficult for Rick, but the important thing was that he was trying his best.

Still, Don telling Ruth meant that Rick could no longer drink a beer occasionally as he'd looked for jobs. Don tried to get him a job at the council, doing whatever labour the council felt inclined to delegate, but the council didn't want to give him a job either. There was no reason given except that others were more suited than him. By then he'd already understood that he was not suited for a job. He was simply not someone worth paying to do something.

Rick spent part of a dole cheque getting a Responsible Service of Alcohol certificate, but then no pubs would employ him. He did a coffee-making course, but no cafés were interested. He'd investigated studying at the TAFE, but it was far too expensive—and anyway, to earn just a little bit of money it was surely not important to have a qualification. He was simply a deadbeat adult who didn't even feel like an adult, and he supposed employers must have sensed that he still felt like a teenager, and that he had yet to properly cross the transformative threshold.

Eventually he'd presented a bold idea to Ruth: they would need to move away from the town. Rick was not so audacious to recommend the city, but surely another town would have people willing to employ him, especially since they had not seen him wandering the main street for many months with CV in hand. He would appear to be a regular person with a strong work ethic applying for a job that he was more than capable of carrying out. Chances are, he'd told Ruth, that he would get the first job he applied for, since people would not associate him with the inability to get a job.

Ruth had agreed to move, but only if Rick arranged a job in advance. This was far from easy, because looking for a job is hard, Rick said, and he didn't have a car. The only bus in town didn't leave the town, and there was only one train that passed through the town, the freight train, and it never stopped. He did consider leaping in front of it one day, he chuckled to me, when feeling especially fed up.

He'd put notes on noticeboards around town requesting lifts to the next town in case anyone commuted on a daily basis. He'd never received a reply. He'd investigated potential bus routes at the terminal, in case there was a bus that passed by even the outskirts of town, but there were no buses leaving or arriving anywhere near. The only option was to drive, except he didn't own a car, nor did he have a driver's licence – and he had money for neither. Meanwhile, as he resubmitted CVs to all of the businesses that had already rejected him, he'd become more and more tense about not being able to have a beer during the day. He was still drinking at home, of course, every single night, but he was lost for things to do in the town while ostensibly looking for a job. He'd reacquainted with an old high school friend named Shane who lived in his mother's shed and smoked marijuana. Since Rick smoked cigarettes, he'd doubted Ruth would be able to smell marijuana on him if he smoked it too, especially since she had never smoked it before and was probably unfamiliar with it.

For several weeks he'd only visited Shane after a solid five-hour stint of looking for work. He would start looking at nine in the morning, visit Shane at two, smoke two bongs, leave Shane's at four, and then wander around town until the effects wore off. Shane sat in his shed and smoked bongs all day while watching television or playing video games. When Rick was there he'd done the same, and enjoyed it because the marijuana made him more analytical, and more sensitive to the subtleties of entertainment. It seemed to make time pass slower too, which was a blessing, as Rick was finding it increasingly difficult to arrive home while still under the influence of the drug. Giselle's screaming would seem more piercing, and Ruth's exhaustion more depressing and alienating.

One day he'd been so fed up looking for a job that he'd visited Shane at ten in the morning. He had planned for it to be a one-off, but it had quickly become a habit. And under the influence of the drug the prospect of wandering the town in search of a job seemed even more undignified – pathetic even. It was true that Rick had been hiding at Shane's house. He'd waited for each day to pass so that he could finally go to bed.

It had taken Ruth several months to realise that there was something further wrong with Rick. She'd certainly known that there was something already wrong with him before—depression, anxiety—but she soon suspected he was doing drugs also. She'd asked about his red eyes one evening and he'd lied that he had been crying on the way home. This had worked as an excuse for that one evening, but it couldn't continue: he couldn't keep telling her that he was crying.

So instead of smoking marijuana with Shane all day, Rick had decided he would do so only at the beginning of the day: from ten o'clock until lunchtime. Then he would wander around town until it was time to go home. This way the drug's effect would disappear entirely before he saw Ruth, and his eyes would be clear.

Giselle was one year old, and Ruth was becoming more worried about Rick's wellbeing. She was very supportive, and eventually compromised on the matter of moving towns: that they would do so without his having arranged a job first. But by that point the prospect of moving to another town alarmed Rick, because what if he couldn't find work there either? He would be alone wandering in a new town, with nowhere to hide during the day.

In the end, moving towns was the only thing left to do. Despite Rick's reluctance, they'd decided to move to a town sixty kilometres west. At first he was anxious, but as they'd begun packing away their belongings he'd started to realise how much he had grown to hate the house they'd lived in, and how much he had lost faith in the transformative threshold of which he had always dreamed. All of the events prior to that—leaving school, becoming an official adult, marrying Ruth, and rearing Giselle—were only steps along the way to true transformation, and this move to another town would be the element that sealed the deal.

On the day of the move, Don had helped them pack all of their belongings into a council ute. They had already secured a flat in the new town, thanks to a friend of Ruth's family. All they'd needed to do was drive, arrive, unload, arrange, and then Rick would spend two days enjoying his new life before getting serious about finding a job.

He'd been a bit nervous about the drive, though—nervous about the way Don had packed the council ute. What Rick and Ruth had anticipated being several trips had turned into one, as Don had made it a game to see whether all of their belongings could fit onto the one tray. And fit they did, but only just, and not properly at all—because as they'd been leaving town, picking up speed on the highway, out near the old abandoned car yard, three lounge chairs strapped to the top of the load had come loose, causing a great imbalance. The truck had skidded off the road.

Don, Ruth and Giselle: they'd all died. Rick had received not even a scratch; he awoke several days later to find that he was back at his parents' house, lying in the same bed he had slept in as a teenager, under the same linen he had snuggled up to for the entirety of his childhood. His parents told him not to worry, that he was living back with them now, that everything would be okay.

Rick said that he had experienced nightmares like this all his life: where, after a period where he was certain he had crossed the transformative threshold to adulthood, he would wake up one day to find himself back at home, in his pokey old bedroom, with his parents pottering around in the next room. In his nightmares he would have no immediate means to escape the situation – it would be months, even years, before he could escape and become an independent person again, and all the while the people around him were enjoying their freedom, and making the most of their lives.

Rick packed his last column of tuna tins onto the Woolworths shelf, and looked upset when he saw there were no more left. He told me that after the car accident it took months for him to want to leave the house again. Clearly adulthood was not for him. He hadn't wanted to face the world, nor had he wanted to take drugs or drink beer and become more miserable. He'd only wanted to go back to being a child, or a teenager, when the world did not seem so horrible.

That's why he came to the supermarket every day: it was a sanctuary. He was overcome with many beautiful memories when he visited it, and if he focused enough, he could pretend that he was there with his mum. The nostalgic songs played over the loud speakers had not changed since he was a child, nor had the harsh fluorescent lighting which accentuated all of the loud colours on each of the products. The sound of the checkouts beeping as products are registered to the bill was intensely musical to him.

When he was a kid Rick had loved nothing more than to go shopping with his mum. Even on occasions when she did not buy him a treat he told me he was happy, because the supermarket for him was a showcase for domestic comfort. It's arranged perfectly: when you enter you are immediately hit with the smell of fresh fruit and vegetables, and to the far left of this area there is the cold meat section. Then, if you take the aisles as they come, up and down accordingly, you are exposed to the breakfast cereal section, the bread section, and then the spices and condiments section, then the Asian and Italian cuisine sections, and then it gets serious with the stationery section, and then the magazine section, and then the toiletries section, followed by the fragrant laundry section which always morphs into the cold foods section, where the ice cream and frozen pies are kept. And each one of these sections, Rick said, is evocative of a strange memory from his childhood. Each section is a warm anecdote, or at the very least an image, of a time when all he needed to do in the world was be good for his mum. And so as an adult there in the supermarket, he was as close to inhabiting a non-volatile world as he was ever likely to get.

Rick pointed to the stacked tuna cans. He said that if I was impressed by the work he had done, then he'd appreciate my putting a good word in to the manager. He was uniquely passionate about the environment.

Rick handed me his CV, and asked that I give it to my manager alongside a personal endorsement. I told him I would see what I could do.

———

Each year the town had its own special day. On this day the main street was cordoned off from the bottom petrol station all the way to the top petrol station, and market stalls lined the streets selling Pluto Pups and other types of deep fried food, or else novelty T-shirts and cheap toys. At one end of the street near the top petrol station, a band played in the park, and there was a jumping castle too.

The day celebrated the fact of the town being a town. For one day in autumn, just before the biting morning frosts set in, people were invited to acknowledge that they lived in the town. It was an opportunity to feel warmly towards the town, and given the festivities, and the coloured lights that criss-crossed the main street at night, and the thousands of litres of beer involved, few could resist being part of the occasion.

I attended the town's day because I was having trouble writing my book about disappearing towns. Adult couples, teenagers and troublemakers milled the streets, browsing keepsakes they could purchase at one of the dozen or so stalls set up in the area. The stalls sold shirts, stubby holders, flags, stickers, plush koala bears and car decals, all decorated with the Australian flag and the name of the town. In the park there was a special cordoned-off area where people were permitted to drink beer from tin cans. It was necessary to line up to gain entry, but since few people left the special cordoned-off drinking area once they had entered, I was not able to enter, and so not able to have a beer. Instead, I bought a can of Coke and sat on the grass as the band played a cover of 'Electric Blue' by Icehouse.

Jenny from the pub eventually called over to me. She was serving beers inside the cordoned-off drinking area, and motioned that she could get me inside. Soon enough the security guard manning the entry waved me over and I was welcomed in.

In the cordoned-off drinking area customers lined up, bought their beer, and then joined the end of the queue again. As she opened beer cans for townspeople, Jenny explained to me that it was her biggest business day of the year. Her pub hardly did any business anymore, aside from mine, so it was lucky that her father was friends with an organiser of the festival. The money she made on this one day was enough to sustain the pub, so I should be grateful that the festival existed, she told me, since I was the only person who ever drank in the pub.

Jenny was always making comments to me like this. But I wasn't about to complain – I was privileged that she spoke to me at all. Especially on this day – there was no need for Jenny to speak to her customers in the cordoned-off area, as there was only one variety of beer, and it was not permitted to buy more than two beers at once, as per council regulations. Jenny automatically served two beers to each customer. If asked for only one, Jenny would insinuate that this person had consumed enough for the day, and should get some fresh air, i.e., leave the cordoned-off drinking area to make room for someone eager to buy and drink two beers at once.

I watched as Jenny served the beers. At one point Rob rattled at the fence nearby and motioned me over. He wanted to get inside the drinking area. He said he'd do anything to get in, and besides, I wasn't drinking anything so there was no reason for me to be in there.

He was right that I wasn't drinking any beer, but I liked watching Jenny work. Also, I did not want to exploit my privilege by requesting a swap. I told Rob that he might as well drink at one of the pubs on the street, two of which had a view of the stage, but he was not satisfied with this solution. The line into the cordoned-off drinking area was blocking the view of the stage, and besides, he really wanted to drink with his friends, who were already inside. I explained that it was impossible and he marched away.

At that time of evening, as the sun was starting to go down and the band were becoming a little more upbeat, the line to the drinking area was snaking around the perimeter of the park, to the extent that the whole park was enclosed by a wall of thirsty revellers, none of whom would ever have a beer this year in the cordoned off area—they would need to wait until next year.

But on closer inspection it was obvious they were all drinking. Many, if not all, of the queuing revellers were sipping from small flasks, and hidden cans and bottles, and probably becoming more drunk than anyone in the official drinking area. I explained the situation to Jenny, who was amused.

Of course they're getting drunk, she said. No one was going to not drink, even if it was against council regulations to drink outside of the cordoned-off area.

I wondered aloud why the people wanted so badly to enter the area, since they were able to drink outside of it anyway, albeit illegally, and Jenny made a gesture with her head which suggested I had already made her point.

You're exactly right, she told me. To be in the official drinking area was to be officially drinking. Then she waved vaguely at the queue, and suggested it would be safer for me to stay in the cordoned-off area.

The mayor was scheduled to give his speech at 8:30pm. When the time came he ascended the steps and waved to the audience at the front of the stage, which comprised only twenty or so men, women and children. Everyone else was lining up at the perimeter of the park. He stood in front of the microphone, tapped it, and made what must have been a joke, because he laughed loudly. And then he spoke at great length.

I asked Jenny whether she enjoyed what the mayor was saying, but she was too busy serving beers. She probably couldn't hear either; amid the noise of the cordoned-off drinking area it was impossible to make out his words. Occasionally there was a moment when his voice stopped echoing around the park, and these magisterial pauses were met with ironic hollering from the queues. From a safe distance, the people of the town were demonstrating to the mayor that they believed he wasn't very good.

The mayor is a prick, Jenny said. I asked why she disliked the mayor, but she motioned that she'd not be drawn on any political topic during work hours. Just look at him, she muttered.

As the speech was delivered, those lining for beers inside the cordoned-off drinking area settled into a murmur. They faced towards the stage with neutral stares, letting the mayor's platitudes wash over them like a television commercial. It annoyed them to have the mayor speak during an event designed for drinking, but they were resigned to it, and might have believed the mayor was entitled to his moment, since they had been lucky enough to gain access to the drinking area.

As he droned on, I gestured to Jenny that I might have a can of beer after all. She handed me two and I edged towards the cordon to survey the festivities. From there, it was easier to understand what the mayor was saying – his speech centred around how the town was good, how it had always been good, and that it was the hard work of its citizens that made it good. The few teetotalers sitting in the grass were packing up their picnic blankets and mustering their children, squeezing between the fences of queued drinkers on their way to parked cars. Finding nothing but the queue and the evacuated grass, I wandered back to the bar and watched Jenny dole out her beers. After another fifteen minutes there, with Jenny refusing to be drawn into any light conversation, I inspected the grass again. The mayor was still offering the same commentary as before: that the town was good, and that it was the townspeople that made it good.

Jenny glared at me when I asked if the mayor's speech would ever end. It was an indictment on my character that I noticed the speech at all. The line for cans of beer inside the cordoned-off area was longer than before, snaking around in double queues. It seemed at that moment that just about every attendee at the town's day was lined up for something.

And then the mayor's speech ended. A stubborn quiet lingered for a minute or so, as no one wanted to be seen to have enjoyed the mayor's speech. A defeated animosity seemed to pervade the main area, but the official drinkers in the cordoned-off area soon caught a second wind. Many started to sing improvised songs about the town. Outside of the area, queued people dispersed and let their guard down as the band returned to the stage.

Jenny pointed as the mayor left the stage. See, she said. Now the queues will fall apart.

I could see that several men were removing their shirts despite the autumn chill. Two collaborated in the removal of a park bin from its metal frame before tossing it aside, the bin and its contents spilling across the green grass. Many other men and women started to roam around the park in search of things to destroy, while the rest stood cross-armed at the outskirts, still in rough queue formation, ready to witness the spectacle. Empty cans of soft drink were pegged, picnic mats were torn apart, celebratory banners were dismantled, tree branches were cracked from their trunks, and shirts were set alight, twirled and thrown. A monotone hymn erupted from the dispersing cordoned-off drinking area queue, resembling a more religious version of the improvised songs about the town.

It was a yearly ritual to destroy a bulk of the park's facilities after the mayor's speech, Jenny explained. After a full day of drinking in the sun, it was the only gesture the people could muster.

The destruction was carried out in a jovial fashion. There was no anguish in the eyes of one man who, climbing a nearby electrical pole, removed and set alight a cardboard placard celebrating the town's day. Another woman smashed a glass bottle against a floodlight encasement, but she did so with tears of joy in her eyes, and her efforts were rewarded with encouraging hoots and hollers. No one made an effort to conceal their prohibited alcohol any longer. Instead, the people flaunted their public drinking by skolling conspicuously from two-litre bottles of bourbon and vodka. These bottles were dutifully smashed against a nearby surface once finished with.

There wasn't actually much to destroy. According to Jenny, no one dared destroy anything which might land them in prison for a night. It was enough just to be seen to be destroying something, preferably of low value, and ideally belonging to a friend, or no one at all.

A couple of brawls had erupted in the crowd among the shirt-less men. These did not appear to be good-spirited fights—the blows landed with impact and no part of the body was off-lim-its—but people watched with a strange, languid calm, as if only out of a sense of duty.

Jenny pointed through the chaos towards a man jeering a group of wrestling boys, a tin of some or other alcohol in his fist. It was Steve Sanders.

Now would be a good opportunity to get the bashing over with, she said. It would be sensible because, according to Jenny, fights at the town's day were more likely to be light-hearted. I might even get off with just a few hard punches to the gut. There were too many other people—and she waved at the drunks—eager to put up a solid fight. Steve Sanders would quickly get fed up with me and go for someone stronger and more combative. He might even respect me for wanting to get involved in the fights. She added that she would call an ambu-lance if he made a mess of me.

I could not make out his face from that distance, and his clothing or posture didn't stand out among the other men of the town. He wore a blue shirt, presumably with a national flag on its front like so many others, and a pair of blue jeans.

I knew it was inevitable that Steve Sanders would bash me if I approached him. Though I was about to go seek out the bashing, I secretly knew that I could hide among the patrons in the cordoned off area if I lost my nerve. As I pushed through the queue and out of the cordoned off drinking area, Rob tried to approach me. I ignored him, fixing my stare on the man Steve Sanders.

As I reached the wrestling boys a large tattooed man picked

another up and dropped him on his head, prompting horrible jeers from the crowd. The band stopped, leaving a shameful silence. Those who had witnessed this act of violence levelled accusations at one another, shifting the blame, and the mirth turned ugly. Four policemen emerged from nowhere and started to corral the drinkers who were closest to the incident.

Someone always has to go too far, Rob said, suddenly by my side. He was drinking from a longneck of beer, but did not seem very drunk. He told me things went too far every year, each time in a different way. The year before someone had thrown a broken bottle at the band. Before that, someone had set a tree on fire. Ten years ago, someone had tossed a dog onto the roof of the petrol station. Rob waved towards the closest petrol station. Destruction and chaos is in their blood, he said as I took a sip from his beer. But mostly they're a tranquil bunch.

Soon enough the park was deserted, save for those in the cordoned-off drinking area.

———

On subsequent visits to the townhouse Ciara never mentioned my book, but we still had meaningless discussions in the kitchen as I prepared dinner. Usually I ate boiled spiral pasta with grated zucchini and some mushrooms. Sometimes I would also add cheese.

Ciara hosted a weekly show on the local community radio station. Every Thursday night at 10pm she would sit alone for two hours and play what she termed "mysterious music". She was open to requests if anyone cared to call, but no one ever listened to the community radio station, she said, and besides, its music library only featured obscure country music performed by elderly Australian men.

Hers was the only show hosted by a young person, she claimed. Everyone else at the station was old and they all played the same music. Between the playing of country music songs they all spoke at length, very slowly, about each of the country music songs they played. Or else they would play popular AM radio classics, the likes of which were permanently playlisted on the local commercial AM station.

Little wonder no one listens to 2MCL FM, Ciara said.

The community radio station was rife with internal politics. Ciara was caught between factional disputes: one side was adamant that the radio station should remain exactly as it was, while the other faction, despite hosting shows no different to their opponents, believed the station should welcome young people in order to secure the frequency's future. The latter happened to boast the station president among them, Wendy Rogers, and it was this detail that secured Ciara her show in the first place.

It quickly dawned on Ciara that no one listened to the radio station. Not even her friends would listen to her show. For a while she would call her friends and relatives at random to plead for them to tune in, just so she knew she was talking to someone. But it was obvious no one did tune in, and fair enough too: the station's signal was very weak. Ciara could only receive it at home if she held the aerial of the radio in her bedroom at an uncomfortable angle towards her ceiling.

Surely it is worth fiddling with an aerial in order to hear someone you know on the radio, Ciara said. If she could hear someone she knew well on the radio—someone aside from the old people at the station—she would listen very closely every week. Imagine all you can learn from listening to someone on the radio, she sighed. You might discover a secret side to them.

Ciara had no ambitions to be a professional broadcaster. Her applying for a voluntary hosting role was the result of a particular radio show that had aired at midnight every Friday when she was a child. This radio show, she said, had specialised in music that was impossible to obtain. It was the most mysterious music she had ever heard.

The announcer had never shared his name. Ciara would spend an hour before the show fiddling with the aerial in order to listen with the clearest signal possible. Talking to me, she could barely remember anymore the way the music had sounded, mainly because there was nothing now to compare it to. Some people would probably argue that it wasn't music at all that he had played, but instead just noise.

The announcer hadn't sounded mysterious, though. He'd just sounded like a regular town man with a regular nasal local accent, probably in his fifties, maybe even older. He'd had the same lazy, benevolent air of all the other elderly broadcasters, except the music he'd played was alien. As a girl Ciara would sit on the carpet next to her bed and listen with her eyes closed. It had been possible to visit unknown lands with the aid of these strange sounds. She'd been able to see locations and structures the likes of which her own mind, even in dreams, could never conjure alone.

The announcer had never talked about the music, or even named the songs. Ciara could remember what he'd said between each song: "You're listening to 2MCL FM, the program is Friday Night Sounds, the time is after midnight and I'll be with you until 3am. I hope you're having a pleasant Friday evening." If there was a supporter drive going then he'd explain the fees and benefits, and if there happened to be a major town event, say the Grosvenor Street fire, he'd make small mention of it – maybe dedicate his strange music to whoever was affected, but that was all.

It's very easy to know everything there is to know about the town, Ciara told me. She knew every street and who lived in all of the houses. She believed it wasn't possible to learn anything new about the town at all. Apart from regular gossip about men cheating on women, pub brawls, and who did and did not do drugs, no events ever occurred that were likely to be remembered.

She sometimes doubted Friday Night Sounds had ever aired at all. Had she imagined it? When she'd described the music to the manager at Sanity, he'd said the music couldn't be real. The sounds she had described were not the type people bothered putting on a CD, he'd said. When she'd tried talking to Wendy Rogers about the mysterious show, the station manager said it was before her time and that the former manager, Reg Gardner, had died five years ago from a stroke. None of the old people at the station remembered Friday Night Sounds, Ciara said, because they were all too old.

During the first few weeks doing her Thursday night show, Ciara had spent every spare minute rifling through the station's files for evidence of Friday Night Sounds. She'd never found anything. She'd even appealed to listeners for information regarding the host but the phone never rang: no one ever listened to 2MCL FM, after all.

During the first two months of her show she'd played music from CDs she'd brought from home, music popular among young people of the town. She would reference happenings in the town she believed might be of interest to young people, and she would occasionally invite local bands to send their demos in. None did, until she put up a notice in several of the town pubs. After that she received a handful of cassettes, mainly by metal bands, and mainly featuring cover versions of popular metal songs. For a long time she played these tapes exclusively, despite their unlistenable quality, because they were something she could play that no one else would. There was no objection from the other members of the station to what she played, because none of them ever listened to it.

Eventually Ciara got to talking with a man known around town as Raz. He played guitar in a metal band called Folical Dysfunktion. He was happy that she played his cassette regularly, and Ciara was happy too. If there were strange new things to learn in the town, she would likely learn them in the company he kept.

No one in the town's metal music scene ever performed live in public. Instead, they rehearsed in their bedrooms or garages and sometimes recorded themselves onto cassette using the built-in microphone on their stereo systems. One night Raz had invited Ciara to a house party at his, where he promised she would be able to see at least two of the town's metal bands in action.

Raz lived in the poor area near the gasworks. When Ciara arrived, the Sepultura album *Roots* was playing, and nearly a dozen men and three or four women were sitting around on couches smoking and drinking rum and Coke. Some of the men were much older, in their late twenties and early thirties, but they'd still behaved like she had always expected metal enthusiasts would. They'd stood with cans of liquor in their fists, swaying to the music, occasionally air guitaring and very regularly bursting into headbanging motions when especially heavy parts of a song came on.

Ciara said she was made to feel welcome, because the metal people were eager to get the message out about their bands. They had a theory that record industry representatives from the city listened to regional radio stations in order to uncover hidden talent.

She'd doubted this, but was young enough at the time to take their word for it. And anyway, there was no way to gauge how many listeners she had, despite the always-silent studio telephone.

As the house party wore on the metal people had become more and more drunk. They'd huddled in circles and banged their heads to songs they liked. Raz had went into the backyard and smashed a plastic chair to pieces while everyone cheered him on. One woman had scratched an inverted crucifix into her thigh with a razor blade, and then got naked. Glasses were smashed regularly, whether purposefully or by accident Ciara couldn't be sure. It was a very wild party, the likes of which she had never known could occur in a town like hers.

The group had gotten drunk quickly, their voices growing louder and the conversations more affectionate and antagonistic. Feeling out of her element, Ciara had retreated to a bean bag and gazed up at the strange gothic posters which hung from every wall in the house, advertising bands she had never heard of, playing in towns she had never visited. The smell of marijuana and the sweet scent of rum, emanating from the pores of each of the men, had made her feel like she was transcending the town.

Raz had closely cropped black hair and many piercings on his face. Ciara said that he was a violent man. It wasn't that he was physically aggressive to other people, she said, but he was very eager to destroy things. Sometimes in the middle of a group hug he would become so emotional that he'd reach out to the nearest empty bottle and throw it out an open window, then cheer when he heard it shatter on the concrete. It was something the music seemed to prompt him to do because it was so powerful. It was not enough for him to passively listen to it: he needed his body to reflect it in some way. He would often grab the skin around his eyes and pull downwards during very intense moments of songs. During calmer moments of songs he would tap his leg nervously as if urging the louder parts to arrive sooner. He would sometimes sing along to the screaming parts of songs, but in a whisper, and watching his face was like watching a madman bludgeon a person to death. When he smoked bongs he did so in a manner that suggested he was going to die if he did not inhale as deeply as possible.

Ciara didn't fall in love with Raz, but she'd been interested in being his girlfriend because she had never met someone so intense. He was not handsome, and they would no doubt have a terrible life together, but she'd wanted badly to be involved in things she did not understand. When his band Folical Dysfunktion started playing at the house party, she'd been careful to watch his performance as a fan, and not as someone trying to assess the group's suitability for airplay.

She said she'd never forget one thing Raz told her: that when he got drunk he would eventually come to the realisation, late into the drinking session, that he could not inhabit the feeling forever. Eventually the party would end, and he would need to stop drinking, and eventually he would stop being drunk, and this truth would instantly drain his happiness. He would look around the room at the other people having a good time, and he would know that later in the night they would leave, go home, fall to sleep and then do other things. He wanted nothing more than to delay this moment, but its certainty haunted him.

After that first party Ciara would sometimes visit Raz's house. Although he lived alone there were always three or four other people having a smoking session in the lounge room, either listening to music, watching TV or both. Ciara smoked bongs too, and for a long time it was her favourite thing to do. It made conversations more affectionate, she said, and it made music sound more intricate and otherworldly. The world outside of Raz's house seemed even more boring, but it was fascinating in its boringness. She'd been able to see the whole town from a different perspective. All of a sudden, the streets and houses she had seen and known her whole life appeared to have secrets. She'd felt she understood a profound, underlying logic to everything, and figured that if the townspeople saw this logic too, they might make an effort to subvert it, somehow.

Raz would always talk about going to the city to see some or other touring metal band. On several occasions he'd promised Ciara they would go, but then as the weeks drew closer he would renege and say he had no money, or that there was no point spending money on seeing bands when that time could be better spent improving Folical Dysfunktion. Raz always talked about the city and how familiar he was with its venues and even with some of its bands. He had not been boastful, but he would often make reference to things Ciara suspected he knew little about.

Meanwhile, she'd been starting to make her show exclusively about local metal bands, which meant that the bulk of it was dedicated to the primal tape recordings of Folical Dysfunktion. It was during this period that she'd started a small magazine about the town's metal music bands. She'd reviewed each of the demos she received, and had treated them with the same care that proper, studio-recorded music would receive in more established music magazines. She'd printed off copies of her magazine and left them in pubs, and sometimes she had lingered at the bar in order to witness someone pick up a copy and read.

Though touched, none of the metal people had taken her magazine seriously as it was too amateur, but they'd been happy to be interviewed for it. Her first interview was with Raz, who she'd described in the magazine as "the father of the town's metal scene". It was a very personal and revealing interview. They'd discussed many controversial topics, including Raz's attitude towards the people of the town, the town culture, drugs, and globally popular metal bands he believed did not pass muster. But when she'd printed the magazine he'd insisted she not distribute it, because he'd been too drunk during the interview to know how silly he sounded, and he did not want to offend the global metal bands in case they should obtain a copy. She also interviewed another band, friends of Raz's called Septic Rape, and also several other musicians in the circle who had never even recorded a cassette or played an instrument during one of Raz's parties.

Lacking the material to sustain a regular magazine based solely around local metal bands, Ciara had started to make things up. She'd created whole scenes and communities which did not exist, but which she'd dreamed about. This had a knock-on effect, as she'd needed to play the music created by these scenes and communities on her radio station in order to verify they were real.

Eventually she'd tried to distance herself from Raz, as she thought he was too much in love with her. She had learned all there was to know about the local metal scene, and none of it seemed very promising.

To corroborate the fake reviews and interviews she'd published in her magazine, she would play strange instrumental songs on a practice organ belonging to her parents, straight to air, without any rehearsal. Then she would back-announce each song, pretending they belonged to a cultish underground society in the town. She did not name the scene, nor the band names, as in this imaginary music scene the bands refused to have names, because they refused to believe they were entitled to exist. For each song, she would choose a different sound on the keyboard and run it through an old reverb pedal found at the second hand shop. Using this method, the music would sound ghostly and distant, she said, and somewhat similar to the music played on Friday Night Sounds back in the day.

Raz wouldn't let go. He would always call her at the radio station, even though she had told him to stay away. He had become obsessive, Ciara said, and would often raise his voice at her, frustrated that she refused to be his girlfriend. Raz believed this new "keyboard scene", as he'd termed it, had "stolen" her from his friend group, and he wanted to know who was in the scene and where they hung out. She'd lied that these tapes were sent to her anonymously.

Inevitably Raz turned up at the station premises. Being a community station that no one ever listens to, or even knows exists, there was no security nor any locks on the door. He'd stormed in and immediately saw Ciara's practice organ set up next to the mixing desk. Her secret had been discovered, but Ciara said she didn't feel ashamed. In fact, she was glad someone would finally see that it was her behind the keyboard scene all along. No one had ever suspected anything anyway, she supposed, since no one ever listened to her radio station or read her magazine.

Raz called her a slut, since he was very poor at expressing himself despite regular assurances during their relationship that he was in touch with his emotions. He did not lay a finger on Ciara or her keyboard, but instead left happy in the knowledge that she was not potentially sleeping with anyone in the keyboard scene, since it did not really exist.

Ciara thought it had all blown over until a couple of weeks later, when she'd received the first cassette ever submitted directly to her station pigeonhole. The cassette featured music very similar to her keyboard songs—simple childlike melodies made dreamy and dark thanks to lots of reverb and echo. She'd known it was Raz. She'd known he was trying to ingratiate himself with her because he loved her more than even his own life, as he never failed to remind her.

But the tapes had kept turning up, she said, and the handwriting on the mailbags was always different. The keyboard settings also seemed to vary dramatically, and she'd noticed slight differences in the amount of reverb and echo applied to each. In short, if Raz was pulling a trick on her, he was doing a very good job. Ciara didn't think Raz was smart enough, or musically talented enough, to pull off a trick that well.

It all made sense, or made even less sense, when Raz died. He'd thrown himself in front of the freight train and that was that: no more Raz. Nevertheless the cassettes kept arriving, and the music seemed to become more intricate and refined, until she'd started to believe that people might enjoy listening to them. Despite weekly attempts to contact these musicians directly, both on air and via fliers left in the pubs, Ciara had never made contact with any of the creators. Nevertheless, an endless supply of atmospheric keyboard music kept pouring into her pigeonhole. It could only have been produced by people in the town, she guessed, as it was difficult enough to find the frequency downtown, let alone anywhere else.

Ciara still reviewed the tapes in her magazine, except she was no longer making the artefacts up: they actually existed. She said she was capable of finding things in the music not already in her mind. Since none of the tapes had artist names or song titles, her magazine had become a catalogue of images and descriptions for music that was not accessible to anyone except listeners in her town. Someone, or many people, had heard her strange keyboard songs and chosen to follow in her footsteps. They must have been in the town, she said, but where?

Ciara had known everything about the town. She'd known each of its streets and every single one of its faces. She'd known what everyone liked, and she'd known what kind of things they did in their spare time. She'd known the types of cuisine they preferred, and she'd known what made them happy and the things that made them sad. The town was boring and annoying, Ciara said.

But she still hadn't known who was sending her the strange music. Might there have been other people out there trying to transcend the town? Or else, maybe people from the city were playing tricks on her. Maybe Ciara was famous in the city, or in another town with industrial-strength radio signals.

She never received requests or telephone calls during her radio show, but she continued to receive new tapes every single day. She said it was statistically likely that hundreds of people in the town were sending her tapes, but she didn't know who they were, nor why they did it. She couldn't even imagine what kind of house they would live in. Did they shop at the Woolworths or work at the McDonald's? Statistically, some of them probably did.

But I doubt they drive cars, she said.

———

One afternoon as I drank a beer Jenny made a passing reference to what she called the Town Extremists. She was conducting a postmortem on the town's special day, repeating all that Rob had said about the population's innocent appetite for destroying things. The annual orgy did not compare to shadier activities in the town, she said, namely the activities of people who hated the town and wanted to see it destroyed.

Jenny seemed to relish the contempt she reserved for the Town Extremists. According to her, they hated everything about the town, and yet they continued to live there. Not many people knew about the Town Extremists, but she did because she worked in a pub.

Jenny had become comfortable enough in my company to explain the blander aspects of the town—for example the football teams and the goings on at other, more popular pubs—but when it came to matters critical of the town she behaved as if I were trying to trick her into complaining.

According to Jenny the Town Extremists were hard-done-by anarchists. Even though they lived in the town and enjoyed all the benefits of being in the town, they hated it with a fiery passion. Jenny didn't know why they hated the town. They were just punks, malcontents, fools, or criminals.

She believed the Town Extremists were an organisation, rather than a disparate group of disaffected people. They might have held meetings to plot their next hateful move, whether it be petty acts of graffiti or full blown political orchestrations.

There was no doubt that it was a gang of some sort, she claimed. Their main yearly focus was the town's day, where they caused all manner of chaos, and she waved towards where the chaos had occurred. She'd seen a few of them loitering around the cordoned-off drinking area, scowling at the town and all it had achieved. They were always the ones who took things too far.

I was interested in tracking down the Town Extremists, but did not know where to find them. Rob didn't know about the Town Extremists, Ciara said they didn't exist, and Tom the bus driver acted surprised and insisted that he didn't live in the town—only around it—and that he was not concerned with town gossip any longer.

Don't ask me about specifics of the town, Tom said, because I no longer live there.

The librarian did know about the Town Extremists, but was adamant they didn't exist. The people in the town dream of resistance, he said. If there was a resistance, it would mean their existence was important to some other people, and that is what the town wants above all things.

Seated at the Michel's Patisserie across from the Big W, the librarian motioned at the people in the town, explaining. When someone dared mention something nice about another town, the people of the town would devise a response that made their own town seem better. If you pushed them hard enough, they would become violent in their defence of the town. It was only the young people who suspected the town was not all it was cracked up to be, but once they realised the rest of their lives would be spent there they'd rethink their attitude towards it.

It's true that there's no reason the town is here, he told me. There was no founder, there was no strange or noble history that the people could marvel at. The earliest recorded memory of the town was that lots of cattle died during the drought of the 1930s.

Whenever there was a drought, he said, people liked to point out that it could not possibly be as bad as the drought of the 1930s, even though droughts were getting worse. A drought could almost be as bad as the one from the 1930s—it could threaten to rival this worst drought—but no one dared suggest that it surpassed it. To do so was considered disrespectful.

As far as the townspeople were concerned, he told me, the town was more perfect in the past than it appeared to be now – in its ability to withstand tragedy and thus be noble. It was a comfort that events had occurred deserving of being remembered, if only by them, and if only this one particular thing. The librarian believed there was nothing noble about the town any-more. No one believed the town could have any new milestones. It could only become weaker, less charismatic, more remote from whatever made it supposedly respectable to begin with, and it was outside of their control. Who knew what kind of fate the rest of the world would impose on it, the librarian said. And yet, the more remote the town's so called legacy became, the more passionate the townspeople were to protect and evangelise it.

The librarian was adamant I'd never understand, since I was not of the town. On the rare occasion the national news cited the 1930s drought as an example of an especially severe drought, the townspeople were proud. When the MP who died of lung collapse was mentioned as a footnote in this or that political documentary on the TV, they were relieved to discover that somebody outside of the town—maybe someone who had never even visited—was thinking about them. It proved that the town was a town, a part of a greater area or country, somehow integral to something bigger than itself. It proved that the town existed. It proved they were a component in something which could be seen from afar. And their demonstrations of pride were cries to the rest of the country, or the world, that yes, we are here, and yes, we are important, but also, that they were in no way com-plicit in whatever terror awaited us all.

How would the town survive without this notion that it is important, the librarian wondered. How could it survive if the truth were known, and accepted? And anyway, he believed the truth of the town was uglier than we could imagine, even if no one knew what it was.

I asked the librarian if he was a Town Extremist, by dint of his negative opinion of the town, but he only frowned at me. No one could ever actually ruin the town, he said. Town Extremists or anyone else. The town would be there forever. The future of the town is that it will just continue to be a town.

———

Originally I had hoped to drink coffee in the Michel's Patisserie every day. It seemed to be the kind of habit strangers would keep in a town. I had hoped the waiters would remember my order and tell me stories about their day, and call me by my first name. I had hoped locals would initiate conversations about major events, and that they would draw me into their conversations with other locals, until finally I was part of a clique of decent townspeople. But I was not interesting to the people in the town. No one wondered where I had come from, and no one asked why I was there. I was just someone they didn't know. I did not meet new people in the Michel's Patisserie as I had hoped. Instead, I listened to people I had met elsewhere complain about the town while sitting in it.

One particular time at the Michel's Patisserie is memorable, because it was the afternoon before the first night I spent drinking beer with Ciara. She came to where I was sitting, bearing a plastic bag full of cassette tapes which she was distributing to secret locations around the town.

Ciara took a seat but did not order a coffee. It was silly to drink coffee at the Michel's Patisserie, she said, as the shop's specialties were pastries and cakes, not coffee. She carefully hid a cassette under a pile of coasters, then placed a sugar jar on top, and then shielded the tape from view with a plastic menu.

I told Ciara that Rob was drinking with his friends at the Grosvenor Hotel. I knew that they would not stop drinking until the game was over, at which point they would have post-game drinks. Ciara was aware but not interested; she was browsing the social pages in the local newspaper. The spread was packed with images of similar-looking men and women, all smiling at the camera unguardedly, dressed casually but in a manner which suggested they had put much thought into how they appeared. If the photos were real, then the people in the town had their nights in a jovial yet civilised fashion. Sometimes a man or woman would look more inclined to joke about the situation than others, but for the most part the people in the photos were politely attentive, as if in some form of dialogue with the next day's reader. You couldn't imagine them being anywhere else and they appeared to believe they belonged there, during that moment when the photographer decided they were emblematic of the town. Their faces inadvertently mocked me. The photos consecrated their belonging: made them historically and verifiably of the town.

I finished my coffee and accepted Ciara's invitation to help distribute the cassette tapes. We placed tapes in the central park's pergola, in the Commonwealth ATM foyer, at the foot of the Coles plaza escalator, between bowsers at the bottom BP, next to the windscreen wiper bucket at the middle Ampol, and among the newspapers at the Parkview pub, where we also picked up some longnecks from the bottle shop. Ciara wanted to have a beer after a job well done, and I wanted to stay with her in case she had anything to say about my book.

On the way to Ciara's house the sun went down and a light rain set in. Though it was Friday evening, there were few people in the pubs or restaurants and no one else in the street. At night, when the shop signs shone and the traffic lights blinked, the town seemed unusually alive, even though no one walked the streets. The night lights, scarce though they were, encouraged the idea that there were secrets to be learned about the town in the hours after sunset.

Ciara lived in a second-storey flat at a cross-street overlooking a petrol station. She poured us both beer into schooner glasses and we sat on the balcony, looking at the desolate town. For a long time we didn't talk about anything interesting. Ciara talked about the petrol station across the road because that was what we were looking at. Then she talked about the church opposite the petrol station, and then the small park opposite that, and then the pub opposite that. There was a lot she had witnessed in this small vicinity, during her life spent in the town.

When there was nothing left in our field of view to describe, Ciara fell silent. We replenished our glasses and I drank deeply, hoping to find the courage to broach the topic of my book. Ciara slouched in her chair, studying a loose thread on her sleeve. She did not look like anyone else in the town.

I bet Rob is roaring drunk by now, she said, lighting a cigarette.

I asked her why she was in love with Rob, but she said she wasn't. She was only experimenting with what it was like to have a boyfriend.

Men are depressing, she told me, if I didn't mind her saying so.

I agreed.

She intended to break up with him in two months. It was her plan to be his girlfriend for exactly six months. If no compelling reason to stay with him emerged during that time—which it hadn't yet—then she had promised herself she would break up with him.

I thought that was fair enough.

After a while, she asked me where I was from. I thought about it for a while. I tried to trace the highways east and west of the town in my mind, but my memory faltered at the shimmer. I could see the fields of canola but not the roads, and I vaguely remembered sadness in shallow hills and burned-off paddocks.

Thinking deeper, I could sense evidence of contempt inside me that I no longer understood. I had definitely come from somewhere, but where? These were memories just around the corner somewhere, almost within reach of full recollection. I remembered shades but no shapes, feelings but no locations.

I told Ciara that I didn't know where I was from.

She thought that was fair enough.

I went to buy more longnecks because we had run out. Arriving back at her flat, I found Ciara cooking instant noodles in the kitchen. Most of the walls in her flat were covered with makeshift, ceiling-high shelves bolted into the plaster, shelves full of unmarked cassette tapes. Every bench top and table surface was piled with cassette tapes too—boxed and unboxed, some with their dark brown entrails unspooled. Any parts of walls not lined with shelves of tapes were plastered with posters for secret concerts, though I recognised none of the bands or venues.

Ciara admitted to me when I asked that the posters were fake. Each was for a so-called secret show, and each poster invited people to ring her at the radio station for details of the event. She tore one off the wall and handed it to me.

The poster depicted a broad plain under a stormy sky. A large smudged moon floated to the left, near the band list, which comprised four lines of nonsensical text. She said she was always drawing grassy plains. Always a plain, always at nighttime, always with a moon at one side. It was a vision she sometimes saw briefly before sleep, appearing for a split second and then disappearing, and no matter how much she concentrated she could not evoke it deliberately. It occurred to her at random, and had for a long time.

I studied the picture. The drawing was primitive, yet the charcoal lines stirred a faint memory within me.

I wondered aloud if her vision was maybe the site of a disappeared town, gently steering the conversation in the direction of my book. Maybe everyone mourns disappeared towns. Maybe in the disappeared towns everything was exactly as people believe things are now. When you think of a disappeared town you can only believe what is widely held to be true for all towns, I announced. There can be no sordid truths, and nothing can be said by any of its inhabitants to defy the assumption that the town was good. You can deposit your good faith in disappeared towns. You can treat them as evidences that this town, and all of the other towns, and maybe even the city, were born of virtue. And that's especially important for you, I said, since your town has no history or basis for its pride at all. It's why the town culture is, in truth, nothing at all, or everything at once. We might not know exactly what defines it until it disappears.

When I finished my lecture, it was only a matter of seconds before I felt remorseful.

Ciara's noodles were so overcooked they'd turned into a gluggy soup, but she made a point of draining them anyway, and offered me a serving straight from the pan, since she only owned one bowl.

It's just a plain, she said eventually.

2

THE DISAPPEARING TOWN

The town had been getting larger over the years. It had stretched for as long as the people living there could remember, reaching outwards towards the shimmer, but falling short of a breach.

It was possible to approach the town from several directions, but only two counted, and the edges at both sides led into entirely different towns. The roads were the same, and the people were the same—it was the same town—but the vantage point mattered above all else, during the moments when a commuter would form their impressions. The first petrol station encountered would be the town: it would teach you all that was seemingly important about the town.

The petrol stations had changed throughout the years. As the prices increased on the signs out front and as the petroleum company emblems became more lurid, you would expect the town to be there for good. But it was another town on the road to some other town, or maybe a city, in one of the directions. Maybe it was just a highway. Perhaps the town at the edge of the road was not a town at all, but just a threadbare fabric of homes and shopfronts, sprinkled with petrol stations and stitched together by roads, where people happened to live.

———

With the money earned at Woolworths I accrued a pile of books and CDs. Every item I purchased, no matter which genre or style, seemed impossibly remote from my environment. None contained any of the moods or thoughts that might occur to someone living in the town.

The lives I found in these books and the sentiments I heard in the music belonged to regions carefully monitored and understood. The sentences and lyrics referred to conditions one could easily imagine encountering, by accident, at some unspecified time later in life. The existence of these situations in books and songs seemed to render them inevitable, because books and songs are about life — but nothing so crisply logical or neatly profound ever actually happened in the town.

On certain nights after my evening shifts the town would be drunk. The town would be drunk because it was Thursday, Friday or Saturday night, and sometimes I wanted to be drunk, too. The town got drunk in a listless way on these uneventful evenings, aware that every night would be forgotten. Or else the night would eventually meld into a final, vague memory of how it felt to be drunk in the town during that particular period in one's life.

During the moments when I peered into the windows of the main street pubs I wondered whether anyone was truly part of the town. Every weekend had the mood of a last hurrah; everyone drank as though they were departing for far-off destinations the next morning. That's how it seemed — and what else could they be drinking to? They drank like it was their duty. I suppose they were drinking to the fact that they were there.

In books and songs people gather and drink for reasons, and their lives bull-rush towards moments of importance. In these books and songs, meaninglessness is depicted too deliberately, and often hinted to have an origin or logic. The people in the town lived as if they would never die, but they were not heroic or foolish like in books and songs. They were only there. They seemed to understand better than anyone else that they were only there.

———

My book about the disappearing towns of the Central West of New South Wales underwent a series of dramatic changes during the period when I was still hopeful that I would finish it. I had taken to heart the little Ciara had said about my book. For a period I was certain that I could sweep away her opinions, just consider them uninformed, but when I finally assessed the matter I realised it was impossible to write a book about already-disappeared towns.

The path of least resistance was to write a book about the town instead, because it was a subject I was capable of researching first hand. So I started writing this book about the town one evening after my Woolworths shift, and called in sick to work for several nights in order to do justice to the energy I had found. Later, after listening to dictations of all I had written during that period of fervour, I felt elevated by a sensation I had never felt before. I believed that perhaps I would be able to write something correct about the town. Perhaps I would eventually complete a book featuring facts and impressions that not only I, and not only the people of the town, but potentially many other people, would be willing to accept as true.

But as the weeks passed, my vision of what the book would be inevitably soured. I began to feel a sensation of indescribable and unaccountable dread. I could not determine the origin of the dread, and it only seemed sensible to examine it from a distance, while shelving products at the supermarket. Dread seemed an important—albeit absent—feature in my book when I was not actively writing sentences, but as time passed I came to believe that it was important to pursue it in the text itself. After all, maybe everyone shared my feeling that the town was headed towards doom. Maybe the town would need to revise its notion of what it was.

———

A hole appeared in the town. One evening Rob lingered in the kitchen doorway as I was cooking my pasta. Eventually I acknowledged he was there, which prompted him to tell me about the hole.

There's a hole in the town, he told me. Everyone was going crazy about it. In the central park, near the town hall, where the town day's festivities were always held, there was a large hole, roundish, about two square metres at the mouth. It didn't seem to go anywhere.

The police had already gone to study the hole. They had set up yellow tape and would not permit anyone to get close to it. Nevertheless it was easy to see the hole from a distance because it was not a simple hole, not the kind that is dug with a shovel. Rather, it was a blankness in the turf, a blankness which appeared to have depth in every possible direction. It was more of an absence than a hole, neither black nor dark nor any other colour or shade. A part of the world had apparently just vanished.

Jenny was annoyed about the hole. She thought that some-one, or some people, were digging malicious holes. Why would anyone dig a hole in the park, she wondered. Kids and drunks could fall in and break their necks.

When I explained to Jenny that the hole was not a typical kind of hole, she refused to budge. Strange hole or not, someone had dug it, and if someone had dug it, it was because they hated the town. This is what the Town Extremists must have been cooking up, she muttered.

The hole was a talking point around town, and much of what was said echoed Jenny's sentiments: that it wasn't just a hole but something more malicious. A small minority, like Rob, believed it to be something supernatural.

Rob told me, as if referring to the worst of all crimes, that he'd spoken to a couple of people who'd stuck their arms and legs in the hole. They'd reported that it was no conventional hole: they'd said that anything that passed the threshold of the hole demate-rialised. Someone had wondered if it might have been possible to dive into the hole and then swim away and up, far away from the entry point, and never return to the surface again.

It was less a hole than a portal, Rob wagered. It was possi-ble that whatever was inside the hole was bigger than the town itself, maybe even the planet.

Rob and his friends all drank too much beer for me to take their word as fact, so I revisited the hole alone one Thursday night after my shift. The police weren't concerned enough about the hole to patrol it day and night – after all, it was just a hole. Yet when I arrived, many teenagers from the McDonald's car park were pegging objects at it from behind the yellow tape – beer bottles, cigarette lighters, fast food trash, and, at one point, a car radio wrenched from a nearby ute. There was a strange silence as they the tossed objects in. Nothing landed.

When the dozen-strong group realised my presence they fell silent. I pointed at the hole, and they stepped back to allow me a solitary moment with it. I had brought a curtain rod to test the depth of the hole. A voice jeered from the outskirts of the group, and then there were a few awkward giggles, and then there was silence.

Under the dim park lights, shrouded by a canopy of oaks, it was difficult to ascertain the colour of the hole. It definitely wasn't a rich black. It seemed to be like the colour seen behind closed eyelids. The hole's mouth resembled a pool rather than an entry point, in the way it merged with the surrounding terrain, and when I jabbed the rod into the hole the submerged length seemed to disappear altogether. I was not looking at a hole: I was looking at nothing at all. I retrieved the rod, plunged it in again, deeper, and when it hit nothing I almost tumbled in. The teenagers cheered as I regained my balance.

It's not your typical hole, one of the kids warned. Others murmured in the affirmative. I laid down flat at the edge of the so-called hole, shoved the curtain rod in, and then lifted it up towards the sky, but it raised no further than the perimeter would allow. Perhaps the hole was an entry point to something bigger, maybe a wide underground chasm, the dimensions of which were impossible to judge. Or maybe it was nothing at all.

The teenagers seemed relieved that I, an idiot out-of-towner, had dared break the yellow tape to get closer to the hole. One girl pushed through the crowd and tossed a bundle of rope towards me. Give this a go, she said. I grabbed one end and dropped the bundle into the hole. I felt no dull thud; the rope was neatly taut when it had fully unravelled.

It must go forever, then, the teenage girl said.

It took a whole minute to wind the rope back in. It was not dirty, nor did it show any other evidence of having met with a surface of any kind. When I reported this observation to the crowd none seemed impressed or surprised. It's not your typical hole, one said again.

That week Rob would regularly bring up the topic of the hole. He wasn't moved by my experience, and pretended that my discoveries were long established fact. He seemed determined to never know the truth about the hole – he only sought confirmation that the hole was not a typical hole. The question of what could have caused it was never discussed to any meaningful extent.

I've not seen anything like it in my whole life, Rob would say. Then we would stand in the kitchen for minutes at a time, making the same observations and repeating the same eyewitness reports in the hope that one of us might suddenly recall some new detail about the hole.

It's probably an environmental disaster, he would conclude, always seeming relieved.

The police tended to the hole lazily, occasionally replacing the yellow tape and infrequently circling the park in their paddywagons. It seemed that most people in the town were satisfied to write it off as a typical, if unusually deep, hole. It was only the teenagers, and the drunks, and the townsfolk predisposed to wonder, who relished discussing it. Teenagers continued to gather in the park in droves, while drunks in the old man pubs blandly speculated over who had dug it, usually deciding that it was someone who despised the town.

Even Ciara was reluctant to believe the hole was in any way mysterious, until one day when we visited it together after several hours spent distributing cassette tapes.

It's definitely not your typical hole, she said. It was mid-afternoon and there were no teenagers about. Only an old man and his mongrel stood at the edge of the yellow tape.

The hole was not a hole, I told Ciara. It was nothing. It wasn't that the earth had been removed and placed somewhere else: it had simply disappeared. I told her that we might have been looking at the first chunk of disappearance, and that it was unlikely to be the last.

I saw annoyance in Ciara's face. She had probably become fed up with my continual talk about my book. She might have thought I was trying to use the hole to my advantage. She might have thought I was trying to prove the point of my book.

It's logical, I told Ciara. The town had appeared for no apparent or recorded reason, and so it would disappear for no apparent or anticipated reason. Yet despite the town having no reason, somewhere along the way it established a notion of itself, and this endured without resistance. That is why the town is a town. But it's not enough to be in a place for no reason, I said. There must be a reason, and if there must be a reason, it should be a good one. The logic was so foolproof that it was no surprise to me, upon closer analysis, that the town had started to disappear.

That's a very artistic way of putting it, Ciara said, and tossed a cassette tape into the hole.

———

Ciara told me there were other holes in town, but all their origins were known. For many years, a group of teenagers had spent most weekday afternoons excavating a vacant plot of land located between a disused nightclub and one of the highway petrol stations. From the street, graffitied wooden boards hid this muddy commercial lot that had come to resemble a fledgling mining operation. Some of the dirt mounds were so high they were visible from the street, and old enough that grass had sprouted on their peaks. One afternoon Ciara led me through a hole in the back fence into the heart of the operation, where half a dozen boys and girls in their early teens shovelled dirt onto their own personal hills.

Some time before, when Ciara was the same age as the diggers, she herself had spent a couple of months aiding the operation. For teenagers of a certain persuasion, it was the place to be. If you weren't satisfied with the town, but couldn't pinpoint what was unsatisfactory about it, digging holes was what you ended up doing.

The teenagers didn't pay us much attention as we wandered the roped paths between their digs. Each hole had a bucket next to it and each bucket was empty, save one girl near the nightclub who had unearthed a fountain pen.

They're digging for artefacts, Ciara said. They're looking for evidence of something. It's a natural impulse among young people. Before she'd met the metal music fans, and before she'd started publishing her magazine, she had spent her afternoons in the vacant lot digging. It was an interesting thing to do, because no one knew what kind of treasure awaited beneath the soil, although surely there must have been something.

According to Ciara, the elderly of the town were always saying things weren't what they used to be, or else describing great characteristics of the town that no longer seemed to be true. Frowning at one of the vacant lot's holes, Ciara insisted that she had never searched for evidence of any of that. Maybe she had intended to prove that none of it was true, and that things hadn't changed for the worse after all.

She knelt and picked up a shard of cement. She did often wonder what they dug for. Was it possible that everything good about the town was a thing of the past? Ciara first visited the digs when she was twelve, and had hoped the operation was about discovering the secrets of the town, but the truth was different: there didn't seem to be any motive among the teenagers, they simply dug because others had dug before them. The meaning of the digging had been lost along the way, and Ciara suspected there might not have been a meaning to begin with. Besides, it barely mattered anyway—and she motioned towards the contemporary diggers—because there was satisfaction to be derived from it.

Everything about the town rested on belief, Ciara believed, but whose belief could they trust? Certainly no one older than us, she said. The diggers didn't care about Anzac day yet, nor Australia Day, nor the town's day. They would though, one day, and that's why they'd stop digging. Once they'd acquired a taste for less important things, they would become a part of the town.

The girl with the exhumed fountain pen stopped digging. She stared, but was chastened when Ciara picked up the pen. She waited for an assessment, slapping the dirt from her hands onto her thighs.

The pen was marked in gold with the word 'Cadia', with a phone number and a little picture of a gleaming nugget. Ciara surmised that there had been a gold mine around town in the olden days, and this vacant block of land had been its headquarters.

The girl looked disappointed. Obviously various shops and offices had existed there in the past. What else could there have been, she said, between the old nightclub and a petrol station? She didn't believe it was an exciting conclusion at all, but Ciara did, or at least she pretended to. It was a small clue towards solving the mystery of the mines. Though there was definitely no need to stop digging, because there might be even more to find.

It's just a pen, the girl retorted. She retrieved a crumpled document from her pocket, listing a dozen or so business names they'd found on fountain pens. Some business names were accompanied by sketched logos and mascots. Just a bunch of companies: real estates, solicitors, accountants.

When Ciara was a digger she only made one interesting discovery. She'd dug over near the petrol station every afternoon. Sealed in a plastic bag, her discovery was a professionally printed magazine called *Foreseen*. It was full of images of horizons, most likely horizons in the area, she guessed. They were relatively flat expanses, sometimes with a calmly sloping hill.

There was no text in the magazine, but one image endured in her memory. It was the only image featuring a tree. At first she had assumed the images were drawings or paintings, because the emptinesses had an alien quality. This image with the tree, though—a stripped gum standing in the distance slightly to the right—was chilling because it confirmed the images were not illustrations but in fact photographs. They were photographs of plains that seemed too still and featureless to be real. How did the photographer access this environment? And where was it?

And why would someone make a whole magazine featuring only landscape photos, and unremarkably flat ones at that? It did not seem like an artistic magazine. It was not attributed to anyone, nor did the photos seem ripe with some complex significance or motive. It felt like a product of the soil, like the dirt was memorialising itself, relishing ancient examples of its uninterruptedness.

Over time Ciara had learned of some of these mysteries in the town, such as Friday Night Sounds and this *Foreseen* magazine, but they belonged in the past and there was no way to retrieve them. Ask anyone in the town, she said, and they will claim that everything was better at some unspecified period in the past, and while their claims could never be substantiated it was difficult to disprove them. Any effort to make things better again seemed futile. And so she wondered, what was the point in doing anything at all? If she had children they would likely live a life more terrible than hers. If she wrote a book or made an album, or a film, it would not serve to explain the time in which she lived, because, soon enough, everyone would be dead. And before even that happened, everyone would hate her anyway, hate the town, hate everything she and they had ever stood for and didn't stand for. She was an obvious target for such hate, because she had read articles that warned things were getting worse, whereas other people might not have read anything like that at all.

Maybe that's why they dug: because the wick was almost burned to its end and the future would be horror. Based on what was happening on the news and what happened when she started to research the magazine *Foreseen*, that was what she believed. She tossed her chunk of cement away.

When she had showed *Foreseen* to her dad, he'd turned it in his hands and flicked through its pages, before deciding that it was some form of propaganda. He'd agreed it wasn't art, though also believed it must have been. What else could it be? He'd said it was full of subliminal messages, and when she asked what subliminal messages could possibly be embedded in pictures of grassy horizons, he'd replied that he could not know because they were subliminal. Chances were, they had both already been infected with the messages, and while they could object to the magazine as strongly as they liked, it didn't change the fact that they had absorbed something potentially noxious. It was too late. It was already shifting blocks around in their brains. He'd confiscated the magazine from her.

When she'd stolen it back she took the magazine to the library, where the librarian had said it was just some art. It might not be art, she'd replied. They couldn't possibly know the intention of the person who made the magazine. When she'd asked how he was so certain it was art, he'd seemed taken aback.

He'd said it was art because it didn't have a clear meaning. He'd supposed it did have a meaning, but based on Ciara's inability to find one there was no question whether it was art or not: it obviously was. The librarian refused to speculate about what the meaning of this so-called art was. He had to think about it. He'd told her you have to think about art, sometimes for many consecutive days. Ciara had already thought about the magazine and had decided, based on what she could understand after many hours studying it, that it wasn't intentionally meant to be art.

As we walked past the bottle shop Ciara lingered outside, in a manner which suggested I should buy us some longnecks. I bought four longnecks of Sheaf Stout and we walked to her flat.

The librarian had said to Ciara that it didn't matter whether *Foreseen* was intentionally art or not. He'd claimed everything became art eventually. Everything in the past becomes art, but generally not of an interesting kind. He believed it was a person's right to determine what was art and what wasn't. He was passionate about this, arrogantly so, and yet he hadn't been able to explain how he had arrived at his belief, nor why she should feel the same way.

Ciara had no luck finding someone who could tell her what the magazine *Foreseen* was – everyone she'd asked just concluded it was art, as if that ended the discussion. Few were happy about it being art, but all were confident that it was. She'd felt prevented from accessing the truth of what *Foreseen* might have been. Ciara had wanted it to not be art. She'd wanted something strange to exist that wasn't just art.

We poured two schooner glasses of the syrupy beer and sat on her balcony.

Ciara had lost the magazine *Foreseen*. She swore she'd left it on her bed one morning. She'd turned the whole room over looking for it.

———

It became a routine for me to follow Ciara around as she left cassette tapes in hiding spots around town. During the early afternoon, before school broke at three, the town belonged to both the elderly and the nine-to-five chore-runners, who paid us no attention. Mothers roamed the plazas too, but they were too distracted by their young children. No one noticed as we secreted cassettes into the shopping plaza prize draws, in the folds of telephone box Yellow Pages, and among the pamphlets at the Westpac and National banks. Sometimes Ciara would wander away from the central district, into the streets of ancient townhouses and colonial homes that cost so much nowadays, and then into the modest brick and weatherboard blocks towards the tentacle roads. Ciara believed she knew the layout of each of these homes just looking at them. She claimed to know all their smells, the toast and coffee, the bleach, and sometimes the dust. The colours inside, the layouts, the floral furniture angled towards the television, the coffee tables with remote controls and NRMA magazines – it was all inevitable. Looking at the front of homes in the back streets of the town, it was easy to tell what kind of families lived inside. Rather too easy, Ciara believed.

It might be true that the Town Extremists are men and women from houses just like these, I said. Maybe they hide in plain sight, and maybe we know someone belonging to them. Perhaps Rob is a Town Extremist, I joked to Ciara. Perhaps the mayor is secretly a Town Extremist.

Ciara would happily have counted herself among the Town Extremists. There were definitely people fed up with the town, she said, but who was angry enough to sabotage it? She suspected that if there ever really were Town Extremists, they'd existed in the past, during a time when there'd seemed to be more at stake in life. No doubt there had been a handful of reasons to be a Town Extremist, back then. Whatever they had been against then – it had won. What could the town be if it wasn't what it was, right at that moment?

Maybe *Foreseen* was a Town Extremist text, Ciara said. She hadn't given much thought to the Town Extremists. She just thought it was what old people called the young, the ones who drank cask wine in the streets at night, bringing property prices down, stealing road signs and setting wheelie bins alight. They were the only Town Extremists she could point at. Mitch and Debbie at White's Real Estate could have been Town Extremists once, she said, waving towards White's Real Estate. As we walked down a quiet back street she pegged a cassette over a roof and into the backyard of a nearby home. As we stopped to hear it land, something appeared in the nearby gutter, close to the front wheel of a Mazda. A dark absence. Ciara squatted and dipped her arm into the hole, left it there for a moment, and then pulled it back out.

It's not your conventional hole, she said.

Ciara and I wandered to the southern outskirts of town, like we sometimes would, where none of the tentacle roads had been paved. Across the railway line, past the gasworks and through the neighbourhood where the poor people lived, the town seemed reluctant to surrender to the countryside beyond. Past a paddock strewn with rusted old freight carriages and piles of corrugated iron, ruins of ceased construction stretched all the way to the Bunnings Warehouse on the horizon, which squatted awkwardly on the highway leading east.

How do we know when we've left the town, I asked Ciara. Where is the official boundary of the town, and is it visibly noticeable, or just an arbitrary line on a government map? Could it be true that we were all part of the same city, the coastal city, and that this is just part of some remote and forgotten suburb? Ciara knew of an official boundary, though. It was many hundreds of kilometres west, a long and deep stretch of mountain that served to emphasise the difference between the city and everything that lay far beyond.

As we gazed at the Bunnings, Ciara admitted she'd never been to the city. She knew that life was harder there. She knew it was more expensive. She knew you needed to be rich in the city, that you needed to be smart and ruthless, cold-blooded almost. More so now than at any time in the past, she said. That's what her parents had warned, and even though they didn't agree with her apocalyptic beliefs, they still appeared to believe things were getting worse.

We smoked there for a while and watched the cars on the distant highway, thin at that time of day. Then we walked back to town, in silence because it was too hot for any effort. We drank four longnecks on her balcony that night, staring at the petrol station, as Ciara related her dire predictions. An ancient Walkman connected to old computer speakers aired the delicate sound of her music over the empty crossroads.

Later we entered the teenage excavation site. Ciara dug small holes inside the larger dug ones, then dropped cassettes and buried the dirt back in. She also left copies of a small booklet created especially for the teenage diggers, but she wouldn't permit me to read it.

———

Rob finally asked why I was spending so much time with Ciara. I replied in as matter-of-fact a tone as possible that it was because she was interested in my book about the disappearing towns. This did not seem to satisfy him. He asked directly whether I was in love with Ciara, to which I replied that I was not, and that it was offensive he would suspect it. Feigning hurt did not work on Rob, and he continued to press me on the matter, albeit in as subtle a way as he could manage. He asked what Ciara said about him, and I told him that she didn't speak much about their relationship at all, since our conversations were largely about the contents of my book.

Ciara doesn't care about books, he said.

As a matter of fact she does, I replied. Her favourite book was called *Foreseen* – it was something he should know, I insinuated, though if he didn't like books it was only natural that they hadn't discussed it, I also carefully insinuated.

Rob said he'd only been going out with Ciara for five months, so it was unfair to expect him to know every single thing about her. He knew more than I did, though. He knew enough to know that she needed looking after. I didn't know her situation, and it was dangerous that I didn't. He wouldn't tell me her situation though, because he believed it was between him and Ciara. When I said I knew her situation he insisted I didn't, otherwise I'd know it wasn't wise to confide in her about stupid things like my book.

I asked Ciara what her situation was, having realised I'd never done so before, to which she replied she didn't have one. She had moved out of her parents' home a year ago, and since then had squatted in the flat with the balcony. In exchange for a packet of cigarettes she'd convinced an old school acquaintance turned apprentice electrician to connect the flat to the electricity grid, and so lived with little requirement for money. She stole discarded bread from the Bakers Delight loading dock every evening, and that was her diet.

She saw no point in getting involved with work. Maybe if she lived in the city, where it was possible to get an interesting job, she would see the point. In the town people inherited work from their relatives, or else they pumped petrol, or stacked shelves or beeped through groceries at the supermarkets. Or else they dug holes along the highway for the council. What was the point of any of that? She didn't want to go to university—and she waved easterly—because there was no point learning anything that was officially true, anymore.

Rob wasn't actually aware of Ciara's situation. When I repeated what she'd told me he seemed disturbed.

So she's basically homeless, he said.

I replied that technically, Ciara was homeless, unemployed, and a bin scrounger to boot.

Rob said she was lying. Her parents paid her way. They lived in a mansion, apparently, and he waved towards where he believed the tentacle roads were.

Everyone lives in mansions in this town, I said. Though they're not very expensive mansions.

Rob said she didn't seem homeless. She was just off with the fairies a bit, like an artist. He waved at a basket of cassettes sitting in the corner of his bedroom. He found them everywhere, but didn't have any way to play them. And anyway, he didn't mind that she was into all that stuff. He believed he could help her, look after her, all of that. He could have been going out with a normal woman, but instead he chose Ciara. His life was an example for her. It would rub off eventually, and she would see the sense in just getting on with it. He was trying to help her, whereas I—and he pointed at me—only wished to indulge her childish side. Look at you, a man of your age working as a packer at the supermarket and writing a book. You don't even know what your book is about, and half the time you're out talking about your book with Ciara rather than writing it.

He told me I was wasting my life, that I was a lonely person writing a stupid book. No one would ever read it, and I wouldn't even have a wife or a kid who could pretend to like it. And anyway, what if I never finished it? What if I never finished anything? He said I probably wouldn't, because the book was incompletable unless I just made stuff up. No one buys books anymore, no one is interested in non-existent towns, no one is interested in whatever I, in particular, had to say about them. It was just a lifestyle. I was too cowardly to live like everyone else because at some point, someone probably told me I was better than everyone else. I belonged in the city with all the other tryhards, not in the town. We in the town just get on with it.

He asked me if it had been my mum who'd told me to write a book. Or was it your high school English teacher? Fuck them both, he said, and he made to leave the room. Get a real job and leave my girlfriend alone.

I didn't ask Ciara whether Rob's interpretation of her situation was true. I didn't need to, because I believed her. I also knew that she did not want to ever be married to Rob, since she was only experimenting with what it was like to have a boyfriend.

The next afternoon she and I wandered past one of the three northern petrol stations in the town. Even during the quieter hours of a day, the lanes in the stations wore queues at least two vehicles deep. Each car leaked the sound of the regional commercial radio station, with its buoyant announcers offering free petrol and Subway vouchers.

I asked Ciara why she was bothering experimenting with having a boyfriend. She thought she might have missed a realisation that had come naturally to everyone else – that maybe there was a transformation that everyone knew about, that occurred in everyone else, a turning point so obvious it wasn't worth describing. Maybe that's why everyone in the town seemed so unaccountably satisfied, she said. Maybe the routine of partnering up with someone caused the future to be viewed in a more favourable light. She butted her cigarette in the dirt of the nature strip. She had allowed for this possibility, hence her experiment, but as far as she could tell, there was no longer any reason to imprison ourselves.

Anyway, if she were to tell Rob exactly how she felt about the world, and by extension how she felt about him, he would be repulsed. He would try to fix her at first, but then, when he learned it was impossible, he would leave her, but only when it suited him. Rob didn't have the guts to be alone, Ciara said. He was a pathetic man, scared of any waking moments he found himself in solitude. She wondered what he would do when he realised the world doesn't care about him. He's still young enough to think there will always be someone to help. He thinks he's invulnerable. He thinks that life is all about just getting on with it. He thinks he's okay because he's a normal Australian bloke who likes to have a beer or two every night in front of the TV. But his comfort won't last, Ciara said, and he knows it, just like everyone else secretly knows it, most strongly when they are forced to assess the evidence during those moments they accidentally allow their minds to focus on the matter. Who's going to look out for him when things heat up a bit? The government wants nothing more than to shed its liabilities, and everyone else will be too busy surviving, most of all the elderly, most of all our parents. The elderly don't care how happy he is. They only want for him to leave them alone, now that he's an adult. As long as he doesn't disrupt them, they are happy to forget him. But he doesn't yet realise he's an adult. He doesn't realise that in as little as three or four years, his drinking will be seen as a problem, not a mark of youth. He'll soon realise that if he keeps working at the petrol station, he'll feel inadequate and useless around people who have much better jobs. He doesn't realise that his childish optimism will soon run dry.

Ciara knew that if she were to tell Rob that she didn't want children, he would think she was just being a punk. He would think she'd eventually come around to the idea. But she believed that children from now on would not have adulthoods like hers or her parents. They could not move to the city, because that is where things are getting worse faster. People might be wiser to cower in towns. Maybe they wouldn't be so devastated when the sea water rose. Maybe when everything became desperate, a small town would finally live up to the qualities that everyone believed them to have: namely, that everyone would help one another out. Maybe the town would have tea parties during the apocalypse, while people in the city tore each other to shreds.

But Ciara doubted it. Everyone in the town loved a good fight.

———

No one worried about the holes much until the next town disco. Held on the first weekend of each season, it was the town's most important regular social event. According to Jenny, young people in the town would become anxious each time it approached, because it was a dangerous disco: any grievances that had fomented over the course of the previous season would inevitably come to a head at the disco, and for many weeks the town was busy with gossip about who would get bashed up, why they would be bashed up, and whether or not the bashing was deserved. Young people went to hook up and to brawl, Jenny said. Everyone knew that was all it was about. It had been like that when she had been a girl, too.

The disco was held in the town hall next to one of the four central petrol stations. Weeks in advance there were photocopied signs hung on street poles around the town, but they were less advertisements than pre-emptive admonishments: they cautioned that no excessive drinking and no fighting would be tolerated.

The town's disco. First Friday of Winter. Five dollars entry. No fighting and no excessive drinking will be tolerated, the sign warned, decorated with images of cartoon balloons, confetti and treble clefs.

Although I was busy writing my book, and although I mostly kept to myself in the town, it was impossible to avoid the rumours and speculation that surrounded the disco. Everyone spoke about it at the Woolworths, for example, and all of the workers were excited about the potential for an especially charged confrontation between Teresa Mayweather and Stacey Kemp. It was impossible to glean from conversations what had caused the conflict, as explanations were rife with references to many previous conflicts, between entirely different people, for seemingly unrelated reasons. Besides, everyone had their own version of the tale. All I could establish was that Teresa Mayweather had it in for Stacey Kemp, and that Stacey Kemp didn't understand the fuss but that she would defend herself to the death, and so would her friends, and so would theirs, and so on. Town opinion was split on whether Stacey Kemp really understood the fuss or not – some believed she was faking not knowing. Every detail of the conflict was cause for scrutiny. It was sizing up to be one of the biggest fights the town had ever boasted, according to Jeff at the Woolworths.

Ciara said Rob wasn't going to the disco, on the basis that it would only be attended by people of the town. Rob had told her that he thought the music lame, the town hall lame, and all the people who attend it lame too. The town's disco was lame.

Ciara invited me to come along with her instead. I agreed, because I wanted to see the brawl.

As we walked along the unusually alive main street, Ciara explained that Teresa Mayweather and Stacey Kemp had been the talk of the town for months, even before I had arrived. The trouble between them had been brewing for several discos, but the main fight that has been going for years involved a dispute between the Brewster boys and Ken Travis. The Teresa Mayweather and Stacey Kemp situation was related to that conflict, but Ciara wasn't certain how. No one was certain, except maybe the fighters themselves, but she suspected that they had lost track too.

One thing was certain: there was always one major conflict at the town disco. There may have been others, but they occurred between lesser people about whom no one cared. There had been efforts by people unrelated to the Brewsters, the Travises, the Mayweathers, the Kemps, and all their associates, to escalate their own conflicts so that they might be the star attraction of the town disco, but none had ever been successful. The main fight had been going for many years after all, maybe for as long as the town had existed, and no one knew what started it, only that it continued, and that the reasons seemed to change from season to season.

When we reached the hall, teenagers and young adults milled the footpath in front of the disco, slung over vehicles, smoking cigarettes. Most smirked at me because I was not of the town. These teenagers radiated the town from their very bodies, but in the company of Ciara I would not be antagonised. And perhaps she would help me blend in. She told me she was boring to the people at the disco.

We pressed through the crowded foyer into the dimly lit hall. A faded portrait of Queen Elizabeth hung above the entry to the canteen, and a delicately carved list of war veterans was bolted to the wall above the counter. Like all old buildings in the town, the hall smelled faintly of dust and cigarette smoke, and it was easy to feel transported to whichever era the town most preferred that day. The young people gathered in cliques, shouting to hear over the music, but Ciara stood deliberately away from everyone else, in a barren corner by the toilets. It was the farthest from the canteen and in full view of the DJ: a bald man standing behind a tower of CD players. Although alcohol was forbidden at the town disco, it was widely accepted that people smuggled their own in, and illicit substances too. The canteen only sold chips, lollies, and canned Coke, the latter sold at a premium because it was only ever drunk as a mixer for rum.

Ciara yelled into my ear that fights generally occurred in the middle of the dance floor. She said there was usually a bit of preliminary bickering out in the smoking area, but if we went out to watch the prelude we'd lose our vantage point and miss the main event.

It was annoying to have to yell over the loud music, so we stood with our arms crossed surveying the room. Red, green and blue lights pulsed, sometimes illuminating a face among the people gathered, and often shining light on contraband liquor flasks. The young people stood in packs at the outskirts of the dance floor, barely moving at all. Some feigned conversation, while others were satisfied to stare at everyone else. From my vantage point, and in that particular room, the town felt like the centre of the world, or at least it seemed held at an impossible distance from anywhere else. The motives implied by each of the townspeople's expressions seemed driven by desires and secrets that could take lifetimes to parse. The town disco seemed pivotal and they all wanted something out of it. How could the rest of the world not know the town's disco, and what could be got there?

The music at the town's disco was typical of commercial radio at the time, and did not hold any secrets as far as I could tell. It was the same music that emanated softly from each petrol station, from the shopfronts at the plazas, and loudly from the fast food shops along the highway to the city. Whether aggressive, sentimental, or sexual, the songs did not seem applicable to the true condition of the town – though what songs would be better I could not say. I supposed the country albums at the library, full of songs about hard work and living off the land, were ostensibly about the town.

The postures of the men and women at the town disco appeared carved by this universal music. No one danced, but they turned their bodies receptively towards the front of the room, allowing the music to shape them in some subtle way. The music was mostly brash and extravagant American pop: didactic, obscene, and colourful. The reality of the music was remote—whole unthinkable oceans away—but it nevertheless appeared to serve its purpose as a frame for their experience. For the people in the town, music did not exist to mirror them, but instead, for the people to mirror it. Or at least the people seemed to try to live up to it, subconsciously, with their bodies turned towards the speakers, and their faces aloof to the strange ambience. They seemed to try, driven by the unacknowledged truth that no songs they listened to were really about the town, or about them, or about the vast stretches of land that buffered them from anywhere and everyone else.

Or maybe they did not try at all, and not trying was the comfort. They might have resigned themselves to phenomena always skipping over them. The brash American music may have been about the world, but how can a slice of world so tiny as the town be a part of all that? It was a miracle the music had travelled this far without losing any of its lustre, or without losing its form entirely.

Ciara and I took turns visiting the smoking area. In the dark alley shrouded with smoke, cliques drank from their flasks openly, stealing glances at all the other cliques. The air was thick with unspoken politics, and each wore their signature gestures, some subservient to others, others entitled to certain liberties. Some apologised profusely when a toe was trodden in the crowded area, while others simply grunted. The smokers appeared even more of the town than those inside, their accents thicker, their faces redder, their gestures and body language more encumbered. I knew they watched me. At moments when I could see through the smoke I saw eyes monitoring me with a bland curiosity, their postures poised to gain prime position for any spectacle I might be at the heart of.

When I reached the entrance of the clear standing space, I was told I couldn't stand there. A woman pushed me firmly, and then pointed down as every smoker watched. I was standing at the edge of a hole. Everyone casually flicked their cigarette ash into it, like it was a newly installed facility. The woman warned me not to say anything to anyone about it, because if the managers knew about the hole they'd clear the smoking area and no one would be able to smoke.

Back inside, I told Ciara about the hole. It's likely someone will fall into it tonight, I said, because the smoking area was so densely packed that people balanced treacherously at the hole's edges. She didn't really care, though. Wherever the hole lead, it must surely arrive back. Besides, she said, we've got more important things to think about. She pointed out the door at a figure who was now smoking in the smoking area. That's Steve Sanders.

It was difficult to see his face through the wall of smoke, but he appeared to have lost weight, and in a standing position seemed taller than I had estimated at the Railway Hotel. He wore a similar outfit, but instead of a football jumper with an upturned collar, it was a dress shirt with an upturned collar. All these months I had been monitoring my field of view for evidence of a shorter, plumper man, and I had been wrong.

Steve Sanders already knew I was there, because Ciara had seen him spot me. She thought that it was a fine idea to let the bashing happen – the most sensible thing was to just get it over with. But not at the disco – it wouldn't be good for it to happen at the disco because if there was a dispute at the town disco, follow-up disputes were inevitable. By being bashed at the disco I risked becoming the talk of the town, and once I became the talk of the town, I was doomed to an eternal revisiting of the situation.

Before I had a chance to weigh up my options, the shrill beginnings of a fight could be heard over the music. The crowd outside churned in its direction, carrying Steve Sanders out of my line of sight. Ciara held my wrist to stop me from joining the swarm, though I'd never intended to leave our vantage point, for fear of being bashed.

They're having their preliminary argument, Ciara yelled over the noise. For ten minutes it would be nothing more than name-calling and threats. Then one person would storm off through the dance floor, pretending to be above the spectacle of a fight, prompting the other party to chase and punch their foe from behind. Someone always got punched or tackled from behind, Ciara said. That was how it always started. That was the routine of it.

Soon enough a frazzled girl stormed into the hall towards the foyer. Another sprinted in pursuit and tackled her to the ground. The room converged on the event, and so did we, though it was soon obvious only a privileged few would see the fight blow-by-blow. Splinter fights sparked out of the struggle as we pressed our way towards the central conflict, many relishing the opportunity to flail their limbs anonymously. Those not involved in any specific dispute looked ecstatic, eyes bulging and mouths gaping wide, malicious voyeuristic smiles grinning at the audacity of it all. Ciara was not aloof to any of this. She blended in with the crowd, pressing her forearms against the bodies in front, and I saw her jeering too.

Three elderly men with tucked in polo shirts stalked the periphery of the crowd, dragging boys and girls out at random and pushing them away into the foyer. The lights poured on, dousing the flushed red faces in a clinical white, and the music stopped. Muffled screams emanated from the centre of the brawl while the spectating men droned their incitements. I was kicked in the face somehow, and I had no desire to discover who did it, keen as I was to keep pressing forward in the hope that it might happen again. The languor of the town had lifted, and no one wanted to waste the opportunity.

Someone yelled that one of the girls was biting the other, and the pushing intensified.

I was having no luck reaching a prime viewing position, and Ciara had drifted away. Men and women palmed me in the face as they staked their claim on my ground, and as I renewed my efforts to gain a vantage point I felt the tide of the fight carry us away, far from the dance floor and towards the smoking area. I had blood on my left hand and I did not know to whom it belonged.

The fight poured through the smoking area's doorway. Standing back, exhausted and elated, I watched as the townspeople tried to barge through the chokepoint. For those that remained inside, the transformation had already occurred and that alone would have to be enough. Circumstances had rendered them innocent.

For those who did succeed in making it outside, it was only because they were victors of their own lightning-quick and brutal fights, showdowns to determine who was strong enough to stay with the horde. It quickly became impossible for anyone else to stand in the smoking area. Men and women took to climbing the people closest to the doorway. There was so much adrenaline in my body that I considered doing the same, until I saw Ciara curled up in a ball by the empty canteen.

She smiled as I tried to help her, pushed me away, dusted herself off, and punched me hard in the collarbone. I took her shoulders and shook them gently, and then shook them much harder. She punched me in the chest, ran towards the smoking area, climbed the human barrier, and disappeared. I hesitated only for a moment before following her.

No one was surprised or angry that we climbed across their heads and shoulders, and it didn't take long before we reached the edge of the crowd and could mount the roof of the hall, where at least a dozen spectators sat with their legs dangling over the edge. More tranquil groups sat on the slanted corrugated iron roof, arranged in circles sharing cigarettes and rum, seemingly numb to the action below. Even from that high vantage point it was hard to find the Teresa Mayweather and Stacey Kemp fight, so packed was the crowd.

Besides, there was a more compelling spectacle now: over in the far corner figures were blundering into the hole. I pointed this out to Ciara and she laughed, yelled that someone would have to fish them out later. Then she jumped into the crowd below, landed gently on the surface of skulls, and disappeared into the ocean of limbs.

The police had arrived outside the hall. When I peeked over the corrugated iron roof I could see two police approaching the entry, the hapless doormen buzzing in a panic around them. Soon the rooftop crowd noticed the familiar blue and red flashing lights and jumped off just as Ciara had, leaving only me and one other man on the roof. The other man was Steve Sanders, I think.

I pointed to the hole and at the people blundering into it. We should take action, I warned. We should intervene, we should work together. We're better equipped than anyone to plan an intervention, from this tactical vantage point. The man I took to be Steve Sanders snarled, acknowledged that it was just he and I on the roof, that there was no one to watch whatever happened between us, and pushed me aside. He ran and jumped into the smoke below.

I'll get you later cunt, he barked as he dropped, and the crowd cheered.

I crawled to the far side of the roof and dropped into the yard of a terrace below. Then I climbed another brick wall and landed onto the tarmac of a petrol station. From that distance the disco sounded like a party, remarkable only for the cries of terror that rang out occasionally, presumably from those closest to the hole. I straightened my clothing and walked as innocently as possible to the front of the building. There, a small crowd of elderly men and women wondered what the fuss was about. I felt forlorn and excluded, standing outside and away from the action.

One of the elderly women said that it sounded like that Kemp girl got what was coming for her.

The police were dragging random disco-goers out by their necks, pushing them to the curb and ignoring them as they fled. As I started to formulate a plan to gain entry back into the disco, Ciara was thrown onto the footpath by an angry doorman.

Run off, dog, he yelled at her. She grabbed my wrist and ran up towards her flat, and a block or two later the world was silent.

They're all fighting, Ciara cried, excitedly. Not all of them, but most of them.

I said it had been obvious what was going to happen. There would be one woman getting her lights knocked out and she was doomed from the start. It had been a surprise to me that no one had come to her aid, such was her disadvantage.

She was copping it, that was for sure, Ciara agreed. Maybe it was true she didn't know what the fuss was about.

———

The shops in the main streets were all closing. Dust set in thickly, brochures and mail littered stoops, and signs lost their colour beneath the gloom of rusted awnings. These losses did not register with the townspeople: they wandered the air-conditioned plazas, entering and exiting via escalators from dark undercover car parks.

For weeks the council patrolled the streets, boarding up all the holes they could find. At first they tried filling them with concrete from big round trucks, but the concrete never filled to the top, and they wondered whether it was even landing. Then they poured trailers and trailers of sandbags in, but there weren't enough sandbags to fill a single hole. So they resorted to blocking the holes with boards. The thin chipboard planks they used never sat quite flush, instead appearing to float just above ground level. No matter how firmly men secured them or weighed them down, the colour of nothing leaked at the edges. And by the morning the boards had always fallen in.

The council and the town gave up. The holes would have to be a new fact for the town. The ground they had gobbled up and were continuing to gobble up was unsalvageable. They presented no serious threat.

Then they started to consume furniture, and thoroughfares, and places where people might sometimes want to stand. It was no longer possible to enter Fryer's Antiques, near the second central petrol station, because the whole ground floor had disappeared. Not that anyone cared much, for the shop had become useless: the town was stripping back to the bare essentials required to still qualify as a place where people lived.

Any urgency to address the matter of the holes receded after

weeks of hopelessly filling them in, until they were finally cate-
gorised an annoyance. Unexplainable, yes, but something people
would need to accept. On the way to the Woolworths I'd often
find teenagers poking at the absences with sticks. Sometimes
they still dared poke their arms in.

Jenny didn't want to hear any more talk about the holes. She
hadn't needed to worry about them because they weren't inside
her pub yet, though some shimmered on the footpath outside.

Anyway, she said, the world was always getting darker.
Things much worse happened elsewhere, things too terrible for
words. They say there's a growing hole in the sky—she pointed
to the sky—and because of it people will one day burn to a crisp,
or else drown in rising seas. She pointed east. Or there is going
to be a war, and people in cities will potentially be bombed. And
there were incurable diseases borne by wind that resulted in
long agonising deaths to good people like herself. All in all there
were worse things going on than some Town Extremists digging especially deep holes. They could dig them wherever they
wished as far as she was concerned—even in the air, even in
her pub—should they dare to do so. And then she rapped a fist
against her chest.

The largest hole in the town spread at the southern end of
the main street, in a paved pedestrians-only avenue near the
turn-off to the highway. Benches lined the footpath with a view
of long abandoned shopfronts, the windows all covered with
newspaper classifieds from several decades past. For years this
avenue had been a sanctuary for teenagers: you could tell by
the cigarette butts stamped into its eroding pavement, and the
tossed Moove cartons rolling in the breeze. Now it was a shim-
mering abyss and the teenagers were somewhere else, maybe in
the grassy wastelands that hugged the tentacle suburbs, where

the view into the country was uninterrupted. They might have gazed thoughtlessly into the vastness they had yet to confront, and might never have needed to confront, were it not for the fact of the holes. As I passed the avenue one afternoon, a small boy stood at the foot of the huge hole and dipped his leg in. His parents were nowhere to be seen – it looked like he was lost. But it was impossible to be lost in the town.

A front-page story in the town's local newspaper announced that the town disco would no longer be funded by the council. Eighteen people were missing and one was dead. They boarded the town hall up, and the PA was sold at an auction.

———

Ciara left Rob one afternoon as I sat in my room writing my book about the town. There was the sound of severe conversation in the next room, then I heard Ciara leave, and then silence.

An hour later Rob snapped and smashed everything in his room. I heard him tear his magazines to pulp. Then he must have fallen asleep, or else gone on a bender with his football friends, because for a whole day the townhouse was silent.

The next day he woke up or came home and punched a hole in the gyprock, and then went quiet. I was scared to face him, since I was a suitable target for interrogation, or even a bashing. Rather than cook my dinner in the kitchen I climbed out the window and bought a packet of chips at the corner store. Then I visited Ciara's and knocked on her door, but there was no answer.

I made a habit of doing this for several days. On my way home from Woolworths I would visit Ciara's with no luck. Then I would climb into my bedroom window and commence work on my book, even if I knew Rob wasn't home. I started to prefer entering through my window—although doing so would eventually attract Rob's attention and signal guilt.

My chief concern was whether I would ever see Ciara again. I knocked on her door every morning and afternoon, until it occurred to me that doing so might seem strange. For information on her whereabouts I supposed Rob was the only source, so after much deliberation I went home one evening through the front door. Rob was watching a football panel show on the television and drinking a VB longneck. He seemed too drunk to suspect me of loving Ciara, at that point. He asked if I knew where to get drugs, specifically marijuana, since he was still trying to recover from the pain of losing Ciara as a girlfriend. I told him I did not, and that he was more likely to have such connections due to his attendance at the TAFE.

He scoffed at this. All the TAFE students were too fixed to the straight and narrow. Besides, they were all business students. I asked Rob what he studied, and he said business.

Slumped in the lounge with the bottle between his legs, Rob said it was very painful having a person fall out of love with you. Every day when he woke up, it was only a matter of seconds before he remembered that he was in immense pain. The immense pain did not subside until he passed out that night. Before, he could never have imagined what it would be like to feel so much pain. He had not thought it feasible that this amount of pain could affect one person at any given time. It was simply intolerable. Why did people continue living when this much pain was possible?

Rob said he believed that Ciara was going out with another man. He'd been trying to call her all the time on her parents' number, just to ask why she broke up with him. Whenever she deigned to answer—which she didn't, most of the time—he would simply ask questions like: why did you break up with me.

What did I do wrong. How can I fix it.

Rob would claim to her that he had never been as much in love with someone his whole life. He'd warn that it was impossible for her to find someone who loved her as much as he. She would respond that this was possibly true, but she didn't deserve such love, and anyhow, she was going through many emotional issues, most of which he could never begin to understand. He'd reply that he wanted to understand them and help her work through them, but this response did not satisfy her.

And yet, she had never strictly said she didn't still love him. Sometimes he would ask if she was still in love with him, but she wouldn't respond. She would stay perfectly silent. So then he would say to her: why would you want to be apart from me if you still love me? Because he figured she clearly did love him, given her reluctance to say otherwise. Ciara would become frustrated and say she needed to get off the phone for a totally unbelievable reason.

When Rob lied and said that he knew for certain that she was in love with someone else, she became nasty. She would no longer claim that Rob was too good for her. Instead, she would lash out, tell Rob that it was none of his business whether she was or she wasn't, but that she wasn't, and that he needed to accept that.

She told him she was not in love with someone else, but even if this was true, Rob thought she was insinuating that it was possible she would one day. And this was the most painful fact of the whole scenario for him. She would be a girlfriend to someone else one day, and she might even talk about Rob disdainfully, like he was a pathetic man who couldn't accept being abandoned, wouldn't leave her alone, and would never have a girlfriend half as good as she had been.

So Rob changed tack: instead of continually calling her to ask why she broke up with him, or whether she was still in love with him, he started to ask—whenever he could get her to answer the phone—whether it was true that she had a new boyfriend. He would try to trick her into thinking that he already knew about her supposed new boyfriend, even though he didn't know anything. He would say, "I know you have a boyfriend" to which she would reply, "I don't, and anyway it's none of your business." And then she would hang up.

Rob knew that he had already ruined any chance of having Ciara fall back in love with him. How could she, especially when he had cried on the phone to her a lot? And yet, he knew they belonged together. He imagined scenarios of them visiting the city together, sightseeing, having a wine in a bar, meeting each other's parents, and he knew two things to be true: that it was impossible for him to be happy unless these scenarios occurred, and equally, that they never would.

Defeated, Rob decided that he would smoke marijuana every day for the rest of his life. He wanted to degrade himself and ruin his brain until one day Ciara would see him and think it was her fault that he was now a broken man. She might decide that it hadn't been a good idea to break up with him after all. Maybe she would try to mend his life by getting back together with him, despite her emotional problems and his erosive addiction.

It would be partially your fault too, Rob slurred at me, peeling the label from his beer bottle. He sat there mumbling for a while. I could tell that he didn't like me, and probably never had. But I did not feel threatened by Rob, as it was clear that he had no intention of doing me any physical harm.

I sat and watched the football panel show for a while. Although he was in a foul mood, Rob occasionally smirked at the jokes, and grunted derisively at times when the announcers offered their thoughts on how the current season would likely play out. When a particular football player belonging to Rob's preferred team was mentioned among the banter, he would repeat the name enthusiastically. Feeling as though I had been let off the hook, for the night at least, I went back to my bedroom and recommenced writing about the town.

———

In the days that followed Rob's depressing speech, I frequently visited Ciara's flat. Sometimes I would wait at her door for an hour or so, sitting cross-legged at the head of the stairs, waiting for her to arrive. During these periods, when I became fed up with waiting for Ciara, I boarded the bus at the stop opposite her flat. Then, once I had travelled a full circulation of Tom's route, I would disembark at the central park and commence knocking on Ciara's door again, before eventually going back home, where I would carefully avoid Rob.

Once when I boarded the bus, Tom was eating a Quarter Pounder and looking more forlorn than usual. As he turned the bus into a dusty street lined with many abandoned homes, he pointed his burger through the windscreen. It was his old house, or at least, he thought it was. His old house could actually have been the one next door. Tom poked his burger towards the next block. Or it could have been on the next block. It was getting harder to place. Many of the townhouses in the central district had been abandoned. He didn't know under what circumstances, nor could he remember specifically who had lived in them. He'd noticed that more and more of the houses were decrepit through neglect.

He'd never seen a removalist, or any sign of people moving furniture from their homes to some other location. The houses seemed to have become decrepit overnight. It was like a rot spreading through the town. One morning a verandah would be freshly swept, the next it was covered with old envelopes and advertising pamphlets. Refuse would block the garden paths, and the weeds, tangled with old beer bottles and K-Mart catalogues, would have grown knee-high over the course of a night.

We turned into another street of sad townhouses. Tom told me that he still occasionally saw people entering and leaving the properties, but it was clear by the way they walked up the garden paths that they did not strictly live in these places. He said you could tell by the way people swung their arms as they approached the front doors. These people were not people who lived in the town. They were there in the town, and he supposed they existed, but it was clear they did not live in the town, especially since he had never seen their faces before.

As we crossed the border road onto one of the town's tentacles, I asked Tom why The Stern Gentlemen had originally stopped performing, fifteen years before that Raymond person had not shown up for the one-off gig.

Tom came to a stop at the foot of the tentacle road and opened the doors, then he closed the doors, continued up the road for two hundred metres, stopped, and opened the doors again. It always took about an hour to drive just one tentacle road. Tom's adherence to the official timetable had become lax, but I respected that he still pulled in at every official stop. The futile pace of his bus was enjoyable.

One day an out-of-towner named Greg had phoned, seeking Tom's help putting on a show in the town. Few bands from outside the town had ever showed any interest playing in the town: if a band from the country was going to bother travelling for a show they would try their luck in the city. Occasionally a band from the city might charitably play a gig outside of the city, but it would be in a much nicer and more interesting place than the town.

Following the phone call, Tom had organised a show at The Vic on an upcoming Thursday night. The line-up was to feature three local bands plus the out-of-towners. The out-of-towners had agreed that no money needed to exchange hands, because Greg had said they were doing it only to have new ears listen to their music. With the complexity of finances ruled out, Tom had seen no reason to deny helping them set up this opportunity.

When Tom had asked Greg what type of music his band played, in order to make sure he booked similar-sounding bands on the night, the out-of-towner had said the band didn't have a sound. Tom had sympathised with Greg on this point, because few bands ever wanted to admit to having a particular sound. He had pressed Greg to describe his band anyway, at least in terms of genre, for Tom's own benefit more than anything. Tom had asked if they were a rock band and Greg had said that yes, they were a rock band, but only to put an end to all the questions.

The show had been arranged over the course of two phone calls. Once Tom had confirmed the date and time he didn't hear from Greg again until a month later, when the band arrived at his doorstep with all their equipment.

The band hadn't had a name. During their first phone call, when Tom had asked Greg what the band was called, Greg had said that it didn't have a name and that it wasn't important to have one. Tom had to list them as someone though, so on the poster he billed the out-of-towners as The Out of Towners.

The three members of the band had been friendly when they'd turned up at Tom's doorstep, but they'd refused to be drawn on any specifics regarding the type of music they played, nor why they did it, nor why they felt the need to play for free in a town dominated by the already-known rock and country cover bands. Tom had offered each of them a beer when they arrived, but all had declined, and while they had been friendly and smiled often, none had been interested in entering a conversation. It had quickly become a little awkward.

The three members of the band were Greg, Richard, and Ebony. Their instruments were a nylon acoustic guitar, a recorder, and an electric guitar, respectively. The ensemble didn't put Tom's mind at ease, because tastes in the town were conservative. When he'd asked Greg what kind of venues the band usually played, Greg had replied that they'd usually played in their house. When Tom had asked where the band was from, Greg's answer was even stranger: he'd said he didn't know where the band was from. Tom had laughed, because he thought it was typically ostentatious rock-star talk, but Greg hadn't smiled, and his face had even seemed a little offended at the laughter. When Tom had then asked where each of the three band members lived, neither Greg nor Richard nor Ebony could name where they lived, which Tom had taken to mean that they were country people. But he hadn't cared to confirm it, because at that point he'd sensed that Greg, Richard and Ebony were delicately sincere, and that his attempts to banter with them or to initiate conversations were making them uncomfortable. Tom had wanted very badly to clarify that they all lived on a farm together in the country, outside of any town or place with any name, but to enquire any more seemed inappropriate and rude.

The band members hadn't had the innocent air one might expect from country people who'd had little exposure to outside life. Nor had they been arrogant in the way some country people are. Nor had they been scornful of Tom's manner of speaking and dressing. When Tom remembered Greg, Richard and Ebony, he did not imagine childlike adults, but nor did he imagine them being conscious of their detachment: they hadn't seemed to be making any calculated effort to appear any certain way. When Tom's attempts to engage them socially had proved a failure, the band had sat in his lounge room studying the integrity of their instruments. Greg had run his fingers up and down his fretboard, stretching the strings in order to ensure that they were stable. Richard had dismantled his recorder to occasionally peer through the hollow cylinder, and Ebony had occupied herself by adjusting the knobs on her small practice amp. She'd left the reverb and echo knobs at their highest settings. Eventually Tom had gotten fed up sitting there watching them do this, so he'd gone to his room, leaving them alone until it was time to drive to the show. The situation had been especially awkward, because at that time Tom had been always smoking bongs and doing so made him sensitive.

Tom had helped them load their instruments into his van and they'd driven the three blocks to the venue. The Out of Towners had refused to do a soundcheck. They'd said it wasn't necessary, because they had, in Greg's own words, "already checked their sound". Tom hadn't pressed them on this because the simplicity of their instrumentation would be easy enough to mix within a minute of them commencing their performance.

Tom had told everyone ahead of time that The Out of Towners were a little bit odd. And yet, once he had been safely surrounded by familiar people at the venue, he'd become excited by how strange they'd seemed. He'd been able to see them as the novelty they were, and had looked forward to hearing what they did with their unusual combination of instruments.

The Out of Towners were given the headline slot because they were from out of town. As the first three bands had played—two of which Tom played guitar in—Greg, Richard and Ebony had sat at a table in front of the stage, nursing their instruments. They'd not wanted to store their instruments in the small designated room behind the stage. When local drunks had tried to initiate conversation with them, most often specifically with Ebony, the band's reluctance to enter into any meaningful conversation had been interpreted as sinister. Ill will grew among the patrons of The Vic throughout the support acts. By the time The Out of Towners had started setting up on stage, many in the pub had already made their mind up about them.

When the band had finished setting up, ready to perform, they'd stood very closely together but did not perform for several minutes. They did not fidget, had not been busy preparing their instruments or checking sound levels: they had just stood there looking at the carpet beneath them. This had given the audience an opportunity to express how they'd been feeling about The Out of Towners, based on the attempts to make small talk throughout the night. There had been a lot of scattered heckling and laughter during this long moment, but Greg, Richard and Ebony had not flinched. They'd just smiled – not nervous smiles, nor confident smiles. Uncomplicated smiles.

Tom scrunched his Quarter Pounder wrapper and tossed it between his legs. He didn't know how to describe The Out of Towners' music. Many would say that it hadn't been music at all. It had certainly been a very experimental type of music, but that description did it an injustice, because there had been nothing cerebral about it. When the band had finally started, for several minutes Richard had just played two notes on his recorder, over and over again. It had been an awkward several minutes because many at the venue had started to suspect that this was all The Out of Towners' performance would amount to. The two notes played together had been unusually sad, Tom said, but they'd only started to become sad after the prolonged period of repetition. After Richard had played those notes for several minutes the room had been in an austere mood indeed.

Eventually Ebony had kneeled in front of her practice amp with her electric guitar, generating calm drones of feedback. These drone waves had seemed to stand at odds with Richard's recorder playing, but after many minutes it had become clear that she was harmonising with Richard, in a tangential way. Their two sounds had seemed to evade each other, but within every circulation of Richard's two notes the two instruments met perfectly, for only a split second. Richard and Ebony had performed like this for another ten minutes, and it had seemed a miracle that no one in the audience had become restless. Everyone had seemed reverent and focused.

The music had sounded alien, remote, like nothing else the audience had ever heard. More than a mere sound, it had come to resemble a portal, an access point to a foreign region. Ebony and Richard had no longer seemed responsible for the sound; the sound had come untethered from the ensemble, had become its own sad and ghostly phenomenon.

Both musicians had performed their parts without any visible strain. No one in the audience had even thought to sip their drinks during this long, half-hour repetition of sound. Tom certainly hadn't. He'd forgotten that he was even holding a beer, and he'd forgotten that he was watching The Out of Towners, whoever they were. The mystery had become unimportant, and their music had ceased to be a simple mix of sounds – it had inherited an illusory complexity. Sometimes faint melodies had emitted from this repetition, faint phantom melodies that were perhaps not really there.

Greg had eventually intervened into the sound with a simple guitar chord, played over and over. He'd strummed freely, hitting gently on each string, and that's when things had taken a peculiar turn. Tom had felt himself begin to cry, and he'd seen John at the sound desk begin crying too. Old Warren behind the bar had sniffed and turned his back, and all the people standing against the walls on both sides of the band room suddenly had small specks on their cheeks, each tear reflecting the orange lights of the stage.

And then Tom had realised that he was shaking, and that he could not stop himself from shaking. The sound in the room had been the most unutterably sad sound he had ever heard in his life. It was the sound of everything that he had never been able to gain control of. It was the sound of his complete lack of dominion, and in this way the sound had seemed to travel directly backwards in time, briefly capsizing during its passage on each spectral memory. It had brought to life sensations which had been forgotten. Each and every time Greg had played his simple guitar chord in conjunction with the strange drone Ebony and Richard had gradually shaped, Tom's body had been less in his control.

The Out of Towners had played for several nights and days without pause. Everyone in the audience had cried for several nights and days while The Out of Towners had performed their very simple and very beautiful music. Nobody had exited, and The Out of Towners had never seemed to tire. The sadness had not been a phenomenon that could tire anybody. That sadness, and its manner of revealing the limits of their control over the passage of time, had not been a sensation of which anyone in the room had been prepared to let go. The sadness had liberated them, rendering them innocent. There had been nothing they could do, and in some vague way they'd all been victims of something far beyond their ability to fight. It had made them want to live more, and that seemed so naïve, now, to Tom.

Passersby had peered inside The Vic and had wondered what was happening inside, though no one ever tried to enter for fear of the unknown. Eventually the media had turned up, but could not find a way inside. It had only been when the police forced themselves in and switched the mains off that The Out of Towners had finished their set.

Tom didn't know where the three band members went. Amid the confusion of the police's entry they had disappeared, and no one ever saw them again. And no one had wanted to, Tom added, turning the bus back towards the town proper. Once they'd all shaken off the stupor of those days and nights in the pub, everyone had felt deeply ashamed.

I disembarked the bus at the terminal and wandered the short distance to Ciara's flat. She still wasn't home, but I found a cassette tape in the stairwell outside. I had no way to play it, so I left it there, and bought two longnecks of stout on the way home.

—

Weeks later I found Ciara in an undercover car park. She was trapping cassette tapes under windscreen wipers, tossing them into ute trays, and wedging them under front tyres. It was a late Sunday afternoon, and fewer than half-a-dozen vehicles were parked in the underground complex.

Ciara flinched when I approached, and then we exchanged hellos. She asked how Rob was going. I told her he wanted to become a drug addict. He might as well, she said.

For the first time I noticed lines beneath her eyes. She had not bothered to brush her hair or do up her shoe laces, and she moved dispassionately, hunched from one chore to the next. She sat on the bonnet of a Holden station wagon and lit a cigarette.

She told me she didn't know why she bothered with the tapes anymore. No one wrote to her. No one ever called the station. There was no one in the town except her.

I told her that wasn't true. I was there. Her breaking up with Rob was no reason for us to stop being friends, because Rob was an idiot anyway. It was a surprise to me that she had bothered with him at all, I said, but it would have been inappropriate for me to say so before. Now you're free to find someone better, or to find no one at all, and in the meantime I could be someone to spend time with. I could even help you make contact with the mysterious keyboard musicians, and with our efforts combined we would surely find them. There are mysterious people everywhere, I said, making strange keyboard music in their homes, probably right at that moment. I didn't believe it, but it must have been true. Ciara's chaotic flat had confirmed it.

Ciara said it was impossible for the tapes to have come from the town. After all, she knew everything about the town. She even knew who owned all the vehicles in the car park we were right then sitting in. This one belongs to Denise, she said, tapping on the Holden's bonnet. Denise who works at the Subway.

She placed a neat tower of three cassette tapes on Denise's roof and lumbered on.

She might as well stop doing the tapes and her radio show, she said. It would be much more sensible to get married to Rob and have some babies. If she did that she would be so busy that she'd stop hoping to find secrets in the town. Maybe then its familiarity would be a comfort instead of maddening. The town was just there and that was that. It was a bunch of people living in houses who all just get by. I should just get by, she said.

Ciara was only repeating what I had been led to believe many months previous: that there was nothing special in the town. Nothing ever happened in it to warrant the attention of anyone else. Assess the matter closely, and it wasn't logically possible to be proud of the town, nor upset about it.

But even if some cruel underground syndicate was responsible for sending Ciara strange keyboard music—possibly composed *en masse* in a shady warehouse on the outskirts of a distant city—then surely she herself was the start of something interesting about the town. She believed that she could only create illusions of mystery, though. No one would wake one day and believe the town was interesting because she had made stuff up. If they did then they would be kidding themselves, she said, sliding off from the bonnet. Or she would be kidding them.

She started walking away in a manner which suggested she didn't mind if I followed.

She said she had tried to be satisfied with the fictions she'd created. Maybe it was possible for some people to enjoy their own fantasies unreservedly and forever, but not her. Even when her fantasies breached the threshold of her mind and seemed to become real—she shook her plastic bag of cassette tapes—they were still impossibly elusive. Someone was playing a trick on her.

The town was deserted. When we emerged from the car park into the orange afternoon no cars were parked along the street. The Mitre 10 and Pizza Hut were shut, and all was silent except for the cicadas. We kept our eyes to the ground, on the alert for any new holes that might have emerged. Some old ones were still draped lazily with yellow tape. They were all small holes, barely the width of a small child's waist. The town had ceased to be outraged by them.

The year before, Ciara had tried to make contact with a man who wrote the music column in Australia's major national newspaper. She had sent him five cassette tapes, with a note asking whether he had heard anything like it before, and if he hadn't, whether he could identify the specific keyboard model that might have created it. She had written five pages explaining her predicament. She'd told him she considered herself the pioneer of the strange keyboard music, and that her initial broadcasts had prompted many others—many hundreds, perhaps thousands—to follow suit. She'd told him the cassettes had piled up in her pigeonhole at speed, but that none could be traced to a source. If he couldn't help her, then he might at least be intrigued enough to write a story about it for the newspaper.

He'd not replied to her first letter, so she had sent a briefer, more urgent letter with even more cassette tapes. Then she'd sent a third letter, and then a fourth, and then she'd finally stopped sending letters. She had still sent him cassettes, though, on a daily basis, partially out of spite, but also because she'd needed to get rid of some cassette tapes.

Finally she'd received a reply — not from the music columnist, but from another person at the paper. They'd urged her to stop sending tapes because the paper only reviewed professionally recorded and distributed music. Ciara had been happy because she'd gotten someone's attention, so she had written back explaining that she was seeking information, not publicity.

She'd not heard back. Instead she'd received a giant box returning all of the cassette tapes sent over the course of several months. Deflated and angry, she'd spent nearly fifty dollars sending an even larger box of strange keyboard music to the newspaper. In fact she'd sent two.

The music columnist was someone who would sometimes write very negative things about music, Ciara said. Sometimes he would blame music for all the bad things in the world. He was a writer able to make readers feel frightened on behalf of the artists he demolished. She used to read him for that reason, really: to see what music he thought was ruining the world. When he'd never responded, she'd wanted to make him so angry that he would demolish all of the strange keyboard music. Maybe if she flooded him with hundreds of kilos worth of cassettes he would become so angry he'd feel compelled to write something about it.

She'd finally received a terse letter written by the music columnist himself. He'd written that if she didn't stop sending the cassettes he would call the police. What she was doing could be classed as harassment, the music columnist had claimed.

We turned onto the highway and walked towards the McDonald's. Naturally Ciara had written him back. She'd repeated everything in her response that she had written in her first letter. She'd also added that no one ever went to gaol for sending cassette tapes to a newspaper. His articles were trash anyway, she'd said in her response – he should try creating something of his own that he wanted to exist, rather than just destroy others' efforts. Along with her response letter she'd also sent him several editions of her handmade magazine about the strange keyboard music, hoping this would enlighten him to the urgency of her queries.

She'd never heard from him again. It made her think cities weren't so special after all. But how would she know, she added, having never been to a city.

There was a crowd of teenagers in the McDonald's car park. They smoked their cigarettes and stared out at the highway, waiting for something to happen. I told Ciara about Tom the bus driver, how he had once seen a performance by some out-of-towners that had caused him to immediately stop pursuing a career as a musician. Ciara was not surprised at all. Old people always blow things out of proportion, she said. They always make it seem like very important things happened in the past.

We went inside the McDonald's and each ordered a McValue meal. We ate in an important silence – I did not want to trivialise Ciara's frustration. Then, after binning our wrappers and skolling the rest of our Cokes, Ciara led me to a back street on the outskirts of the town. As afternoon faded, the houses in those distant streets seemed older than they were. Each home emanated the indeterminate colour lights of shifting television screens, and the smell of meats and boiled vegetables drifted towards us. After a few blocks walking along this back street we reached a clearing with lush overgrown grass and an electrical tower standing in the evening light. A deep gully ran through the centre of the clearing, and in the direction of the town it ran beneath a rickety bridge, towards which Ciara wandered.

The passage under the bridge led to a narrow open-air tunnel, and then finally to the mouth of a stormwater drain. Ciara did not walk purposefully but I knew she was leading me somewhere significant.

We walked into the mouth of the tunnel and stuck to the left side of the concrete passage. Light gradually receded until it was pitch black. We continued for several minutes, using only sound to guide us, before Ciara stopped, grabbed my hand, and pulled me down a small, barely perceptible passage. We needed to edge forward at an angle down this passage; if it had rained we would have drowned. After a while the passage opened up into a space I could sense was much bigger, and Ciara lit a lantern that she must've known was there.

We were in a large room, apparently chiselled out by hand. Stacks of water-damaged cassette tapes lined each of the four walls all the way to the ceiling, and more piles of tapes were sat throughout the centre of the room. Sodden bill posters covered the ground, all handmade by Ciara, and I could tell at a glance that many depicted her featureless plain. Even when a portion of poster revealed only a straight line, I knew it was a plain. This is the only secret in the town, Ciara said.

I tried to look impressed by Ciara's secret room. I was impressed, but it was difficult to look any certain way when I was also doing it for Ciara's benefit.

She had been trying to entice people there for years. At first she had left subtle breadcrumb trails—empty beer bottles leading to the mouth of the tunnel, and texta hieroglyphs on the walls just inside the mouth—but still no one had ever broke the fragile string she'd tied across the entrance to the room. No one in the town had ever thought to explore the stormwater drains, and she supposed there was no good reason to.

Then she'd started writing articles in her magazine about a secret room somewhere beneath the town. She'd placed great emphasis on how incredible it was that there was a secret room somewhere beneath the town. It needed to be seen to be believed, she'd written – it was the only part of the town left to be discovered. She'd tried to depict the secret room beneath the town as a satisfying destination that also contained many other secrets. She knew that if she had found herself reading about a secret room under the town somewhere, the first thing she would do was try to verify that it was truthfully there, even if she suspected it was a lie. And if it turned out that she was indeed being lied to, the fact of the rumour existing would have been its own reward.

But no one had ever tripped her string. It came as no surprise really: her magazine was only printed with a photocopier and she wasn't sure anyone ever read it. There were millions of officially-printed books more reliably interesting than her amateur magazine, she said—though none of those books were about the town. She had thought for a while that her magazine's focus on phenomena specific to the town would encourage people to read it, but she'd been wrong. No one wanted to learn new things about the town. No one wanted to learn old things, either. She supposed people really did only want to read about why the town was great now, or why it wasn't as great as it used to be.

We were silent for a while. I wanted to draw parallels between my book and Ciara's efforts to lead people to the secret room, but I could not formulate sentences in a way that would suggest camaraderie. Instead, I resorted to advice. Perhaps you should make a magazine about the holes, I told her. Maybe you could write an exposé on the origin of the holes. You can make it up: if it's printed on paper and the only source of information then maybe you will end up driving the whole agenda, since no one else was. Maybe you could claim that the secret room had in fact been chiselled out by a hole. Maybe you could claim that the tapes containing the mysterious keyboard music had been fished from the holes. Whatever the case, it could do no harm to alert people to the strangeness of the holes.

Ciara was not comforted. She lit a cigarette and we stood in silence. It was impossible to know what to do. Soon she kicked at one of the walls of cassettes, and grabbed more cassettes and tossed them aside, continuing to kick and grab and toss until a clearway had formed where there had once been a wall of tapes. The room extended in that direction much farther than I had realised, and it was jam-packed with cassette tapes.

I helped Ciara dig a tunnel through the cassettes. Our tunnel burrowed deep beneath the town, under homes and streets, curving slightly at times. We dug without speaking, our entry point plugged with plastic and unspooled tape. It was like we were digging our own cocoon. Cassettes crunched beneath our labour, echoing so loudly that the tunnel might have lead beyond the town's shimmer. Maybe it would end at a cliff by the ocean. Maybe in a cliffside hole near the coastal city, people tossed all their cassette tapes in, unaware of the hole's extent, believing their waste forever discarded. Maybe it didn't matter where the tapes came from: the fact of them existing was enough, like a coastline leveed with message bottles, lids screwed too tightly.

We reached a cavern on the other side of the tapes, where a ladder on the far wall lead upwards to a trapdoor. Ciara mounted the ladder, pushed through the heavy wooden panel, then held it open for me to follow. My legs and arms were tangled in shiny brown cassette ribbon, and so were hers.

We were in a shed, the walls lined with rakes, brooms, and paint cans. As I ripped the ribbons from my limbs Ciara opened the shed door, and night air dispersed the musty smell. We were in the shed behind her flat.

———

Though I had not seen Rob for many weeks I eventually thought it wise to move out of the townhouse. After an afternoon spent inspecting the abandoned houses Tom had pointed out, I opted for the least vandalised one, situated on a street leading to the central park, opposite a BP petrol station. There were four bedrooms, each branching from a wide, high-ceiling hallway at the front of the house. Beyond the hall a cavernous lounge room lead to a kitchen, laundry and bathroom. I swept the wooden floorboards and dusted the cobwebs, but there was little I could do about the graffiti left by teenagers and local drug addicts. There was no electricity, so I used a pen and paper to continue writing my book.

Ciara was impressed that I had found such a nice home – maybe even a little bit jealous. She said she might as well store cassette tapes in the house and I agreed that she could. The next day she lugged half-a-dozen bin bags through the central park, then emptied them in a pile under the master bedroom window. She offered to arrange electricity for the house via her apprentice friend, but I was not brave enough to break the law to that extent.

I browsed the newspaper for legitimate places to rent, but none were available. Demand could not have been high in the town, and yet there was no longer any supply. After a matter of weeks I became accustomed to my circumstances. I showered in the staff bathroom before my shift at the Woolworths, and dug a hole in the large overgrown backyard for my waste. After a month, I could no longer see any point paying rent in the town.

One day Ciara helped me drag a mattress to my house. We dropped it in the master bedroom near her piles of cassettes, adjacent to the open fireplace. I made a desk with cement bricks and a piece of chipboard I found in the back shed, and bought a cheap camping chair from Kmart. Once I purchased the camping chair it was official that I would live in the abandoned townhouse for the foreseeable future. I didn't need a candle or anything because at night the lights from the petrol station flooded the room with a harsh, surgical white.

Ciara suggested that some day maybe we could connect my house to the storm drains, via a tunnel. Maybe then we wouldn't need to walk above ground at all – we'd just connect the tunnels to wherever we needed to go.

She was happy that I was no longer living with Rob, but she was also happy that there was someone else squatting abandoned dwellings in the town, following her example. Most nights we would drink longnecks in my overgrown backyard or on her balcony. We would share hot chips and sometimes even some fried chicken or a hamburger if we were especially hungry. Ciara would talk to me about her world predictions, and I would try to bring the topic around to the subject of my book. It was easy to seize upon these most pertinent subjects in a town so silent. On Thursday, Friday and Saturday night there was occasionally the sound of drunk people arguing on the footpaths, but otherwise the town slept silently as soon as the sun went down.

It seemed that we felt the same way about most things, though I never dared to think on the scale that Ciara did. It never occurred to me to worry about her. Her outlook was bleak, but she did not seem depressed, nor was she eager to do anything that might lead to change. She knew she wasn't in control. She was born too late to make any meaningful difference. It was all already decided for us, she always said, and when I asked who exactly made the decisions and what the decisions were, she pointed to the town, and then told me I should listen to more of the cassette tapes. The mood of the world is in this music, she said. People don't listen to it because no one wants to be a Town Extremist: listening to cassette tapes, found beneath the soap dispensers in the women's bathroom at the plaza, or buried in the sugar satchels at the McDonald's, was not of the town enough. It was a huge risk. Who knew what kind of horror might be contained on a tape?

Ciara said that if I listened to the music closely, I would hear a reflection of the world outside. Then she waved in the direction of the mess of brambles and discarded corrugated iron at the far end of my backyard. Ciara had listened to so much of the strange keyboard music that she could recognise popular melodies in the decayed sections. It was like eavesdropping on the world from a vast distance, or like hearing the poorly recollected memories of a once vibrant, hopeful world. She said that when the prospect of finding the creators of the strange keyboard music seemed even more remote than usual, she liked to imagine it was the music of aliens witnessing us from afar, offering their sympathetic elegies.

After three weeks living in the derelict house I wandered past Rob's one day. The grass was overgrown but the grass had always been overgrown – though it was now strewn with tell-tale pamphlets and bill notices, and the curtains had been removed revealing empty rooms within. Peering through the windows, I could see no evidence of a sudden move. The layout of the house—the way the open doors lead into the darkness of the narrow halls—seemed different to the house I had once inhabited. The townhouse had become mysteriously vacated, just as Tom had described. I suppose it was lucky that I left when I did, though maybe I had passed up an important opportunity to go wherever those people went next.

———

One afternoon before my shift at the Woolworths I retrieved Rick from the cereal aisle and offered to buy him a coffee. Since our initial talk he had always nodded hello as I packed canned foods, but he never dared stop for fear of affecting my shelfing targets. I won't interrupt the workers in the supermarket, Rick would always say. It's disrespectful to the supermarket.

I had never cared to study Rick's face closely, but when I did over coffee it occurred to me that he no longer really lived in the town. Yes, he was there, and presumably his home was too, but he had breached the shimmer long ago. It was no epiphany that had set in motion his extrication: the town itself had squeezed him out. What remained was only a body.

For a while I'd presumed Rick would have a big part to play in my book about the disappearing town. Without thinking about the ramifications, I'd long believed the story would resolve itself in this direction. When I flicked through its pages in my imagination, Rick's name appeared regularly. But in practice, I was not having any luck including him, or a version of him, in my book about the town. There was something too conclusive about Rick at the supermarket. I feared he might prove something I did not want to prove.

Rick told me over our coffees that some of the happiest days of his life were spent loitering in this Michel's Patisserie, including when he had been a teenager. He and his friends had often waited here, in order to pounce on any passing eighteen-year-old who might agree to buy beer for them. Once someone had agreed, they had always met this buyer in the underground car park to transact the goods. Then Rick and his friends would get drunk in private at the weekend, behind the grandstands at the football ground.

Visiting the plaza after school, it had been impossible not to find people to hang around with. It had been just as impossible to not be involved in some controversy, and it'd been enjoyable to witness the controversies play out. It had been especially fun to be at the heart of the controversies, said Rick. These had commonly involved a love interest, and the question of whether that love interest loved you, or loved someone else. Ultimately everyone had always loved someone; every moment had been suffused with import. It had been a time of major heartbreaks, but also of talking to girls and maybe even having sex with them, but in reality, never having sex with them at all.

Sometimes Rick and his friends had sat in the food court eating chips and gravy. They had talked endlessly, and everything had been interesting. He told me that each person had always hoped the conversation would land on a topic of special interest to them – for example, whether or not a love interest was potentially reciprocal or not.

Now that he mentioned all this to me, Rick admitted that finding a lover was the motivation for everything he and his friends did. That's all anything had ever been about, though getting drunk at the weekend had been a close second priority. Every Friday and Saturday night Rick and his friends would get extremely drunk behind the grandstand at the football ground. At the plaza they had made their plans, both vocally and secretly, but the football ground was where the plans had been executed.

It had been an uncomplicated joy for Rick, getting drunk as a teenager. Everyone had become more receptive, more sentimental and warm. Monday and Tuesday was for studying each hilariously drunken moment from the weekend, as well as every sign of possible blossoming love. Then Wednesday and Thursday was for planning and anticipating the upcoming weekend: arranging alcohol and cigarettes, and determining who would be attending the grandstand gatherings.

Life had felt like an episodic drama, a drama that could not end bleakly, because it had been impossible to imagine life becoming bleak at all. There had been difficulties of course, but Rick had thought back then that no one was deserving of agony. That no one was deserving of misery. That eventually they would all leave school, get jobs and get married, just as their parents had done with ease, and they'd all still get drunk but in pubs instead of parks. Nothing could go wrong with these plans, because that's what everyone seemingly did before them, and if everyone did it then it couldn't be difficult.

Life had turned out to be very difficult for Rick, he told me. He didn't know why, but it had. He had marched up to the transformative threshold but was denied passage. When everyone else had begun working at their menial jobs, which would grow to be managerial jobs, and maybe then something even more important and lucrative, he had still been wandering the plaza, looking for a way in. Even when his job prospects had seemed the most hopeless, towards the end of Ruth and Giselle's lives, he had still wandered the plaza, CV in hand, hoping to encounter one of his high school friends. But on the rare occasions he had, they had been performing some or other duty related to their job, and could barely stop to say hello.

There had been nothing left to talk about anyway, Rick said, since he'd gotten married.

I was taking notes as Rick described his torment. I did not feel intrusive or voyeuristic, because he spoke in a cheerfully fateful tone of voice, as if he were surveying his life from a vast, impersonal distance.

He said it was now impossible to enter the plaza without remembering those warm years, and yet, he did not feel compelled to contrast them with his current situation. Maybe if he had left the town and returned, the plaza would be sad. But he'd never left, never stopped going to the plaza; the best way to ward off sadness, he believed, was to make any environment permanently commonplace, to bury the place in daily logistics. In this way, he could keep layering on new meanings. It wasn't a foolproof enterprise, but it was true that he now felt ambivalence rather than nostalgia whenever he passed through the plaza. It's hard to feel sentimental about a place that had never become unfamiliar.

The best way to plug memories is to distort them with the present, Rick told me, in the same way that it's possible to erase meaning from a song by repeatedly listening to it. For example, if Rick bought a pull-apart cheese roll at the Bakers Delight every single day for the rest of his life, then he was increasingly likely to forget the time he had bought a jam tart for a girl he had adored. The Bakers Delight would lose its significance. In the same way, if he visited the football grandstand every Friday and Saturday night now as an adult, and found it empty of drinking teenagers, surely he would eventually forget that once it was bustling with them. In this way, slowly, Rick had been asserting himself against his fondest memories, dimming the contrast between now and then. He was continually reconfiguring the town. Repurposing it.

The most resistant location to his method was his home. He had spent his entire teenagehood longing for the day he'd leave home, and yet there he still was, still waking every day in that same bedroom, his mother in the next room, the spectre of his father omnipresent. It was impossible not to seek perspective in that environment, impossible not to trace the causes of circumstances. He had always been conscious that he should have moved on to more. And so he would leave the house, every day, all day, and come to the supermarket.

Rick told me that the supermarket reminded him of being a child, and that he gained some small satisfaction from that feeling. But in truth, he found the supermarket the most attractive location because it lacked uniqueness. It was possible to be in any Woolworths and imagine being in a Woolworths in the city, or a Woolworths situated deeper in the country, or even a Woolworths abroad. There was nothing inside the town's

Woolworths that could remind him that he was in the town. Woolworths was an embassy for nowhere and everywhere. As Rick went through the checkout and out the doors every evening after a day in the town's Woolworths, he could imagine he was emerging into a different town altogether.

Rick loved how the Woolworths in the town was forever changing. Its corporate branding changed, its slogans pushed new perspectives on homely sentimentality, its sale sections at the end of each aisle proffered new bargains on a weekly basis. One week it'd be $4.00 extra-large boxes of Coco Pops, the next week it would be Kleenex, and then Vegemite. He could dive into the intricacies of how products are displayed, the subtle hierarchies and manipulations, and therein was a world of distraction. Even the workers constantly changed. The staff turnover was relentless, and yet I—and he pointed at me—was among the only constants. Rick could be distracted thinking about the days when I wasn't yet there, and those days seemed blessedly similar to now.

While I completed scribbling down my notes on all Rick had said, there was silence. When I looked up he was wearing the bland expression of a man immune from surprise. He didn't seem at all interested in looking at what I had written down. He asked how I'd gone with the CV that he'd given me. I told him that the Woolworths had recently let go of several staff with no intention of replacing them, because the town is disappearing. Besides, there were holes everywhere; he wasn't seeing most of them because he spent all of his time at the plaza, and the plaza was impenetrable to the elements. It was unlikely now that he would ever get a job at the Woolworths, or the Coles, or the IGA for that matter, or anywhere else. He told me that he thought our coffee was a job interview. I had to tell him that this was an interview, but not for any job.

———

Excessive public drinking soon became the norm in the town. There had always been excessive drinking, but usually inside the pubs, and usually on Thursday, Friday and Saturday nights. Now at all locations and at any time of day, men and women could be seen sipping from longneck bottles, wine bottles, and sometimes even spirits, as they weaved between the holes.

There was more violence too, but the biggest change was how strangers would mingle in the streets, intoxicated and uninhibited. The town resembled a depressed country festival suspended in a 2am lull. Life had taken on a drowsy and aggressive sadness. It was possible to eavesdrop, but no one addressed any pertinent matter directly, instead focusing their conversations on the most general examples of the town's decline. They seemed careful to explicitly avoid the topic of the holes as the cause of the decline, instead seizing on other, more rational phenomena: that the town was too big nowadays, or else that it was too small. That the town was too far away from elsewhere, or maybe too close. That it was the fault of Muslims, though there wasn't even a mosque in the town, let alone an organised group of practising Muslims. That kids play too many video games. That giant mutant subterranean rabbits had wrought erosion of the soil. That something bad had happened long before the holes were holes, that this unknown something was somehow connected to the holes.

Ciara told me that people were mourning the loss of the town – even though they'd been actually doing that for many years. The town had never been in people's eyes what it used to be in the past. Perhaps the moment the town was founded was the very best moment it ever had, and ever since then it had been in decline.

Ciara and I still had coffee at the Michel's Patisserie sometimes, where normal life continued. I would drink a coffee, and she would watch me do it. She would listen to me hold forth about the progress I was making on my book without offering feedback or advice. She did not like my book. I suspect she might have hated it. Even when I said I had changed tack on my book about the disappearing towns, preferring instead to focus on her town—since it was clearly disappearing—Ciara did not seem especially interested. She only asked how many pages I had written, or what the word count was, or whether I had thought about my prospects of having it published. I told her I had not bothered checking its length, nor had I thought about it being published. I assumed no one would, since the subject matter was obscure.

It's true that my book about the town was not as factual as I had originally intended. I had started writing about Ciara's town because it might offer opportunities to verify claims. When writing about disappeared towns I had needed to make do with my own speculations, based on scant primary sources. In theory, writing about Ciara's town did not require any speculation, since it was there.

But it was impossible to write about the town in any factual detail. Instead, I found myself writing spontaneous, off-the-cuff observations, and then later, as I wandered the honeycombed streets in the evening with Ciara, silently corroborating them. At times it took great effort to corroborate what I had written, but I always managed to stretch the truth of the town around my assertions.

For example, it was possible in my book to write that the town was suffused with "a barely perceptible sadness", and it was possible to feel confident, as I was writing this sentence, that it did. But it took concerted effort to observe this quality in the people of the town. It was just as possible to write, sitting in seclusion, that, to the townspeople, the highway did not "represent a proper route out of, and away from, the town", yet it was impossible to verify this without interviewing actual townspeople. The sight of the shimmer on the horizon seemed evidence of my claims.

The truths I aimed to discover about the town changed from day to day. As the town disappeared, so did my grip on any particular town truth. When I dared explain this to Ciara she did not appear surprised by my admission. She wasn't actively hostile towards my book, but nor was she able to feign enthusiasm – she was just unmoved by the possibility of a book existing about her town. She might have thought I was unqualified, having not been reared inside the town culture. I asked her whether she thought me writing a book about her town was a bad idea, but she told me she didn't know. She said that I wouldn't know until it was finished, that I wouldn't know until it was a book.

Despite my continued efforts to prompt the question from her, Ciara never asked about what town truths I had aimed to arrive at in my book. As time passed, I started to pursue conversations with her about my book more aggressively. I would mention that I had just finished an especially difficult section—even if I hadn't—but Ciara would only express a vague pride. Then, when my efforts could no longer be mistaken for idle conversation, she invited me to read an extract from my book on her radio show.

Nearing the day of the show, as we stood buying cigarettes at the western petrol station, Ciara reminded me that no one ever listened to her show—but that if they did, they might well call to offer me some feedback on the direction of the book. She couldn't

147

offer any feedback, she said, because she had never written a book. Nor had she read any classics that struck her as relevant to her life, because old classic books were old and new classic books weren't written anymore. Life wasn't classic, anymore.

I was enthusiastic about the prospect of reading an extract from my book on live radio, but only because I would be reading in the presence of Ciara. Maybe she would have a change of heart. Maybe when she heard me reading it aloud—with me taking pains to dwell on certain well-constructed sentences that I was proud of—she would come to believe my book had potential. So I spent many days choosing the passage I would read, and then many days reading it aloud in my lounge room. The writing did not seem as evocative when read aloud, nor did it seem as interesting or consequential. In the end I rewrote an entire section of my book, stitching together the most resonant phrases I had written.

I told Jenny at the pub that she should tune in for my interview, but she did not even know the community radio station existed. She didn't believe me when I said that it did. She said that the town had only two radio stations: the AM and the FM.

When I told the librarian about my radio spot, he wasn't impressed. He reminded me that I hadn't even finished my book yet – how could I feel good reading on the radio when I didn't know what it was about? I told him that I did know, that it was about a disappearing town in the Central West of New South Wales, and that besides, surely it is impossible for anyone to embark on writing a book without knowing what it's about? The librarian shook his head, told me that I was completely wrong. That the sole reason why a person wrote a book, in his view, was to figure out what it was about.

The community radio studio was in an old office building

across from the Rec Street petrol station. Inside, shelves of old twelve-inch records lined one wall, and smaller shelves with CDs lined the other. Photographs of Australian country singers decorated noticeboards, all of them brandishing their guitars in authentic rural environments. Their presence felt at odds with the fluorescent light – and with Ciara, who was the only person on the premises at that time on a Thursday night. She said that old people were in bed by seven, although they didn't listen to the station during the day either. The radio frequency was hers alone on a Thursday night, which was why she could get away with playing the strange keyboard music. She offered that maybe when I'd finished writing my book I could read the whole thing on air. I could read it from beginning to end, every word, perhaps with the backdrop of strange keyboard music.

Ciara's pigeonhole was stuffed with unmarked cassette tapes. None had artist names or song titles, nor any label artwork to differentiate them. I wondered aloud what Ciara could say about the music during her back announcements, since there was nothing to factually report. She said that I'd obviously never listened to her radio show before.

She carelessly scooped a pile of cassettes into her satchel, leaving debris on the carpet surrounding. Then we entered the studio: a harshly lit cube, the inner walls covered with sound-proofing egg cartons and more posters of country music singers. Ciara pulled the cassettes from her satchel, stacked them neatly, picked one from the top of the pile, and slotted it into the tape deck. As she prepared, I scanned my handwritten notes. It was important to get my reading right tonight. Reading to Ciara was like reading to the whole of the town.

Ciara warned that we were to be on air in thirty seconds. She waited for the previous show's pre-recorded closing track—'Ain't No Sunshine' by Bill Withers—to finish, her finger poised on the pause button. Then, at exactly 11pm, she lifted her finger and a quiet hiss emanated from the studio speakers. Seconds later a single synthetic piano note resonated throughout the room. It trailed off with the faintest trace of repetition before a second note sang out, lending a sad clarity to the first. Then a third, brighter note sounded, before the trio became acquainted amid the hiss. They interacted at a graceful-yet-lazy pace. The echoes caused each note to smear together, before even more notes joined the fray.

We sat in silence. Ciara spent minutes re-stacking her cassettes in possible orders she could play them, but eventually she could no longer feign distraction. She shot me a brief glance and then stared up at the soundproof padding behind me. I stared at the Chad Morgan poster behind her. The music had seemed to erect a barrier between us. As I thought for something cheerful to say, Ciara looked embarrassed.

It should have been easy to say something admiring about the music, but it was impossible to do so as it played. The synthetic piano notes stripped speech to its core banality. The thought of anything other than the music and Ciara made me feel small, but the music and Ciara made me feel smaller still. The music did not evoke images, but instead a hazy indeterminate colour. Its familiar components did not culminate in familiar qualities. It was sad, but not for any graspable reasons. It felt like an absence, but a warm, preferable absence. It did not mean anything at all.

If only I could make music about the town instead of writing about it. Then I could bypass the explicit assertions I puzzled over, those ephemeral obstacles that prevented me from making any meaningful progress.

When the song ended Ciara allowed the silence to linger for

minutes before speaking.

You're listening to Thursday Night Sounds, she said into the microphone. She moderated her voice on air, sharpening the otherwise loose trails of her rural accent. If you're listening, she said, please call up. There's nothing to be ashamed of and I would like it. Ciara recited the phone number and said that she'd be there all night. And then she played the next tape.

This music was not dissimilar to the first composition, with stretched notes, except that a synthetic horn instrument carried them further. And the notes were pressed more deliberately, and the echo was stronger, driving the simple melody into fractured, dissipating circles. The colours the music evoked were colours absent in the town – or absent from the physical world entirely. These foreign colours, serene and sad, only brought a stifling clarity to the studio around us. It was painful that we could not somehow inhabit that sound, yet it also seemed impossible that we couldn't.

After dozens of unchanging repetitions in the song, Ciara said to me that she knew she had listeners out there. Why didn't they call? I told her that it might be because they had nothing to say about the music. It was music that elicited a profound sense of hopelessness, that revealed a critical failure of language. The music might have contained its own existence because it bore the complications of one. It could not be adequately discussed during a telephone call, nor politely bonded over. If words tried to live up to this music, they could only fail in their attempt to compensate. What could anyone say, I said to Ciara. She said that they only needed to say that they were listening. They didn't need to admit they were responsible, nor did they need to talk about the music at all. It'd just be nice to know someone else was hearing it. It seemed important.

Hearing her say that made me think about my book, and how it was not important at all. The music seemed to contain everything that was important to convey, and my book was a mess of clumsy, off-the-cuff observations that frequently contradicted each other and never arrived at any truth, real or imagined. The music seemed at peace with meaningless, and my book strove to find meaning where none existed. Or at least, it fumbled with a meaning I lacked the capacity to understand. I was writing my book because it hadn't been written, and beyond that there were no reasons to write it. I was writing my book to lend substance to myself, and to all the spectral people to whom I figured I might potentially belong.

You're listening to Thursday Night Sounds, Ciara said quietly again into the microphone. My guest tonight is writing a book, and he needs your help to complete it. She left a long silence, and continued: It will only take a moment to turn your radio down and call me on the number. She announced the number. Make a request, please. Share a comment, tell a story, anything is welcome. I urge you to call the number immediately. Everything you have to contribute is relevant. We can discuss anything you like. I can try to help you, if help is what you need. Or you can tell me a joke. Ciara paused, and then said, I'm afraid I don't know any jokes.

There was another tense silence. I will wait a little while for your call, she said. I will not let the music play for two minutes. You will not miss anything if you leave your chair, or bed, and walk to wherever your phone is situated. We can then speak on air or off — whichever you want. The studio fell silent. One minute left, Ciara said into the microphone.

I dared to look at Ciara, who was staring at the light on the telephone. Feeling temporarily brave, I let my eyes linger on hers, but they evaded me as she moved to play the next song. Then she slouched back in her chair and stared up at the ceiling. A funereal major key melody stretched over a booming, barely audible drone. I gave up wondering about Ciara's mood for a moment and let the music absorb me. When I did, I soon needed to pull back, gasp for air, before the undercurrents pulled me permanently in. I fixed my stare on the cassette player, eager to rationalise the music, eager to reduce it to a composition deliberately recorded onto tape. But the dread was insurmountable, and its source could not be unpicked to any extent that would explain the feelings it wrought. I wanted to leave the room but felt crippled by the strongest desire to make Ciara forget I was there. The music rendered all my efforts pathetic, and nothing I could ever do would live up to it.

The composition ended as abruptly it had started, with a jarring fade and silence.

I might not read an extract from my book after all, I said. Doing so did not seem in keeping with the spirit of her program. Whatever you want, she said. She supposed her radio show might not have been in keeping with the spirit of anything. It's not, I said, relieved. It's definitely not at all. And then I laughed.

I went to the bathroom and flushed my extract down the toilet, and then climbed out the foyer window onto the roof and smoked one of Ciara's cigarettes. The town's lights seemed more static than usual, as if the world had paused to contemplate the music. The black stretch of countryside at the edge appeared more foreboding and unknowable than before. If anyone listened to Ciara's radio show, they likely lived out there.

When I climbed back into the station Ciara was mopping the foyer floor. I wanted to say something intimate, but more than ever before I felt unqualified to speak.

She gestured at the mop and told me that she needed to take a break from the music sometimes. I told her that I understood. She smiled. Thanks for listening to my radio show, she said.

I left her there alone. Men and women argued on the footpath outside, drunk and frustrated. None could convey their message. They were all trying very hard to be heard. I could not make sense of anything they argued, and I wondered whether they might at some point stumble across a realisation otherwise too sentimental for my line of thinking. But I felt sentimental too that night, and their arguments, drunken though they were, seemed born of more critical symptoms. The town was coming to an end – that much could not be ignored, not even by them. The nature of the ending, though, was harder to know. I drank a longneck of Sheaf Stout and went to bed in the shadows cast by the lights of the petrol station, still open for business, despite everything.

———

The town's train station was exactly as Jenny had described: a so-called museum inside a train station, ostensibly a tribute to a closed stop, but in actual fact a shop selling artisanal dolls, crockery and landscape paintings.

I arrived a bit before 5pm and explained to the man at the counter that I was there to see the freight train. I lied that I intended to board it, just to see his reaction. He said I absolutely could not board the freight train, that it didn't stop, that he didn't know where it went, and that besides, it was a freight train.

I bought an Anzac biscuit and found a seat on the platform. The station retained all of the qualities one expects of an historical train station: lush potted plants, quaint wooden signage, and ornate metal park chairs. At 4:59pm I could see the freight train trundling closer to the station. Then, at exactly 5pm, its engine entered the eastern side of the station before the series of rusted metal containers it pulled shuttled through, revealing nothing of their contents as they passed into the western distance.

So there you have it, the museum operator said. He had arrived at my side without me noticing, giving off an odour of coffee and cigarette smoke. He told me that now I'd seen the freight train I could imagine what it might have been like during the time the train station operated at its full capacity. Maybe I could even imagine what it had been like to board or alight the train here, he said, in a voice intended to evoke wonder. He thought about this all the time.

As Jenny had warned, the museum operator knew nothing of when the station was built, nor when it was officially closed. He and his wife had opened the shop many years ago with the council's blessing, and it was possible that the station had operated during their lifetime, only how could they know the finer details when they themselves had never harboured any desire to catch a train anywhere? For details on the history of the train station, the museum operator advised that I try asking the elderly people of the town, though he doubted I'd find an answer for such an obscure question.

The freight train's destination was also obscure information, according to the museum operator. He did not mention the man who had once jumped onto the train, possibly to avoid spreading bad publicity about his business.

Oh the train goes somewhere, he said, returning to his evocative tone. It no doubt transports produce from the city to the country. I suggested to the museum operator that normally produce would also travel from the country to the city, and that perhaps the freight train travelled back towards the city in a round trip. The museum operator denied it. The freight train only travels from east to west, he said. That means somewhere west there is a town or station with a field of terminated freight trains, I speculated aloud. It's possible that there are many acres, hundreds of square kilometres even, of terminated freight trains with nowhere to go. The museum operator agreed that this was probably true, but claimed it wasn't his job to oversee the state's infrastructure, it being a task more complicated than he or I could possibly imagine. He walked away.

When the museum operator left the platform I climbed onto the tracks and walked in a westerly direction. After five hundred metres the track curved away from the station, winding its way between the back fences of residential houses, before running straight for a kilometre in what I took to be a south-westerly direction. The grass on the track side of the sagging neighbour-hood fences was thick with trash and Paterson's Curse. The houses looked sad and decrepit from this vantage point, but I could not have been in the poor area of the town: the gasworks façade was nowhere in sight, and besides, the poor area was east of the train station.

My disorientation really started in earnest when the train line I was walking on passed beneath a bridge I had never seen before. A certain vantage point to the left of the track revealed signage for a tyre warehouse on the street above—Mick's Motors and Tyre Warehouse—which was presumably part of a small in-dustrial neighbourhood I had never encountered before. Neither my frequent exploratory walks in the town, nor the bus's ex-haustive route, had ever taken me there.

Past the bridge, the lines of residential homes were replaced by the looming cement backs of two- and three-storey build-ings, visibly aged and grey. It was impossible to discern the finer

SHAUN PRESCOTT

details of the town's layout from there, but I was certain I had never seen the front of those tall buildings − nor any other tall building for that matter. A crest of land started to emerge at both sides, gradually ascending until I was walled in by old rocks. The sky seemed much further away now, more remote, in that tunnel-like valley. I had never felt so tightly pressed in by the town.

Though afternoon was fading I did not feel compelled to turn around. I began to suspect I had entered another town altogether, or else a secret district inaccessible by road or footpath. It was true that the town's grinding mood of over-familiarity had lifted − though I only recognised the mood in retrospect, once it had gone. Wandering the enclosed train track, I felt like an explorer treading beyond some impenetrable threshold for the first time.

After a while the tall cement buildings were behind me, but the track remained sunken in the earth. The rocky crests at either side were too steep and unstable to climb. Traffic sounds had diminished; cicadas droned in their place. Far ahead, the crests gradually fell away into a bleak, dark-green countryside. When I finally emerged, the track continued in a straight line to the horizon, through half-a-dozen paddocks and over a hill. No other features were in view except the silhouettes of distant trees, and the early evening shimmer of a muddy dam. It was impossible to tell how far the hill on the horizon was in the dusk, but there was no need to investigate − it was obvious the track's destination was too far away. The earth in those fields radiated loneliness.

Yet I felt compelled to follow the track anyway. I had nothing to lose, and it had been a long time since I had seen an uninterrupted expanse of land, let alone walked across one. The sun had fused pleasantly with the distant hills, suffusing the dark blue with an orange glow. Ignoring the track, it was possible to imagine that no one else had set foot on these plains before.

There was no evidence of country homes or improvised dirt – no farming, no campfires, no disappearing towns. I walked for nearly half-an-hour before it dawned on me that the sun had made no progress in its decline: it sat permanently at the cusp of the horizon, and the track was as faintly illuminated as it had been when I exited the makeshift railway valley.

Meanwhile, the sky behind me—the sky above where the town must have been—was not illuminated at all. There was no light pollution, no distant ambience and no gasworks tower. Either the town had disappeared, or I had.

At that remove the town existed only as a memory, and not a very vivid one. I was unable to remember the specific layout of its streets with any clarity. Only certain building façades came to mind, completely at random, and when I thought about Ciara I couldn't picture her. She was a name and a series of barely connected facts, and none of these cohered. It was difficult to stay rational under the potent impression that I had never been in the town at all. My memories were like those of locations in books – locations born of the imagination's impulse rather than any painstaking description on the author's part. Though stars festooned the sky thicker than in the town, and though the moon was close to full, the surface of the land I trod was sunken in darkness, and I needed to step carefully.

At that moment it seemed impressive that the town existed at all. In a world of famous landmarks and major cities, of globally-felt phenomena and apocalyptic prognostications, it was a miracle the town was there, even if it was now invisible to my eyes.

I was walking across the type of land often described as 'wild' and 'indifferent'. Close though I was to a well-established town, my instinct was to believe that the land was not to be known. It was the slate on which a certain variety of logic and meaning

SHAUN PRESCOTT

could be drawn, and it seemed inevitable that some day, someone would. But this land was not as wild and indifferent as I
had come to expect. It was at the edge of a town, after all, and
just over the nearest hill there might have been the highway,
raging with its own indifference through the lay of the land. The
town was wild and indifferent, I was wild and indifferent, but it
seemed during that suspended moment at the edge of the town
that the land was anything but. From the town, it was impossible to see the land stretch this luxuriously. The town shunned it,
repurposed it, shielded it with terminated developments, distant
edgeland warehouses, and the waste that accumulated at the
side of the never-ending westerly highway.

For the likes of me it was only possible to either be in the
town, or at the edge of it, or very far away − somewhere specifically else. At the crest of the distant hill the remains of the sun
illuminated what appeared at first to be nothing at all. When my
eyes adjusted, I realised I was standing on the last hill. The only
horizon left was the one that lead to more identical horizons,
and I supposed the desert was out there, maybe hundreds of
kilometres away.

To the far east of this view lay the unmistakable silhouette
of the town's gasworks, and then the glitter of the lighted town
surrounding it. I did not question the logic of the train track
I had walked along. There was no use thinking about the lost
freight trains. The gasworks and the town lights beckoned me
on the horizon.

When I got back to town I told Jenny what I had found. She
shook her head, said it was harsh and dangerous out there. God
knows how the likes of her lived at the edge of this harshness
and danger, but she did, they all did, and she supposed that was
what made them of the town.

I told Jenny that the town should not be thought of as brave simply by dint of sitting where it does. It was arrogant to consider the land outside the town as wild and indifferent. If this is the land we all claim to belong to, then surely a more charitable view was owed. She only laughed when I said this. She didn't belong to the land at all, she said. Some of it was hers, she owned a piece of it, but she did not belong. It seemed more than ever that she believed herself a frontierswoman, one braving a ruthless soil. In fact all she did was live in a building, buffered by other buildings, buffered by the barriers the town had either inadvertently or deliberately put in place.

The land outside the town was beautiful, she said, but it was an ugly beautiful. The misty green fields in England, she said — now that is beautiful. The beaches in Bali, that's beautiful. The land outside of the town there is a dry wreck—and she gestured towards out there—but it's an ugly beautiful. It was like the people of the town, really.

It wasn't like us at all, I thought, though I dared not press the point with Jenny. There was nobility in ugliness. The town, by comparison, was a dreary simulacrum of somewhere else, somewhere not belonging to here.

———

If Ciara's predictions are correct then the end of everything is looming as I write, many months after we parted ways. Ciara's apocalypse is closer now than it was back then. I've reason to believe that she is right, as do many others. Evidence is emerging. The newspapers and pundits cannot escape it anymore.

But for some the end of everything is daily. I know who was displaced, that they experienced their own terminal crisis not too long ago. Some live in the aftermath. Now I know that I shouldn't have tried to write any book. I know that the books that are worth writing already exist somewhere, buried in the most inaccessible chambers of labyrinthine state libraries. No book is mine to write. At least, none that describe this.

———

During the weeks before I lost all hope of writing a book about the town, I laboured to find its essence. It's true that I had never properly understood what an essence might be, nor was I certain that a town should always have one.

For a time I would ask the people I had met, with deliberate bluntness, what the essence of the town was. Jenny at the pub said the town's essence was being a town. Ciara said the town's essence was not a characteristic she was qualified to define. Tom had already said the essence of the town was that nothing was complete. That there was always a fraction missing. That maybe the fraction missing was the essence.

The streets were changing. The central park of the town was grown over, wrappers tangled the lawn; you didn't enter for fear of snakes and well-disguised holes. The shops on the main street operated on strange schedules. It was like a giant hand had lifted and shaken the town, scattering its logic, severing all of its threads. For days the linen boutique would be shuttered but then, on a muggy evening towards midnight, the door would be open and the counter manned – but only by a shadow. There was a new essence in this—and I hoped at the time to arrive at it one day—but it was too late to diagnose the essence that was gone. Maybe there was never an essence, and this was the town's punishment for having never established one.

I walked aimlessly in search of the former essence, supposing a perfect angle on a specific setting might illuminate it. I supposed the essence might be in the language of the townspeople: not what they said, but the way they said it. It's true there was an attitude and a certain way of holding one's body in the town, but I didn't know what they believed, or why, nor the origin of these. I only had my suspicions.

My book was following the same trajectory as the librarian's. It didn't seem possible to write about the disappearing town, nor towns already disappeared, because there was nothing true to observe in them. The town is a patchwork of strange fictions, I told the librarian, though it wouldn't be entirely true to make that observation either. Who would understand it? I suppose few would care to verify it, and even fewer would read it in the first place. I had forgotten why I wanted to write the book. What had I been searching for?

That's brave of you to admit, the librarian told me, seated during his lunch break at the Michel's Patisserie opposite the Big W.

After becoming a failed writer of books, the librarian had aspired to be an exceptionally good person instead. Seated one day in the park in the centre of town, eating his packed lunch, he had brainstormed how he would do so. He had lost all hope of revealing the depth of his character in book form, so he would need to demonstrate it in some other way.

No available options had satisfied: he had not wanted to and nor was he able to make an extraordinary donation to any charity, and he had not wanted to help the elderly cross roads, or house stray dogs. Strategies like these promised neither elation nor pleasure, and he had wanted his goodness to be widely acknowledged, because, he had thought, there was no evidence that the town being good automatically made him good. He told me that this is what everyone else believed: that they are each and all good because the town is good – or, at least, they believe that they are not bad. Those who actually are bad, he said, are said to be possessed by some force atypical of the town, possessed by some foreign contagion, perhaps.

The librarian had believed that in order to assert himself publicly as someone good, he needed to do so under circumstances that were not just a matter of rote benevolence. It had to be sudden, and seemingly born of some brilliant instinct. He had decided that he needed to save someone's life.

The librarian had never devised a plan for how this would happen. Instead he had just wandered the streets after his shifts, on the lookout for any seemingly dangerous turn of events. He'd visited pubs with the hope of intervening in brawls, and he'd lingered in the central park at night in order to interrupt any muggings. Occasionally he'd sit for a minute or two near the busiest intersection in town, on the slight chance that someone would crash their car. No one ever did – or at least, they never did while he'd been there.

His plan had never worked. Now, he told me, he still had no idea what qualities those people most respected in the town possessed that he didn't. They're all successful businesspeople, he supposed, but he could never run a business, for he was bad at maths, bad at talking to people, and bad at accepting that he was not a writer of books. He was, it seemed, bad at everything—especially bad at being a part of the town—so there was little point in asking him, he said, about the town's so-called essence.

The librarian checked his watch. It was time for him to go back to work, where he would sort and file books written by other people. I told the librarian that it might not be long before everything in the town changed dramatically. The holes were spreading quickly, doubling overnight, and it would come as no surprise if they started appearing inside of people too. This possibility of holes appearing inside of people had never occurred to me until I said it. Now I wondered if the holes had been appearing inside of people for years. What if the librarian had a hole inside him? What if I did?

The town won't disappear, the librarian told me. But he said that if it did, it would allow him to create something more accurate in its place. He would write with meticulous detail about this new beginning, so that in the distant future people could trace the trajectory of the town from beginning to end. In a whole new town the librarian might even have a say in establishing what the town was about from the start. He could make sure there were never any factual errors. The old people of the town—and he waved at the current town—would have no say. They had forgotten what this town was about, selectively, and he'd never forgive them for doing so. In his history, the elderly would be prehistoric, inscrutable, so far removed from the truth of his new town that no one could possibly grasp the extent to which they had lived. From that distance, he said, history might suppose that they had never lived at all.

But he told me he'd never given a new town any close thought, since the current town definitely wasn't going to disappear. And he shrugged his shoulders and left the Michel's Patisserie without saying goodbye.

———

The next morning, three blocks of the main street had disappeared. The absence was so large that it was no longer just depthless or devoid of colour. Instead, it had become a glimmering mirror, towering skyward, as high and wide as the missing buildings. Viewed from any direction, the mirror—it could no longer be called a hole—reflected the land in those directions. At least, it appeared to do so. No one dared prove it. People saw with their own eyes, amid the softly drawn world inside, a reflection of a region in which they no longer lived.

Early risers pottered the streets at its edge, staring into the reflection of the vacated landscape in which they stood. This disappearance could not be contained with chipboard or any other material. Someone called the police, and they came, but they only joined the witnesses. By nine o'clock, hundreds were spectating from adjoining roads, careful not to stand on the yellow-taped pieces of chipboard that had long consumed the footpaths.

I heard someone ask out loud: what could have caused it? Many people were saying similar things, at first mildly and remotely, and then, as the hours passed, with an impatient tinge. None had answers, but the most common belief was that it was an environmental disaster. By midday that theory was widely believed to be true, and there was an atmosphere of relief, as now someone powerful would no doubt come to their aid. Someone in the town had surely appealed for help. Probably the police had already done so, or the mayor, or a town busybody.

The site came to resemble an impromptu carnival. People gathered on the fifth remaining block of the main street, near the air-conditioned entrances to the two shopping plazas, eating from bags of chips and even drinking beer as they gazed at the mirror. Policemen put up police tape along the edge, lending spectators the courage to wander closer. It was a mirror, but not one that reflected perfectly. Some things in the reflection were missing. None of the witnesses saw themselves. If there was any concern for who might already have been lost inside, I heard none express it. The shops had long closed anyway, and the strip rendered useless, were it not an avenue for cars that, despite the seeming danger, still drove in wide detours around the phenomenon.

Ciara's flat was located in one of the disappeared blocks. But I soon found her among the spectators.

I found her, hand on hip outside the Rivers clothing store, eating a cheesy bread roll from the Bakers Delight discards. She said she'd fallen to sleep in her secret room, and then when she'd tried to climb up into the shed, she'd peered up into the chamber and it was an infinite ladder. It had climbed towards a ceiling in an impossibly large room.

I had emerged from my abandoned home that morning to my normal view of the petrol station across the road. But the bowser boys were not in sight, and no cars lined the lanes. The air was different. When I turned into town on my way to Ciara's flat there was no road and no park. Instead there was the towering hill of reflection, and I thought at first it was a trick of the light. But approaching the emptiness of the browned spectral fields within, no buildings or roads emerged.

Ciara had followed her tunnel back to the stormwater drain entrance. From there, she had edged through the holes, between infested houses and vacant lots, until she arrived at the highway. She waved towards the highway. Business was carrying on as usual there. The cars were driving through like normal, to the city or the country, and the petrol stations there were as busy as they always were. She thought at first that it was an early morning hallucination, except she could detect a strange shade clouding the town centre – and she waved at the sky. Then, when she had marched up the main street to fetch me, her way was blocked by the disappearance.

By early afternoon the people in the town seemed happier, because they were still alive. It was agreed that death by the mirror-hole was unlikely, and it had also been agreed that the problem was now big enough to warrant calling for a government representative to help, or maybe even the military. Such officials would ensure that whatever had been lost would be found, and whatever destroyed fixed. In the meantime it was sensible to make the most of this phenomenon while it lasted. Everyone wanted to be a part of this event because it would surely go down in history. It was something in the town, finally, which would.

There were fights, of course – a natural consequence of having many people in one place in the town. Long lines emerged from the Domino's pizza shop, and the Subway, and a smaller line from the Red Rooster. The main street was legally an alcohol-free zone, but the circumstances prevented the police addressing such minor concerns. Instead they just stood cheerfully at the makeshift barricades to the mirror, posing for photos and exchanging banter with small children.

The festive mood turned volatile when someone penetrated the mirror. A young boy, shorter than the police tape barricade, only five or six or so, wearing shorts, a blue football jumper, sand shoes, and with cropped blond hair, sprinted through the morass and disappeared inside. Loud yells of reaction were followed by the howling of his mother, eerily late to arrive. She made to follow him, but a policeman held her back. Men and women scampered along the edge of the police lines, pretending to be eager to follow the boy in. Bottles and other useless objects were lobbed into the mirror, disappearing instantly. Sensing they were losing control, the police appealed for calm, for quiet, and even experimented with the mirror, dipping in their arms and prodding their feet at its edge, failing to mask their dread as the tips of their limbs momentarily vanished.

Ciara and I stood alone a distance away, at the entry to the clothing store. Everyone else pressed closer to the giant mirror-hole, making unreasonable demands of it and each other, and struggling to compete with the mother. She knocked two policemen over and bull-rushed the mirror, prompting five others to barge after her in pursuit. They all disappeared. Many people were whipped up by their momentum, and followed them.

From our vantage point this entire moment did not seem to be real. Our viewpoint wasn't perfect enough to lend the stampede the sense of gravity it deserved, and the scene wasn't glazed in the manner of a television broadcast, nor was it commentated. Dozens of people, maybe a full hundred, seeped into the mirror, and it didn't feel like it was the most important thing we had ever seen.

Fights broke out among the remaining crowd, with inevitable results. Ciara and I climbed onto the awning of the Rivers clothing store and watched as crowds of men and women fell or were flung or simply marched straight into the phenomenon. Ciara told me she didn't think they were dying. She thought they were just disappearing. I told her that she was probably correct, for if they were going in their hundreds to their deaths, the street would have had a more convincing sense of occasion. It would have felt like an historical moment. It didn't. It all just seemed ridiculous.

Workers at both the Woolworths and Coles heard about the event, finally. We could see them in their near-identical uniforms filing out of the sliding glass doors and onto the footpaths, hands to brows, other hands pointing. I asked Ciara whether she had recognised any of the people vanishing into the phenomenon, and she told me that of course she did. She had recognised every single one of them. She pointed at the crowd and said that it was unlikely however that they recognised each other.

Soon the afternoon sun shone too hotly on the corrugated iron awning we were standing on, so we climbed down and went into one of the big shopping plazas. It was quiet under the fluorescent lights, except for the distant ring of cash registers and barcode scanners at the Woolworths. I bought us a longneck of beer each from the adjoining BWS, and we returned to the street.

Things outside had quietened down. People weren't fighting or marching into the hole anymore. They were all just looking at it again, with a new, strange calm. Although, their focus had indeed shifted. There seemed to be growing resentment among them towards the crowd of people all the way on the other side of the void, who were gathered up near the northern-most petrol station. Perhaps what annoyed them was that there were other people involved at all, watching from an entirely different angle. Maybe the version of events from these other people would prove to be the definitive one. And it did seem that there was no way to get to these other people, for due to holes all the roads in the town were now impossible to navigate (though the wide roads circling the central district were intact), and the only other way was to pass through a fire exit in the plaza with the Coles. But no one did, because it was rumoured that using the fire exit was illegal.

Despite the resentment, or perhaps because of it, people on our side were eager to establish a mood of solidarity among themselves. They chanted the name of the town, and the odd ruffian threw bottles and other rubbish at the mirror. Some people chanted the name of the nation while throwing their trash, as if the mirror were an invading foreign power or something naturally—but not actively—hostile to the town. The number of ruffians in the crowd seemed to grow: shirtless and red-faced, drunk since the morning hours and swollen with gestures. These men, usually tamed by the rules they took for granted in the town, wanted nothing more than to thump somebody amid the new anarchy. They roamed the crowd in packs, targeting the few who did not look perfectly of the town. They had a special instinct for strangers, and before too long four men marched up to the closed Pizza Haven in front of which Ciara and I were standing.

Ciara whispered into my ear that this was Steve Sanders.

I drank deeply from my longneck, and asked which one.

All of them, she said.

My instinct was to flee, and so I did. I ran into the plaza and down the hall that culminated in the fire exit to the other side of the giant mirror-hole, but someone had locked the door. The four Steve Sanderses followed, moving with excruciating calm as they neared me. One of them asked what I was running for. The others laughed. I mentioned my complete innocence, sounding very harmless and pathetic, but in that moment I didn't sound innocent, even to myself.

We just wanted to say hello, one Steve said. You never say hello. Why don't you ever say hello?

I told him I was too shy, and that I had heard rumours that Steve Sanders wanted to bash me.

Each Steve moaned in mock sympathy. One told me that they wanted to bash me because I never said hello. Another said that in this town everyone says hello.

I told them that I didn't know that.

Well it's true, one said. You're writing a book about the town but you don't even say hello.

My book isn't about this town, I told them.

They didn't seem to believe me. Why would you write a book about our town, a Steve Sanders said. There's nothing to say about it.

I agreed that there was no reason to write a book about the town, that there was nothing to say about their town.

So our town isn't worth your time, then, another Steve Sanders said. What's a better town to write about?

There is no better frigging town, another said, the rancid smell of beer on his mouth. What's your problem with this town?

It's not good enough for him, another said.

What a cunt, another added.

You come to our town, take our jobs, and you don't even respect it as the best town in Australia, a Steve Sanders said. Do you see us coming to your town, writing books about it, talking down about it?

Another told me to think carefully before I answered. But I didn't think it wise to make them wait for a considered answer. I told them no, because I didn't have a town of my own.

Bullshit, one said

I saw Ciara behind them, standing at the entry to the hall, signalling at me. She was pointing to her mouth and shaking her head, and making gestures with her fist.

The thinnest Sanders stepped forward, making me flinch. You realise no one in this town likes you? he said. Everyone thinks you're a piece of crap. Why do you stay?

I protested, told them that I actually adored the town. That it was so peaceful and idyllic, that I did not feel good enough for it, hence my lack of saying hello. This prompted Ciara to make her gestures more urgent.

You're taking the piss, one said.

You're only saying that, another said, feigning hurt.

No book exists to just describe how great a town is, the most articulate Sanders said. Books about towns always describe how bad they are, how bad things have happened in them. But what has happened that is so bad in this town? Nothing, because there is no book about it.

We don't have a book, the last Sanders said, and we'd like to keep it that way. He told me that there is no reason to have a book. That if I did write a book, they hoped it'd be about how they punched my lights out. Then they made to attack me, but didn't, like bluffing footballers who don't throw punches because they don't want to get in trouble.

I told them my book wasn't about hidden bad things, but rather the current condition of the town. I told them, warming to the subject of my book, that no one really understands why towns in the Central West of New South Wales are the way they are now. No one has captured their essence in an historical book, nor even a fictional one. Wouldn't it be good for people to understand how excellent things are? Why should you be denied a reason to be here, I told them, thinking myself at that moment to be a cunning manipulator. My book wasn't refuting any history, nor attempting to create one. It was simply an acknowledgment, lest the town disappear. Which it is, I said, pointing towards the giant mirror-hole. I told the multiple Steve Sanderses that they might some day regret antagonising the sole person willing to write a book about their town, and anyway, that there were arguably more important problems at that moment than me and my book.

So you are writing a book about the town, one Steve Sanders said. So you were lying before.

I'm not writing about this town specifically, I said, but about towns in the Central West. I supposed aloud, in a manner I believed to be humble, that their town might share certain characteristics with all the towns I truthfully wanted to write about.

So you think our town is just like any other town, one Steve Sanders said.

I could not think of a correct response to this question – and by correct, I mean a response that would keep them at bay. Being similar to another town might have appealed to them, but it might have angered them too. I responded that I had no conclusion, that I was still studying the other towns, but definitely not this specific one. It made sense for me to stay in this town, given its proximity to the other disappeared or disappearing towns. I used it as a base, as an access point to my real sources.

So our town is just a base for you, one of the Steve Sanders said.

Yes, I said, exhausted. It's a base. But a very pleasant base. A beautiful one, with its own local culture.

For us it's a way of life, another Steve Sanders said. And nothing bad happens here anymore. Nothing happens at all here anymore. There may have been things that happened in the past, but as for now, things definitely do happen, but they're not historical. He dared light a cigarette in the plaza, and continued: does everything that ever happens need to be made into a book? No, he said, I don't think so. Nothing that happens now here is historical. History is in the past. He pointed to the floor and said, this is what history worked towards. This is the result of it. This is what people worked for. Farmers, builders, Anzacs, the lot. This is how things are going to be from now on. This is how they're going to stay. History can end, you know. It doesn't need to keep going. We now have everything set perfectly in place, and so nothing needs to happen anymore. Interesting historical things don't always need to be happening. It's better when they don't.

Yeah, another of the Sanders men said, so even if you were writing a book about the town, it wouldn't be very interesting. No one would care about your book.

Just admit you're a fuckwit, mate, another said.

The fire alarm went off, and we stood there, confused. Within a few seconds all the Coles employees arrived at the head of the hall, sweeping Ciara up in their panic. The Steve Sanders that was smoking stubbed out his cigarette, turned around, and told the Coles employee evacuees to use the main entry because the fire exit was locked. The store manager jangled a chain of many keys in a show of authority, and none of the Steve Sanderses could resist it, so they stepped aside. Amid the fuss Ciara grabbed my arm and pulled me back inside the plaza. We ran, and the Sanderses ran after us. As we turned the corner towards the sliding exit doors to the street, one crash-tackled me from behind.

You can't run from us, a Steve Sanders barked as he pinned me to the ground. If you do, there's always others out there ready to pounce. He punched me in the collarbone and then stood, pressing one foot against my chest. I had hoped the Steve Sanderses no longer wanted to bash me, that a simple dressing-down would suffice, but they started to kick me with increasing force. Ciara stepped outside and lit a cigarette.

Moments later she yelled to the nearby crowd outside that there was a fight. Dozens rushed to witness the spectacle: a proper brawl. I can't recall how many people because I quickly passed out, probably from terror, more than the pain.

—

The next day when Ciara arrived at my house I was sitting in the dusty lounge room writing my book. Although I had decided my book would never be completed, there was no other way to spend the time. I also felt like not writing a book would render my whole existence pointless.

I was surprised to see her, as she had appeared to abandon me the day before. Before I could say anything, she asked what I could possibly be writing under the circumstances.

I told her that I was in the middle of a chapter I had never previously thought to include in my book. It was an important chapter, and it was requiring a whole new approach. I would need to write a second draft after all, I told Ciara, because I believed I knew why the town—her town—was disappearing before our very eyes.

The evidence has been there all along, I said. I'd thought about it deeply: if you scrutinise anything for longer than a moment, nothing is really complete. Everything is missing at least one component — sometimes something negligible, at other times something crucial. All of these absences, the cavities, are the empty spaces where important structural elements would normally exist in order to support the ongoing truth of anything. It is the same for a town.

From above, I said, the town may appear to be an island, but upon closer inspection it is just an accumulation of flotsam, bobbing this way and that, and it is a surprise to me that anyone has ever managed to set foot upon it, much less walk safely on it. And it is extraordinary that many actually believe it to be an island: a location, especially a location with a purpose.

That's a very artistic way of putting it, Ciara said. She laid on my bed and closed her eyes. I suppose she had not slept for many days, considering the circumstances. But I interrupted her efforts because I wanted to know whether she thought my view on the town held any truth. She sat up and said she did not know. All she knew was that the next day she was going to breach what was left of the shimmer. She couldn't stay once the whole town had properly disappeared, because she was certain that if she did, she would disappear too.

I told her that I thought this was both sensible and true.

She said we ought to go to my town. Maybe there we could live with my parents until she could sort her new life out. She could pretend to be my lover if necessary. Perhaps she could get a job and settle in my town, and make some friends, and one day start to belong. Maybe she would grow to understand the culture of the town I came from, and she could perhaps even one day be indistinguishable from the local people. She could become so accustomed to my town's culture that she'd make it her routine to visit a Michel's Patisserie every morning, where the people would look up from their coffees and newspapers to greet her warmly. Then she might gossip lightly with the barista while sipping on a coffee of some kind. Then she might have children, born to the town, who would be so unambiguously of the town that it would prove to the townspeople, beyond a shadow a doubt, that she too was officially of the town. Maybe they would forget that she was not truthfully of the town.

Her plan was impossible, but I didn't say so, or begin to explain why.

She said it would be sensible to visit a new town and to find people with whom she felt comfortable. She had always considered doing this, she had to admit. But such a thing was inconceivable, she said. Maybe she could trick people into believing she was of the town, but forever she would know that she was from somewhere else. And even if she forgot, and even if no one else knew, the truth would be that she was from somewhere else.

Or even worse: since her town was currently disappearing, she would soon be from nowhere else. She was becoming someone from nowhere, and that was unthinkable. How would people tolerate it? Any town culture she could imagine would not permit that, she was sure. They would be suspicious of her. She would be the woman from nowhere. She envisioned it like this: she would arrive in a town, even my supposed home town, and stay at my supposed parents house, and we would pretend to be lovers, and she would visit a pub with me and meet my supposed old friends, and they would shower her with warm greetings and compliments because they were happy that I was in love with someone, but soon enough they would ask her where she was from, and she could not simply say "I don't know" or "I've forgotten"—she would need to say she was from nowhere, for she would have no option but to tell the truth, and under those circumstances I would need to break up with her due to pressure from my town culture, and she would end up in the stormwater drains or in the abandoned buildings in my town, and she would need to kill and eat pests for sustenance, and she would be jeered at and spat on by men and women warm in the embrace of their town culture, and she would become addicted to drugs.

So these are the best and worst case scenarios, Ciara told me. But she knew that more than likely what would happen is that she would miss her town culture, despite it not being much of a culture at all. And so she would eventually reveal too much reverence for her disappeared town culture to my town's people, and they would detest her for seemingly having a different culture at all. They would try to compare town cultures, and they would be worried that hers threatened to be better.

Ciara laid back down on my bed. She added that none of it made sense, because she suspected all the towns in the country were the same.

I didn't know for certain whether all of the towns in the country were the same, but I was able to imagine they were. The city is probably different, I said. There were surely great mysteries in the city. And it was almost certain that we would be able to uncover secrets about Ciara's town in the city, as the city is where knowledge is kept. It is where the important libraries are, full of books written for their own sake. These books, I told Ciara, were only written to allow someone to be certain they existed. They only existed to verify that certain events and phenomena existed. They were not written for the joy of reading. Besides, I said, we can't go to my town. I don't have a town.

The city it is, she said.

3

THE DISAPPOINTING CITY

The town was only a memory during my final days living in the abandoned house. It had mostly disappeared, and what remained could not have been mistaken for a town.

It was difficult to decide whether to leave the remains of the town. When in my mind reasons to leave seemed obvious and logical, reasons to stay would soon follow. This is where I belong, I would say to myself. I belong here, to something that has never been anything. Other towns, or the city, or even the drowsy plains beyond the breach, might only serve to demonstrate that I, and Ciara, and everyone else in the town, are not real. We were there, but none of us were real.

In the big coastal city they might ask who we are, and we might not have an answer. Everyone there would be already comforted by their own reasons for being. They might have rituals and customs which they could explain by history, serving to assure them that they are real.

They may not ever need new vantage points to know that there is more in the world. They may only need to cross the street, or to catch a train from home and travel three stations.

Their city might keep them occupied forever, and even if they were barely as real as us, they might never have cause or time to wonder why they're barely there. They might never have cause to wonder about their bearing to the soil, having barely ever stood on soil proper, having barely ever seen it at all.

During my final days in the town I became frustrated with the townspeople in the plazas. Nothing they had lost was real. None of it could be substantiated. No one could accurately define their town's essence during the rare occasions they were lucid enough to try. The truth of their town culture was only that they were there. The town culture was the belief that they were meant to be there.

———

Rick lived in a small fibro home at the edge of the town. What remained of the road's tarmac had worn grey and patched. It might have been the oldest part of the town, given the rust on the Tonka trucks that lay tangled in weeds, and the barbed-wired gasworks looming in its centre. Most people in the town had long recommended against visiting these particular few blocks.

I knocked for several minutes before Rick answered. The house smelt of cooked pasta, tobacco smoke, and dust. He took a moment before he realised who I was. Then he dropped his arms resignedly and walked up the hall. I followed.

On a television in the lounge room an elderly woman was remarking on some stainless steel trays. The lounge room was dark save for a dim yellow lamp in the corner, a lit cigarette in the ashtray, and the fluorescent green indicator of a rotating air conditioner. A mattress leaned against one wall, a makeshift couch with pillows propped as backrests. Four plastic bags rustled in the air conditioner fan. Receipts were piled atop a makeshift coffee table.

Mum's asleep, he whispered.

He beckoned me into his kitchen. There were no appliances or utensils or anything in there except a toaster. Rick was cooking some toast, and offered me some slices with Vegemite. I declined, since I was in a rush. I've already eaten my breakfast, I said. Rick told me he couldn't eat breakfast first thing. He needed to feel starving in order to eat. Especially in the morning – and he pointed at the television screen. He knew it was unusual to wait so long to eat. His mum was hungry the moment she woke up.

He went about his business making his meal. It took several minutes. Then he turned and faced me, and sunk his teeth into the toast. He was ready to hear whatever I had to say.

I told him that I was going to drive to the city, and that I would stay there permanently, and that he should join me and begin a new life. There would be hundreds of supermarkets in the city, I said, and he may even get a job in one. Or in the city he might feel inclined to never set foot in a supermarket again. He would no longer need to repurpose his town, since he would no longer be living in it. The town had never shuffled to make a place for him, and so going to the city seemed to be the only natural thing to do for someone in Rick's position.

The Woolworths is still here, I said, signalling towards the town's centre, but it now would take a great amount of effort and luck to get there. You can't simply march to the supermarket anymore. You have to know the exact route.

Rick told me that he already knew the route well – he'd already figured it out. There were parts that would never quite disappear entirely—and he pointed towards the street—on certain roads. Stick to the right roads, and you were unlikely to vanish.

Besides, he said, the Woolworths definitely won't disappear. They were still cycling through this quarter's sales. Prices on a particular brand of muesli bars were scheduled to plummet next week. He told me that he knew this because the supermarket always left obscure hints about its future sales: breadcrumb trails for the dedicated bargain hunter. If the powers that be at Woolworths suspected something as sinister as complete disappearance, Rick surmised, they would not bother planning a major sale.

I knew for a fact that in a fortnight the Woolworths was planning on rolling out a two for \$3 sale on Sanitarium muesli bar packs, and so perhaps it was true that the entire premises were unlikely to disappear. But I told Rick that he had missed my point: that it was not important what was happening at the supermarket. He did not approve of my tone.

He said he knew he was an idiot, that it was idiotic to be addicted to supermarkets and unable to see life beyond them. He said he could detect in the tone of my voice that I thought I was conversing with someone much stupider than myself. I must have thought I was acting noble, he told me, trying to save someone far less capable. He said that he was well aware he was as stupid as it was possible to get as a grown adult. He'd already proven himself incapable of living like an adult, and yet, he'd not sought escape and gratification like so many wiser stupid adults did. He was stupid in a way that I could never understand. He supposed I tore my hair out, witnessing his missed opportunities to escape stupidity. If only he could see this very simple solution, I must have thought to myself. There were so many better ways to lead a stupid life, not to mention all the ways he could stop living a stupid life altogether.

Rick told me he thought he lived the stupidest life possible.

He saw drunks on the pension who couldn't hold their bladders, yet they seemingly lived lives less stupid than his. He saw infants, unable to talk or stand up straight, unable to articulate themselves except to cry, and yet his life was clearly much stupider than theirs. Infants and drunks... their lives weren't determined every step of the way by stupidity. But his was. Everyone who had ever looked at him thought he was too stupid. It wasn't that he'd done stupid things, it was just that he lived a stupid life, even though he'd attempted nothing different to what his friends or parents had. He gestured towards his mother's room.

Rick insisted that he was not trying to elicit sympathy from me. Why would he bother, when he knew the first thing I felt laying eyes upon him was sympathy? I must have known he lived a stupid life before he'd ever uttered a word.

There had always been many options available to Rick in order for him to stop living such a stupid life. If some sequence of stupid events guaranteed that he could not live a satisfying life by the measure of the town, then why not live an emphatically stupid life? Why not be irrational? Why not live an evil life? He had no family. He could wander into the horizon and happen on a house and burn it to the ground, or he could catch a lift to another town and seduce every woman in his path. What would be the point of doing otherwise? He wasn't getting what he was promised. He might as well.

It would be satisfying to do both of those things, and if he were to do them, there wouldn't be much at stake. But he could only think. When he considered deviating from his set path, his muscles would not let him. He could not convince his limbs to do what his mind would like, but the same held true in the opposite direction: his mind obstructed his limbs. There was a vast gulf between them. Both were frightened at their opposite ends of the chasm. They bickered relentlessly in search of a solution.

He said he supposed this just made him normal. But he was a normal person in a stupid life. There was nothing stupider than when he awoke in the morning. He would be tranquil for a minute or two, and then he would remember: this is the stupidest existence possible. It almost felt like a responsibility, Rick said, to let life continue to ladle stupidity on his head. I was lucky—he pointed at me—because I'd only ever witnessed people with stupid lives, but I didn't live a stupid life. What type of life did I live?

I told him that I didn't know. That there was no specific mood to my life. That I did not awaken into stupidity, but nor did I awaken into something satisfactory or serene. That I just woke up and the first thought that occurred to me defined my day. I said this to Rick on a whim, though it wasn't true at all.

Rick told me that if the town was disappearing, then so was he. After all, he had felt both happy and wretched there, and that is the most anyone can ask for, especially an idiot. He didn't get to decide the ratio, and nor did I. But he knew one thing: he didn't want to set the process in motion again. There may be happiness elsewhere, but there would be wretchedness, too. The ratio would not change.

I was growing tired of listening to Rick philosophise about his life. I told him that the town was disappearing, and that it might be impossible to leave by conventional roads by the time he had finished his speech.

Why would I leave now, Rick said. Perhaps things were changing for the better, because soon enough the town would only be the plazas. It'd only be the supermarkets. He wondered: why shouldn't he stick around to watch his memories advance into their purest forms? There was relief to be found in that large absence at the centre of town—and he waved towards the absence—because everything he had ever wanted was impossible for everyone, now.

I did not want to be drawn further into one of Rick's speeches, so I accepted his desire to stay, and left his house via the back door. As I did, Rick instructed me to climb through two blocks of backyards, swing through the canopy over Rozelle Street, and then walk along a certain low brick fence that I could take the rest of the way to the plaza.

———

Tom's bus route had ceased to exist. The main bus terminal was lost in the mirror.

On the footpath outside her disappeared pub, I told Jenny about Tom's bus route, as a means to demonstrate that it wasn't only her livelihood that had been ruined by holes. She didn't agree.

What do you expect? Jenny said. Who would catch a bus now, anyway? No one would catch a bus under these circumstances, even if they could. But everyone always needs a drink.

The holes were a matter of serious inconvenience to her. She was waiting for an intervention, or maybe she was waiting to disappear too. Jenny had lived her life at the frontline of logic, barracking for it. There on the footpath at the edge of her disappeared pub, she may well have been wondering how anyone or anything could restore the town's face value. I don't think she even knew: her stubbornness blocked any conclusions at which she might have arrived.

I asked her to come to the city with me, but she refused. It was barely Australian there, she said.

I spent six hours searching for Tom. I searched at the

McDonald's—still bustling with commuters and oblivious townsfolk—and I searched at the recreation ground too. He might have been eaten up at the bus terminal, lost inside the mirror. He might have driven straight into it, perceiving no difference in the empty reflection.

Eventually I found his bus on the edge of town, by the monolithic Bunnings, parked at the edge of a weeded gully with doors open and hazard lights on. You always put hazard lights on in a stationary bus, Tom had once said to me solemnly. Even off-road. It's about safety.

Tom was in the bus. He had been sitting there at the edge of the town for days now, with a dry petrol tank and a view of the shimmery horizon just over the crest of a nearby hill. He said he'd considered walking back to town, but had already sworn privately that he'd never return. Not for any practical matter, anyway. He felt he really should head to the next town—and he pointed towards the horizon—but to walk would take days, probably weeks, if there was even another town at all.

I ducked back into town and returned with a jerry can of petrol. But by then Tom no longer wanted to drive to another town. The renewed possibility cast doubt on the project. Instead he wanted to recommence driving the circular road around the town. Life wouldn't be any different in the next town, Tom insisted. He said that if I thought any differently then I had clearly lived a very different life to his. Everything was the same everywhere, even in the city. Tom speculated that it was probably even worse in the city, and waved towards the east. It was barely Australian there.

How could he possibly know, I asked, if he had never been to the city, or even another town? In a new place he might form another band and potentially become famous. He could sing songs about being a bus driver in a disappearing town. There aren't songs already about that, I said. To my knowledge there are no songs about this town at all. Why couldn't he be the pioneer of songs about the town? People might warm to them, now that it had disappeared. He could even channel the moods he had discovered in the music of The Out of Towners. But he said he'd already tried to copy The Out of Towners' music, but never with any success. When he played in their style it sounded like music created by a child, even though he had more experience playing music than any of them. No matter what he did, he could not reproduce the sadness of their simple music. Even though his life had grown sad, he was just not able to.

Tom only wanted to make music that recognised the town wasn't what it used to be, but he wondered: why should there be new music about that? It would do no one any favours, he said, and anyway, he was certain it was impossible to do it deliberately. It happened naturally: even happy songs, completely unrelated to the town, composed abroad in state-of-the-art studios, contain the message that the town isn't what it used to be. Sadness was the fate of every song.

He had once tried to deliberately write the saddest song of all time, but it only sounded like the most pathetic song of all time. And anyway, there was no chance it would ever be heard. The reason there are no songs about the town, he said, is that the town isn't anything anymore. It's just a place where lots of people happen to live. People have thought for a long time that the town was unique, in ways they could never articulate. But it isn't.

Back when Tom was still playing gigs he thought he might one day become a pioneer of the town's music. It would take time, though, and maybe the time would never come. As time passed, Tom had grown to believe that there was no story or theme to the town. It was what it had always been: the super-markets, the cheap mansion suburbs, the diminishing town squares, the traffic, the fast food chains, the dozen or so petrol stations. He didn't know when the town had turned from the fabled paradise of old into a place like everywhere else. It had no centre—he waved towards the mirror—but perhaps it never did. Not for as long as he could remember. He suspected that centres were disappearing everywhere.

Jenny was still on the footpath when I passed by that evening. She was standing, hands on hips, facing the phenomenon that had consumed her pub. I tried to offer my condolences, and tried to offer some suggestions, but she only shrugged me away. This country's gone to the dogs, she said.

———

Ciara and I hadn't discussed how we would leave the town, but it was clear we couldn't walk. When I brought the matter up with Ciara she was not concerned: she said we'd just have to steal one of her parents' cars.

Though Ciara had been squatting in the flat near the central park for more than a year, she seemed to believe that her parents didn't know where she lived. But the whole town must have seen her perched on the balcony all the time, enjoying her vantage point.

I didn't press Ciara on the subject of her parents. She seemed certain they had not disappeared, and equally certain that a Commodore sedan would be parked in front of their home in the tentacle edgelands.

We first visited her underground tunnel from the drain entry and bundled as many of her cassettes as would fit into four plastic shopping bags. Then we visited my townhouse, where I made copies of my files and then smashed the computer. I dropped the ruined computer in a hole by the telephone box outside.

It took most of the night to walk to Ciara's parents' home. The holes had eaten large swathes of terrain. Whole intersections were impossible to traverse, and the roads in the old part of town could not be navigated at all. We crept through sleeping properties, some houses now skeletal, our torches aimed down at the grass in case of holes.

As we crossed a pockmarked bridge onto the highway, Ciara said she had left her parents' home the year before. She couldn't figure out a reason to stay with them. Every day had been the same. Her dad would go to work, and her mum would stay at home, cleaning and watching television. Then her mum would eat a sandwich at lunchtime and browse the catalogues that came in the mailbox. Her dad would then come home, drink a bourbon and Coke, and watch four television shows in a row: the news, then two soap operas, then an American sitcom. Then he might watch the beginning of a movie, but would fall asleep before it finished. Then at the weekend they would go to the plazas. She said it had gotten unbearably boring.

I had my doubts about stealing their car, but Ciara said they had three cars anyway: one for her mum, one for her dad, and one for ducking down to the shops.

The tentacle roads—or at least the one Ciara's parents lived on—seemed unaffected by the holes. It was early morning when we arrived at the foot of the street, the sky dotted pink and white. Ciara had watched the neighbourhood grow; she could remember a time when her house and two others were the only buildings on the street. It had seemed like a desert. Her whole early life was lived in a construction zone, debris and materials everywhere, dust and dirt, yellow mesh fences around burgeoning lots. The view from her bedroom window had resembled a war zone. Once a new house was completed, shiny green grass would be laid like an oasis around it. But even now—she pointed to the closest house—they seemed unfinished to her. Nothing had happened inside them. They were built to be as far away from the threat of things happening as possible. They were built to look like nowhere else, or everywhere else.

Her primary school was just down the road, somewhere along the highway towards the town. For years she had been unaware that there was a town proper. In the back of her parents' cars she'd entered the plazas through back entries, via the highway. She'd not seen shopfronts or the central streets; life seemed remote from the car window. The town had been mysterious when she was a girl, full of potential secrets.

These streets were meant to be the future of the town, Ciara said, but they could never catch up. They were built too late. They could never look dignified next to the older streets. There was not enough time left.

Ciara instructed me to wait a couple of houses down. She knocked on the door of a neat two-storey home, indistinguishable from the others. It had a dry stone fountain perched inside a chipwood oval. The door eventually opened and she disappeared inside.

I sat in the gutter. There was no shade. The trees were only sticks, sticks neatly arranged along the nature strip, some of them still tagged with their exotic Latin names. After an hour the houses came alive: venetian blinds slid open and the hum of televisions permeated the street. It was a Saturday morning, and life was carrying on as usual in that neighbourhood. Children watched cartoons and adults fried bacon. Down the road a woman hosed her immaculate lawn. A man pedantically snipped at a struggling hedge. They were as far away as possible from the threat of things happening.

A man emerged from the house across the road, and with a hand to his brow he monitored me openly. He asked if I had broken down. I replied that I had, just over on the highway, and that I had arranged to meet my wife in this location. It's a bugger of a place to break down, he said. He kept staring for a while, waiting for further details. Then, when I remained silent, he shrugged and started pottering around the lawn. He was looking for something. He asked if I had seen his newspaper, and I signalled that I hadn't. I didn't have the patience to explain to him that all town newspapers had disappeared.

———

I dozed while sitting on the gutter, and woke to a much brighter, hotter day than before. Ciara jabbed me with her feet and demanded I get in the car. I tossed the plastic bags into the back seat while Ciara climbed into the passenger side. It was apparently my responsibility to drive, though I had not done so for years.

She said there was no rush. I looked at her for a moment. She didn't elaborate because she was already on the dials, scanning the radio. I started the car and pulled out of the driveway. The car's accelerator was more sensitive than I had expected.

Though the tentacle roads weren't marked on Ciara's map, I knew my way because of the time I had spent riding with Tom. Once on the circular highway that connected all the tentacles, it was only a matter of time before the town's highway strip would appear, where the McDonald's, KFC and several petrol stations were located.

Her parents wouldn't call the police, Ciara said. The police had all disappeared, and besides, she had locked her parents in their bedroom. The only way out was to climb out the window, but they wouldn't—she lit a cigarette—because you're not meant to climb out of windows.

I turned onto the main western highway. Holes weren't a problem on the highway, and the drive-through takeaways and petrol stations carried on like they did every other day. It was impossible to see what consequences the holes had wrought from any point on the highway. Years might pass before a commuter discovered what had happened to the town.

Ciara's cunning was impressive, but I was also aware that we had done something illegal. It was only a matter of time before her parents smashed the door down and called the police in a town further east, where they would intercept us. It would be a huge problem for me, I told Ciara.

They won't break the door down, she said. It would be disrespectful to the house.

——

We drove for hours before we reached another town. Billboards for McDonald's and Great Western Inn marked its border, and petrol company signs warned of approaching stations. Soon we passed the first BP, and then the second, and then an Ampol, a Caltex, a Great Western Inn, and then some golden arches, and then the giant chicken bucket, and then finally a sign with a name, a number, and a council emblem. We were officially in the town.

It was possible to pass through this town without strictly visiting it, but Ciara wanted us to turn right into its wide main street. It was a Saturday afternoon and the town was as busy as it was ever likely to get, because the townspeople were dressed like they were going somewhere specific – most likely the pub. Ciara lit a cigarette as we parked at the foot of the main street.

After some time sitting in the town I worried that we might draw unwanted attention here, or somehow fall foul of the authorities, or else act in a way that might seem offensive to the busy people. Ciara was not worried at all. She sat on the bonnet and smoked her cigarette, making no attempt to hide how closely she studied passersby.

I warned Ciara that it was probably sensible for us to look like we have some reason to be here. Maybe we should go into a shopping plaza and buy some supplies. Maybe we should browse the bookshops, or Sanity, to see whether they stocked any books or music unavailable back where we came from. Maybe we should browse the library, and see if it has any books.

We split a footlong at a nearby Subway, then walked the two large blocks of the main street. All of the shops were the same as the town we'd just left, except there was a BI-LO instead of an IGA. The park where this town's annual festivities might have been held did not contain any holes, as far as I could see. It's true that the town had a different atmosphere to Ciara's town: an atmosphere born of closeness to the swell of mountains that stood a few hundred kilometres east. This town was colder, and the people seemed less concerned about being in the town. It might have been possible to catch a train, but we couldn't be sure. We had come by car.

I was disappointed that Ciara was not in awe of the town, since it was only the second she had ever seen. I had expected to take on the role of worldly chaperone, guiding her through an unknown realm, but Ciara did not care about the town. It was exactly like hers, she said. It was just an Australian town.

And she was right: there were equivalences to everything that existed in her town, exactly as she had suspected. The people walked with the same gait, they ate the same food, they worked the same jobs. Ciara butted out her cigarette. She had smoked heavily since leaving her town, completely fed up with discipline. It's just another boring town, she added. She wasn't disappointed, though. For a while she didn't want to leave. She wondered whether there might be something to discover there, but I warned her that it wasn't possible. I warned her that I had started to learn the truth of towns.

———

We passed through three more towns before we stopped in one again. From our vantage point each town had been aside a flat highway lined with fast-food drive-throughs and petrol stations. Unlike Ciara's town, each town had a claim to something. Some ponied their status as the cleanest town in the area, while others had signs boasting of ornate statues. Some were home to especially interesting shops, like a cottage selling the most beautiful porcelain dolls to be found in the Central West. Others laid claim to famous football clubs, or stunning natural landmarks, or long-dead politicians, or artisanal bread fairs. Some were home to legendary sportsmen, or the last vestiges of a gold rush centuries prior.

Ciara said she didn't think she could live in any of the towns we passed through; she seemed to have forgotten her fleeting desire to linger in the first town. It would be impossible to function, she said. The networks were established too long ago. It was always best to know with certainty what one can't belong to.

The last town of the Central West sat at the foot of swelling mountains, and it was unlike any we had passed through before. As we arrived at night, the silhouettes of cliffs were faintly visible among the eastward stars. It was an ugly town, squat and lifeless beneath the surrounding hills. House lights speckled sharp slopes. When we turned off the highway we saw drunks wandering the uneven footpaths with lethargic, unsteady steps. The town appeared haunted to me. It was too close to something entirely else.

It seemed dangerous to drive through the mountains at night, so we stopped in an empty Woolworths car park. A narrow lane led onto the main street, where a gutterless road curved between empty storefronts and the occasional shuttered restaurant. None of the roads ran perfectly straight. Nothing was gridded, and even the buildings stood at vastly different heights. I lowered the passenger seat and made my bed there, while Ciara prepared her blankets along the back seats. Before settling down we agreed to wander the main street in search of food. Since the town was so strange maybe shops would be open past ten, and some might even be open til morning.

If I had felt ill at ease in the first new town we stopped in, I felt dreadful in this one. It did not feel organised under any council's watch, and the blue streetlights highlighted every smear and blemish on the dust-stained shopfronts. At that time of night it was impossible to imagine the town in the light of day. It was the last town of the Central West, or the first, and it bore no resemblance to Ciara's town. Fibro homes stood lonely on the main street between colonial terraces, and vacant petrol stations were cement craters between square, functional shops made of brick. We passed several abandoned pubs before encountering one that was open, strung with flashing fairy lights and loud Tooheys New signage. Inside the pub it was empty and forlorn.

Opposite was a pitch-black playground where, to our surprise, a fluorescently lit van sold hot dogs. Ciara became animated. We must eat, she said.

Ciara's enthusiasm for hot dogs and her seeming ambivalence towards our environment did not alleviate my dread, but I followed as she crossed the road and marched through the dark towards the van. An old woman stood elevated inside, brandishing metal tongs. Ciara ordered four hot dogs.

The old woman said that unfortunately she was out of dogs. She had bread rolls though, and we could eat them with some tomato sauce – maybe a bit of mustard too, if we liked. Ciara nodded. The old woman placed her tongs down and tied an apron around her waist. Then she retrieved four long white rolls from a plastic bag. She tore the rolls open with her hands and squeezed the sauces. Then she wrapped each roll in a paper towel and handed them to us.

As she filed her sauce bottles away, the woman explained that she always ran out of dogs by ten in the evening. If we wanted dogs and not just rolls, we'd need to arrive earlier. After all, it was late. And there was no point in her overstocking the dogs. She spoke like we had chastised her for running a poor business. Ciara made sympathetic noises, but I stood back, not wanting to be drawn into whatever monologue the hot dog woman seemed about to deliver.

She wanted to know whether we were passing through the town to the city. Ciara said that she hoped so. I added that we were, and that we had better go, since we were expected there by morning. The woman said that it was stupid to go to the city. Things were heating up there, and we wouldn't find a place to stay. The people in the city would eat the likes of us alive. She pointed at Ciara maternally and said that she should go home to her parents. Then she gave me a foul look. Ciara said that it was none of her business, then bit into one of her rolls.

The hotdog woman was angry. Of course it was her business, she said. There was no use having the likes of us driving through the mountains in the dead of night. Her son—and she pointed easterly—had nearly driven to his death off the edge of a cliff, veering from the likes of us. Her index finger panned slowly from the mountains to the earth.

Ciara shovelled the last of a roll into her mouth, and then asked: who's the likes of us? She sounded genuinely curious. The hot dog woman didn't reply, instead retrieving a phone from the counter. She'd only pressed two digits before Ciara jumped up, tore it from her fist, and tossed it into the dark. Then Ciara grabbed my wrist and pulled me, bolting, back towards the fairy-lighted pub, through the ugly winding streets, and down the lane into the car park.

We hopped into the car and I turned the ignition as fast as I could, but Ciara laid her hand on mine. You need to eat this first, she said, passing me a bread roll. She had mustard and tomato sauce dripping down her arm. She was panting, but elated. Her eyes were drawn as she lazed in the reclined passenger seat, monitoring the car park contentedly. I would have insisted we leave, since the police could arrive any moment, but as the thought occurred to me I realised that it might be wise to wait for the police to turn up. We could lie that Ciara had just lost an important member of the family, that she was feeling irrational in her mourning, that it was an isolated incident, that whatever fine needed paying we'd pay, but that it was important for us to reach the city by morning. I was merely a chaperone, called upon at late notice.

We didn't leave. I ate the sodden bread roll and then we slept,

I on the reclined passenger seat and Ciara in a ball at the back. She looked younger in her sleep.

—

Later that night I awoke and found Ciara in the driver's seat. The car's radio emanated calm distortion as she browsed the dial. I studied with interest the frequency display as Ciara turned the thin white column over the orange backlit numbers. Many faint stations could be heard. The radio was receiving many—far too many—signals in the dead of night, all at once, from stations many hundreds of kilometres away, and perhaps even from the city. Drowsy late night announcers spoke amid the hiss of swollen high hats and white noise, while chords of country music were audible in the background. Commercial jingles for the stations themselves poked through at times, but they were shorn of their vibrancy: they sounded sad and remote in that mountainside car park, each one promising the greatest hits of decades past, promises they couldn't keep. All your memories from some golden era, they enticed. The greatest moments of yesterday. It sounded like a traversable landscape full of shadows and gullies, speckled with towers of commanding voices and ensembles, begging to be heard, each separated by rivers of sonic refuse.

Ciara froze at the far right of the dial. A peculiar, droning melody played, and she grabbed my shoulder. It's them, she whispered. My muscles seized as the buried melody competed with 'Ain't No Sunshine' by Bill Withers. The three notes of the melody sounded like foghorns, oceanic in their vastness, stretched beneath the interference. I think Ciara may have shed a tear, though if she did, she managed to wipe it away before the beat kicked in. That's when I dared look her in the eyes, because

I knew what to expect. It wasn't her keyboard music at all. It was only the opening notes to 'Great Southern Land' by Icehouse, and as the first verse started Ciara turned the radio off and went back to sleep.

———

We left the town at 6am. The man at the BP said we would reach the city by midday.

Ciara said she had seen the city in her town. I sensed she wanted to compare notes before we left her region for good. I agreed she probably had seen the city in her town, though I did so reflexively. I knew she had not seen the city at all.

She said that in her town, if she could find a concrete wall of a certain age beneath a blue sky, with no trees in sight, she could imagine she was in the city. But it had to be a certain type of city. It had to be a city she had once imagined to exist. This city might have been at odds with the reality of a city, but it was how she had imagined cities throughout her life, and it was a vision that predated any of her encounters with truths about how cities actually were. It was her city.

As I accelerated up the first ascent of the mountains, she said she knew her city well. In her mind it was an eternal asphalt highway lined with glistening marble shopfronts, diagonal glass chutes for elevators, impenetrable soot from countless different bus networks and clogged commuter traffic, and people marching to their destinations.

There was no shade at all, in her city. The sun beat down on the cement façades with brutal will. There was strange music: many different songs playing at once, both nostalgic and futuristic, and it was the most beautiful sound she had ever known, except she had never really heard it. It was a sound that never ceased, not even at night. It was always present; there was never silence. If she applied all of her mental power she could hear it whenever she wanted to.

The air in her city was alive. The traffic never paused. It was impossible to imagine her city quiet, or still. Everything about her city implied a lesson not yet learned: what a sunburned man in a Ford sedan, parked in front of a corporate building, was thinking at any particular time. Where was he likely to go, what was he likely to do, what had he seen before, and how did this all culminate in a vision of the world. It was possible to be occupied by this speculation forever, Ciara said. You could harvest these speculations at random, and be occupied for the rest of your life.

In her city she never walked. She lay in the back seat of a car and stared upwards at the passing towers. There was an unfathomable number of people inside the towers and they all went somewhere else at night. They all made their way from there to another location, and that location was buffered by other locations, located between many other highways, among millions of other homes.

These people did not live on any particular street, because how could they? When they left the concrete highway they were lost to the mess of locations. They were nothing in particular to the other people in the city, who were all fed up with imagining the finer details of how other people lived. Everyone was fed up with having to think about these things, because it was too difficult to be correct. Even so, they would occasionally feel urged to do so.

Ciara would feel urged to do so constantly in her city, she said, and would never become fed up.

In Ciara's city the people had resolved that there were

mysteries impossible to solve, factors that were unknowable, and they lived with this. The mystery and unknowability of things was a part of their everyday condition. Their environment was far too complex. It was not an effort to ignore their history. They did not try to remember, nor did it occur to them to do so – remembering was not a priority because it was difficult enough to know how to drive home of an evening. Remembering the route, all the turns, the correct lanes and turnpikes, whether to line up for a filter light, whether the approach to a certain round-about needed to be planned for a whole kilometre in advance, the locations of important shops... all of this was enough to occupy them. Their lives were occupied completely by logistics. That was the way she imagined her city to be.

I said that her city was probably fairly close to the truth of cities, though I did so reflexively. I couldn't know what to expect of the coastal city as we moved towards it, as I'd never cared to imagine.

———

Ciara became more reckless as we approached the city. She wanted to steal our McDonald's value meals. She wanted to steal petrol. She blankly stared down men while she stood at the bowsers pumping, and she crushed her cigarettes near fuel-puddled lanes. She wanted to drive every stretch of the journey, and she wanted to push the accelerator as hard as it would go, like we could catch air as we wound our way down each mountain slope, like we could sail or plummet the rest of the way to the city.

She still planted her cassette tapes along the way. She bundled up an armload at one mountainside car park and then spun around, sending tapes unspooling across the bitumen. She left them inside the straw and napkin dispensers at McDonald's, and in the windscreen-cleaning tubs at the petrol stations, and occasionally she'd toss them from the window of the moving car into the mountain forests, and down into the canyons. She left them at truck stops, where at least one man stopped to pick one up.

It turned out the route we had taken was not the conventional one. A man at a BP said that this route was preferable for tourists, since it wound more elegantly around the illogical declines. The other route tore straight through the mountains on four-lane highways. He said it was often impossible to even know you were in the mountains on that road. Though you'd probably be in the city by now if you'd taken it, he added, as we purchased a bag of chips.

When I went to the toilet at the back of the station, I saw, where the trees parted for an electrical tower, the city sprawled many kilometres below. I called to Ciara and we stared at it for a while. From that vantage point it was difficult to distinguish roads, and it was impossible to tell whether the city had an edge. It was impossible to imagine how the winding mountain roads could eventually lead into it. She said that maybe they wouldn't. It didn't look like a city at all. It looked more like a spread of mould.

I told her that it was likely the city was so big that its edge couldn't be seen from where we stood. That the good parts were much further away. But I didn't believe what I said. It seemed impossible that the city could keep pressing past the grey shimmer that shrouded the farthest horizon.

—

Ciara kept playing with the dials on the car radio. The frequencies were weak in the mountains, but as we descended into the basin the dial filled with stations. There were at least a dozen to choose from, with varying degrees of clarity, and all were much busier and more assertive than the station in Ciara's town. There were many references to traffic jams in various regions of the city we knew we would never find. We passed through what must have been a satellite town, different to any we had seen before. This particular town—or maybe it was a suburb of the city, or even its own city—seemed made up of all the edges of other towns. Lining the road were large bottle shops and car yards, factory-sized clothing outlets, petrol stations, and a green, featureless park with dozens of sprinklers. Everything was impossibly new, like the tentacle roads in Ciara's town, except here there was life: families buzzed in paddock-sized asphalt car yards in the shadows of monstrous homewares outlets. Further in the distance, visible only with effort, the green fences of large brick homes stood gleaming. Even the roads were perfectly black and smooth, as if glazed with oil. Ciara was unimpressed. It's nothing like a city or a town, she said.

Once we'd passed through this town of edges it seemed we'd be in the city at any moment. Neither of us knew how it would happen – whether the threshold of the city would be marked in any way. The road felt resistant to the nearby sprawl, and it wasn't long before we were descending steeply again, surrounded by mountain forest.

Ciara was getting impatient. I didn't tell her that once we found and crossed the city threshold it might be many hours before we reached a part that resembled what she had imagined.

And I dared not admit that the city she'd imagined might not exist at all. Though how couldn't it? Surely the city was vast enough to hold any vision that might occur to someone who had never set foot within.

———

It was late afternoon when we turned onto a narrow circular road, and then onto a six-lane highway running endlessly towards a grey horizon of factories and plains. This was the road into the city, I told Ciara. It must be the one that leads into it proper.

She was excited then. Said she was looking forward to drinking a beer when we got to where we were going. So I asked where in the city she wanted to go, but she didn't know. And I didn't either.

The drivers were all aggressive. I stuck to the left lane where no one could pressure me to drive too fast, but vehicles still weaved impatiently around us. It was as if they knew Ciara and I didn't need to be anywhere, especially not there.

Ciara said that we'd need to find jobs once we got to the city. That we'd need to find a house too. I told her that I supposed that was true. That there was not really any other logical thing to do. She said I would most likely work at a Woolworths again, and maybe she would too. But before that we'd need to take it slow. For a while we'd live in the car at the edge of the ocean. We'd print out copies of our CVs at a library and look for jobs during the day, and then we'd drink some beers on the beach during the night. When one of us found a job we would rent a house or apartment right in the centre of the city, maybe even somewhere with a view of the water. Then, after we'd worked for years and saved some money to each buy houses, I could do whatever I wanted—she flicked her cigarette onto the highway—and she'd do whatever she wanted.

I supposed she was only being careful, not factoring me into her long-term plans.

She said she'd go for a walk every day, each time in a different direction. If seeing the city spread out like that—she gestured back up the mountains—had told her anything, it was that you could spend a lifetime walking the city's roads—especially if what I said was true, that our view earlier had not even been the full extent of it.

She wound her window up and turned the radio down. She was pretty sure she hadn't seen this six-lane highway from up there. It was big enough that she would have. She supposed we'd breached the city's shimmer already. She lit another cigarette and wound the window down again. The fumes from the city were so potent that I couldn't smell her smoke.

———

The highway went on for hours. Giant road signs frequently indicated destinations, but none were for the city itself. It was difficult to tell which region of the city was the centre proper.

Night fell, and we were hungry. We deemed it sensible to park in a McDonald's car park for the night, because city centres after hours are dangerous places, so we would need at least several hours of daylight in the centre in order to prepare for it at night.

Ciara was excited to stop. Sitting there, the spectacle of headlights rushing through the highway artery could sustain us for the night. We ate our Value Meals in the blue-lit outdoor area, Ciara smoking between mouthfuls of her Big Mac.

We watched as tired families ate their Value Meals and Happy Meals in ominously lit sedans.

It rained, and we felt lucky that we hadn't reached the city proper on a rainy night. Sitting in the front of the car, we watched the highway headlights illuminate the mist. Approaching midnight, the highway traffic hadn't slowed. Surely with the pressure of so many vehicles flowing inwards the city might one day burst at the seams. Ciara laughed when I said this. She said the city could hold everyone in the country if it needed to. The size of her town was a speck among this spread, she said, pointing back up the invisible mountains again. She seemed like she couldn't believe we were in the middle of it. She seemed to believe the city was impenetrable, that we'd done something special.

At nine the following morning, after shaking off our unspoken reluctance, we turned back onto the six-lane highway. It was a crisp, blue, sunny day. Though we hadn't been able to find any beer the night before, there was a hungover mood between Ciara and me. It was a feeling possibly born of the realisation that the journey was drawing to a close, that soon we would need to face whatever new reality awaited us in the city proper.

Several times Ciara counted our money. We didn't have much, but we had the car. On the radio, a man and woman exchanged banter on popular news topics of the day. Certain celebrities were up to no good, cheating on their husbands and wives. There was some discussion about sharks and whether or not it was safe to swim at the beaches, and whether or not sharks should be killed. The jovial announcers invited listeners to call up and offer their opinion on the matter, then the news bulletins discussed the unaffordable prices of houses in the city, then discussed an impending heatwave, and then discussed several violent conflicts happening in countries that weren't ours.

Then came the sports report, and then an announcement about the traffic throughout the city. There was nothing of particular note about the traffic that Sunday. Clear highways, and a choke-point on some specific road, but nothing that would cause us or anyone a delayed journey.

At that point on the highway the road signs above started specifying that we were nearing the city itself. The signs indicated that it was always straight ahead. For most of the drive our view had been blocked on both sides by tall cement walls debossed with wattle designs and the occasional Southern Cross. Billboards appeared more regularly, promoting brands that never bothered advertising in regions outside the city. The advertisements were louder, more lurid and suggestive, designed for people who spent their money more aggressively. Neither of us spoke.

The hours wore on. Eventually Ciara said that we were meant to be in the city by now. I had been waiting for her to say so. I'd become increasingly worried that we'd missed a turn off.

I looked at the road signs and told her that we could turn left or right onto special roads bound for Liverpool, Strathfield, Campbelltown, Auburn, Blacktown, Ryde, Newcastle, Wollongong or Hornsby – but that the city proper was still straight ahead. The signs couldn't be wrong. She said that the signs had been wrong the whole time.

—

When we did turn off the highway onto a four-lane road, Ciara became animated again. We could see shops and apartment buildings on either side, although it still didn't look like a city.

She said that once we were there we'd need to take a day or

two to get ourselves acquainted. We'd spend those days walking and exploring, occasionally stopping in a park to drink a beer. At night we would explore the concert halls and see the kind of music popular among unusual people in the city.

She lit a cigarette. She'd acquired a habit of doing so emphatically, like it punctuated the arrival of a new epiphany. She pointed forward into the hazy brown horizon and told me that she believed there would be so many people there that the odds of finding someone interesting would certainly be in our favour. We'd passed so many faces already, and they were just the people who had cars. There will be many people who don't have cars, she said. There was no way the city could be united by anything in particular.

She tossed a handful of cassettes out the window. A car beeped, and then overtook us, and a man waved his fist as he sped into the distance. Ciara laughed.

It won't be easy, she said, lowering her tone. I think she was mocking me.

We'll need to find a place to stay, she continued, but not immediately. We'll need to figure out exactly where we want to stay, because the city is vast. Maybe we've already passed the best place.

It was one o'clock when we arrived in the city.

———

We wandered a beachside suburb. I told Ciara that the city was the oceanside. That it was many things, perhaps even everything she had imagined, but that the oceanside was the quintessential region of it. The oceanside was what you saw on the television and read about in books.

We parked the car in an open-air lot. Outdoor showers and food stalls lined the promenade. Beachgoers sauntered in their shorts and bikinis, seemingly oblivious to the spectacle of the ocean. It seemed impossible that a person could ever lose fascination for the water. How could you not just stare?

This is where we will set up, I told Ciara. We'll make it our routine to drink coffee on the grassy embankment, and to gaze at the ocean during lazy morning conversations. Eventually others would tend to join us, and then we would start to feel properly in the city. And once we were employed, presumably at the Woolworths in the nearby plaza, we could rent or even buy one of the apartments facing the water. After that we would just wait and see what happened. I told her that I might even feel inclined to write a book about something. I had not read any of the hundreds of books about the coastal city, but I knew what they were about.

We didn't have swimmers, so we took off our shoes and tiptoed to the shore in our bare feet. There was a shimmer on the water many kilometres out, resembling the edge of the town when inside looking out. This shimmer didn't seem to hide anything − or it didn't hide anything we could ever hope to find. It didn't signal an illusory border, only a true one. Ciara jumped into the shallows and then pranced back out, her ankles tangled with seaweed.

That night Ciara and I drank some longnecks while sitting on the sand. Many other people did the same. Some even swam naked in the calmly churning tide, wading gracefully at the edge of the void in playful temptation. How different would Ciara's town be if it was located here? Water might lend clarity to everything we had determined unknowable.

Ciara said she felt like she was on television. That everything felt so obvious.

We didn't discuss anything for several days. We were too engrossed in the city's finer details. The beachside suburb lived a life of weekends. Monday to Sunday people drank on the beaches. They laid blankets and canoodled on the sand. Their houses held sound systems that burst ripe with the music of cities. They delivered their bodies to the sun in exchange for gold. And the rest of the country also flocked to the shores, the water charitably caressing the edge, permitting the belief that everything was under control.

In the mornings we'd climb out of the car straight into the centre of the world. Beer gardens lined the promenade to the east where shirtless men and bikinied women drank languidly in the sun, tranquilised by the heat and the ambience of televised sport. The road parallel to the sea thrived with cafés and restaurants, with the smell of grease and salt, with the sound of ceaseless life.

Ciara seemed immune from bewilderment – instead, she noticed the small novelties, like the backlit advertisements on the stainless steel bus stops, the fairy-lighted bar district, and the gulls feeding on scraps along the bright green embankment. It was beautiful to be there. It appeared to be a place we might want to stay in forever. But each evening as we climbed into the car after midnight to sleep, careful to drape the windows with sheets, a sadness overwhelmed me. I knew we were only visitors.

———

The following week a man from the council warned that if we didn't move the car it would be towed. The tank was empty and we had no money to fill it, so we sold the car to a group of English travellers. We waved as they drove away, then we lugged our plastic bags of cassettes and clothing to a nearby bus stop. I told Ciara that if worst came to worst we could just ride the buses all night, every night. It was the city.

I immediately regretted selling the car, though Ciara welcomed the change. She said that we couldn't just sleep in the car forever, because the people who lived near the beach had always looked at us funny. I hadn't noticed, but they probably had. Besides, she said, she didn't want to look at nothing forever. She waved towards the ocean shimmer, said that the water was boring.

The bus travelled through residential streets, then long circuitous highways, and then into the city proper. I figured Ciara would never get bored in these parts. Even the sky was littered with sights: hundreds of windows to peer into; the luminous blues and reds of finance institutions and upmarket hotels; the helicopter sentries. We alighted from the bus at the central train station into barely-penetrable crowds of people all marching and sometimes running in our direction. A block away, on a dark narrow cul-de-sac lined with green bins, we entered a building signposted 'HOSTEL' in red neon. The narrow terrace smelled of dust, vinegar, and stale cigarettes, and the European man at the desk was not interested in us. Cockroaches skittered along carpet so threadbare it shone. For thirty dollars a night we rented a windowless room with a single bed and slept head-to-toe.

Sleep was difficult due to the heat. We were forced up and out of bed at dawn, eager to breathe the comparatively crisp air in the park next to the train station. This park was where a lot of the homeless people of the city ended up for the night, curled beneath makeshift tarpaulins strung between trees. Some men slept balled up under coarse blankets, or, in some cases, a wilted piece of brown cardboard. Some sat in small groups and discussed their own matters, urgent arms flailing and voices coarse.

When the park began to fill with rushing commuters we wandered deeper into the city. It was impossible to gain any insight into the way people there lived their lives. All were careful to avoid eye contact, even in pubs.

———

During those first tentative days in the centre of the city we'd pass the toxic heated afternoons in the tourist bars along the city's main street. Even there, right in the centre, where only business was conducted and no one seemed to live, elderly men and women drank their schooners of beer while monitoring some or other sport. Ciara and I did the same, albeit in light conversation. We discussed the city and how, even while in the dead centre of it, it still appeared remote. The city wasn't living up to Ciara's imaginings, and yet it was very typically a city.

One afternoon before rush hour, when the city felt its quietest, Ciara said she didn't feel a part of the city at all. She felt like we were moving from vantage point to vantage point, spectating from the inside. She didn't feel strange; she had expected everything to feel different, for her mind to find another course.

We discussed the origins of the city. Ciara had an idea about it, because everyone did. We drank in pubs that had once held people who'd witnessed these origins first hand, and it was easier for people today to keep imagining that past than to surrender to the present. It was easier to imagine those spectral founders smoking at the bars, wet from a day of manual labour, than it was to think about who was there presently, or why.

Ciara always drank more beers than I – too many beers, though I dared not say this to her. She'd started to resent practical considerations, such as our quickly-dwindling funds and the fact of us not having a home. She drank three beers a session at first, and then four, and then six. For each beer she smoked two cigarettes, until the end of the night when she would puff them ceaselessly, even as she stumbled back to the hostel where the sour European at the desk would shake his head. It was during these routine binges that Ciara would retell the same stories over and over: about her cassettes, about Friday Night Sounds and the futility of Thursday Night Sounds, about her efforts to spread banal myths in her town, about the city paper's music writer, about how the world was going to end. She never touched on what had ultimately happened to her town. She appeared to believe that her town would take her back some day, that it lay inevitably in her future. Such was its grip that Ciara cared little about the motions of the city; she did not seem interested in picking through its impenetrable façade, seemed only eager to witness it through the yellowed glass of sports bars, ensconced safely in the television ambience so reminiscent of her disappeared town, in the company of drowsy men and women who shared our nomadic air. She seemed to be waiting for something to happen.

Just as our financial situation was getting dire, I got a job at the Woolworths across from the Town Hall. This supermarket was unlike any I had seen before: it sprawled across three levels, plunging underground, and no one wandered the aisles listlessly with trolley in tow. People instead cherry-picked goods with the aggression typical of cities. The shoppers did not want to talk to me like they had in the town. Their aloofness was welcome at first, but then alienating.

There are too many people here, Ciara said, seated at the sports bar near the central train station where we always met after my shift. Why would they be interested in speaking to you, she asked me. They don't even see you. I only occupied the space between where they had come from and where they were going. She ashed her cigarette on the floor.

———

Eventually there came a time when I'd arrive at the designated sports bars after my shift and Ciara would not be there. Back at the hostel I would wait for her to arrive home, she drunker than every night before, and I would not hear an explanation because I worked the next day, when she would sleep her hangover off.

At the weekends we would board the suburban trains at the central station and travel their full extent, never disembarking except at the end, only to catch the next city-bound train without ever leaving the platform. These were my most restful times in the city. Only during those listless train trips was I able to discern a truth about the city. It was only one truth among millions, but it was a certain one: the truth of the city was that its dimensions forbade ever knowing it.

The stops on the various train lines seemed mystical, not completely inhabited, maybe just stopgaps between the city and the mountains. Surely no one had ever lived a full life in the neighbourhoods around any of those stops. Lidcombe, Auburn, Granville, Stanmore, St Marys, Hurlstone Park, St Leonards, Lakemba, Macdonaldtown, Redfern, and Ryde: the names were as plentiful as the plains past the shimmer, and if these names only signified places between one true location and the next, what of the vast stretches between them? And what of all the locations not near any train lines? It was a surprise we didn't need a passport to enter. It was a surprise no one was monitoring our movements in the city. For those who dared disembark at these places, who ensured they didn't get lost?

—

I visited a real estate agent in one of the suburbs. I told the man at the counter that I would like to rent a flat, or a house, or anything else inhabitable. The real estate agent was not eager to help. He looked at me with disdain and replied that he had nothing. I protested that there must surely be somewhere to rent in the city, since it sprawled in every direction.

It's true that the city is big, he said, after taking several phone calls. But it's very difficult to find a place to live, because it's very competitive. Living in the city is not just a matter of deciding you want to do so, and then doing it. He said I needed to be of a certain temperament. He straightened his back to demonstrate that he was of that certain temperament.

He told me that if I wanted to live in the city I had to fight tooth and nail, to engage in lies and subterfuge, to mock up false incomes, to be someone else. He said I wouldn't find somewhere in this surrounding neighbourhood on the income I had specified, nor within any stone's throw, nor along the bus route up the road. I was better off getting on a train and going as far as I could before hitting the mountains. There I might find a place I could afford – although I should know that it would be full of poor people and I would no doubt be robbed every second night. I would probably need to get the cheapest flat available, and there would not be much pleasure in spending time in it, so it was best for me to rent a flat near an RSL or pub, and make that my lounge room instead. He waved an arm out towards the west and told me that I would probably become addicted to the pokies and die in debt to criminal elements. Or if that didn't happen, I'd probably be mugged by drug addicts and immigrants every night on the way home. It's just something I'd need to factor in, he said.

Perhaps I should put aside money to give to the criminals. If I was lucky, they wouldn't bash me. But I'd be lucky to encounter even those dire circumstances, because if available properties did pop up, other people in the city would rush to buy them. I'd be better off not bothering. He said it was about time people realised the city was full, and he waved towards a man passing on the street. He told me that I should consider moving to the country and farming food for the people in the city to eat.

One morning when I dared wake her before leaving for the supermarket, I told Ciara about the real estate agent's diatribe. She had heard much the same on her travels, but was less shaken than me. The city is full, she said. People have long thought the country was full. When she'd always told them it wasn't, they'd insisted that actually, it was.

I told her that it was a blatant lie for anyone to say that the city is full. I suspected the real estate agent was making things up – after all, people in the city did not feel obliged to be polite like they did in the country. The real estate agent was just being a normal city man, living true to his position in the world. If I'd laid several hundred-dollar bills on the counter and acted true to the city too, pretending that I was smarter and richer and better than him, and not just a man who works at Woolworths, then I would've found us a place to live within days.

Ciara said that everyone in the city was frightened about the future, more so than in the town. They didn't admit it explicitly, but they all seemed to know that big things were about to happen. They knew that the fewer people around them, the fewer people there would be to attack and loot them when everything collapsed. She gestured towards the water. They only want to protect themselves and their property, she said. She claimed that, unlike me, she spoke to them. None of them dared reference the coming catastrophe, but they all acted and spoke like it was a certainty, like they'd need to hunker down at some unspecified point in the future.

She told me that everyone in the city speaks about the city in the same way people in the town spoke about the town. They say the city is not what it used to be. If she asks what it used to be, they simply reply that it used to be more like a city.

It wasn't always like this, the city people told Ciara. The city was once authentically a city. Now it was only where business was conducted. She was doomed for arriving late, she said, laying flat on the dank mattress. She was too late for everything.

———

We never again discussed moving out of the hostel; instead we just fell into a routine. I would arrive home at 7pm and Ciara would at some time long past midnight. She said she liked to wander the streets at night because some secrets are only fathomable after dark. I wondered what secrets she could hope to find in that city.

Inevitably each night I fell into conversation with the elderly men who lingered in the hostel common room. They were all living precariously, much more so than us. Brian was one: he used to live in the Central West, and when he mentioned the region he gestured far west, with a vague wave that set upon nowhere. He'd worked as a rouseabout on various properties, but moved to the city when he'd injured his back. It was no longer feasible for him to labour, he said. I learned quickly that he loved the word feasible – everything was measured by its feasibility. He was the most assertive in his desire to figure me out, but only to the extent that I desired to figure him out.

Brian listed some of the towns in the Central West that were close to the properties he used to work on. The names of the towns were familiar, but in the dim smoky light of that common area they sounded inconceivable. He'd travelled wherever there was work, hitchhiking the lonely narrow highways between towns, breaching the shimmers. He'd sheared at a station near Dubbo, picked grapes on the outskirts of Orange, built fences along plains to the east of Parkes. His life had seemed typical yet anachronistic, more mythology than real life, too consistent with some deeply held belief, so consistent that it did not feel true.

One evening, as we sipped from cans of beer, he told me that it wasn't feasible for me to live there in the hostel. It was where rooted old bastards ended up, he said. It wasn't sensible to bunker down in a cheap hostel, especially with that young girl—he pointed out into the city—who couldn't hold her booze.

Brian believed that if we had no reason to be in the city, then we should leave. Even if we didn't want to, the city would find out in good time, and purge us.

I spoke about my abandoned book on disappearing towns. Brian did not dismiss it like I expected an upfront elderly labourer would. And he listened deeply to my speculations about the towns that used to dot the Main Western line. I felt no confidence anymore speaking about my book. Its memory tightened my chest, wracked me with fears of tedium. And that held true despite my having witnessed a town disappear, I told Brian. It had been a normal drowsy town of substantial population, and people barely noticed it as they rushed through the highway on the way to the city or the country proper. I had always believed that a town like that could contain certain truths I could include in my book, truths the likes of which everyone wishes to have confirmed. At the very least, I'd believed I'd find a town that suited me.

Brian had nothing to offer in exchange for my admissions. He only nodded in silence, a silence similar to that which I'd noticed all men who thought themselves proper men shared: a noble abstention from speech, averted eyes expressing a stoic empathy.

———

I could feel my grasp on Ciara loosen with every day that passed. Although it had never been my goal to have a grasp on Ciara, I'd come to appreciate her seeming reliance on me. I had grown to regard her as a person I could rely on to feel uncomfortable with.

When I considered the turn of events that had led to our initial meeting, it did not seem feasible that another person could ever replace her. I had not been searching for someone like her – she had simply arrived. I didn't believe she could be replaced. Sure, in the city there were other uncomfortable and dissatisfied people, but whether they were dissatisfied with their lot, or dissatisfied with themselves, was impossible to know immediately. If they were the latter then we might never have the moment when we both recognised an affinity.

The city had a habit of looking old. And the various tourism documents loved nothing more than to draw attention to the areas that were the oldest. When I wandered the parts of the city that were widely believed to be old—near the famous harbour and beneath the famous bridge—the neighbourhoods carried an air of modern prestige that seemed at odds with any reality.

The city had a deep affection for its own history, but only to the extent that it confirmed what many already believed. In the old area, near the famous harbour and beneath the famous bridge, a certain bygone poverty was romantically depicted in oil paintings that hung in expensive bars, bars where straight-backed businessmen barracked for some team or another running about on a TV screen, and tiptoed businesswomen laughed. These people thought they belonged there, and maybe they did, though most certainly they didn't, and neither did I.

What I had been searching for in disappeared towns was a cherished history. In the city the history was barely verifiable, and probably a myth. None of the people in these bars, eating steaks and drinking carefully brewed beer, had ever needed to search for it. They all thought themselves as belonging to this cherished destitution, via the frayed threads of a mysterious continuum. They believed that they had all been poor once, as evidenced by the paintings, and it made them happy.

———

One morning Ciara got home at 4am and vomited in the bed. Then she poured a longneck of beer onto the vomit and started wiping it onto the carpet, which she then scraped with her hands into small heaps. Then she passed out on the floor next to the door.

We were evicted the next day. We sat on a bench in the park near the central station, and she didn't say anything for a long time. When the sun shone too brightly she announced that she would move to another more shaded bench. I did not follow at first but inevitably, after some time, I did.

We'd left her cassettes in the hostel. Ciara hadn't felt like carrying them, and I had my hands full, and the stern European man was too angry to let us come back for a second load of belongings. I wondered how, without the cassettes, she ever hoped to follow more leads, how she could ever play them to a potential ally. But she said she didn't care too much about the tapes anymore. If she did find their origins in the city it wouldn't really matter, because she'd always hoped the origins lay somewhere in her disappeared town, or somewhere similar. Besides, she said, people in the city did much stranger things than record mysterious keyboard music. She waved in all directions, like a veteran of the city. She told me that everyone was living strange. That no one had anything to hide. They all acted on whims. They did whatever they wanted, but only during the night. She curled up on the bench.

Later she explained to me how, during one of her nightly wanderings through the city, she'd entered a basement somewhere to the west of the central train station. There she'd found a small room of men and women watching a young man scream into a microphone. He'd not done anything else, she told me. He'd just screamed. Not even words, just screaming. The audience had sat cross-legged or leaning on the walls, transfixed by the man's abject remonstrations. He'd done this for several minutes, then the audience had clapped politely, and then gone about their socialising.

She told me that I should go see the man scream. That it hadn't seemed like art at all.

I was very interested in seeing the man scream, except I doubted it would happen again. How could the same thing ever happen twice in a city as large as this?

When Ciara had approached the screaming man he'd acted very humbly, and did not appear as anguished as she'd expected him to be. It had all been a performance, he told Ciara. She'd been disappointed that he hadn't screamed right in her face. He wasn't truly anguished to the extent that he had demonstrated. Still, she had been impressed.

Ciara had seen lots of things in the city. She had seen a fight break out among half a dozen men at a bar in the hills near the water. She had been offered drugs several times by elderly men. She had drank with homeless people in poorly lit parks, them giving her alcohol in exchange for her tobacco. She told me that it was only possible to really see the city at night. During the day it hides, is far too coy. She said that during the day the city is occupied with maintaining the conditions that then allow strange things to happen after hours: crafting the tensions it desired to release.

We showered at the train station. Ciara then wanted to walk in the direction of where she claimed the real city was, where she had done all her spectating, and I wanted to find a place to live. So we parted ways and agreed to meet in the park by the central station at seven that evening. I found a hostel similar to the one we'd just been ejected from. A room in this one cost sixty dollars a night. The hostel was mainly occupied by younger people of British origin, who pored over maps in the common room where piles of magazines and atlases were kept. I paid for three nights in advance and then, because my meeting time with Ciara was still two hours away, wandered the main street, browsing bookshops and CD stores. Teenagers crowded the convenience stores and clothing outlets, sipping from tall styrofoam cups of soft drink. There was a cinema, and a video arcade, and each buzzed by day in much the same way they did at night, lights blaring in defiance of the sun. There were too many cross-streets, far too many routes, and none seemed to travel in any compelling direction. Overwhelmed and tired, I returned to the park and waited.

Later, after Ciara had left me for good, my most enduring memory of the city was sitting in the park. I have since learned even more about the city and, like Ciara, suspect it is doomed. I read news articles about men and women brawling in the name of what it means to be a city, or a nation: smashing their bottles on the skulls of others, tearing items of clothing from women's heads on the promenades that line pristine shores. They say it is not really them, but it is, but also it isn't, but who knows. They seem to suffer the same symptoms as the people in disappeared towns did. Their notion of who they are belongs to the past, can only be read about in books or found summarised in certain rare songs or films. I, alone and still searching, can't condemn them for believing they are good. But I also can't understand how they arrived at their notions and their summaries, and why they seem to need those particular ones and not some others. It seemed to me, as a person in the city for no reason at all, that my searching for anything in particular was a futile activity. I only saw people who were there, who existed. The people of the city, and of the country, are united only by the truth that they are there, connected by the dirt they claim to own.

Ciara had stopped searching. I suppose she figured she could get lost among hundreds of others similarly lost in the city, could relish the proximity of history, of meaning, from certain fragile vantage points. Both history and meaning are always within reach in a city, although rarely at the same time or place. Every block in a city holds a crypt of story, locked in cement or on forbidding faces, in the Subway stores and the many Hungry Jack's, places that were all something else before, something truer. Story is in the pubs and plazas, once dens of sepia. Story is in the crooked lanes, down in the old part of town where the darkest secrets are hidden, or on the glass corporate avenues far removed from any past, no matter how shallow the passage of time.

Ciara might not have needed herself anymore. She might have begun enjoying no longer being reflected by anything, neither tapes nor other townsfolk. She was in a city with no reflections at all. A city like any other city. She was an unremarkable force moving invisibly through its streets, finally without a name or reputation, nothing to live up to, nothing to define herself against, tangled in all the competing messages, the sites and sensations that seemed to corroborate widely-held truths, and also those that challenged them. Both satisfying in their own confused ways, but not in keeping with my own searchings.

My own searchings came to an end in the park. I no longer had the energy to comb the streets for whatever I was looking for. Belonging is a condition you are born into, not one won or discovered. The British in their thongs, bantering in the hostel common room, unmistakably British, had no such conundrum. They were complete: a series of events and a true, verifiable culmination. I was just a reluctant notion, a wrong one, an argumentative one. A notion lazily arrived at, the vapour trail of some fleeting condition.

I drank that night with the British. They did not consider me unusual, just someone to whom things must be explained carefully, speech enunciated perfectly, clipped for clarity. I drank more than three beers and I told them about my book, how I could no longer write it, how no book could ever be written about what I had been looking for. My book would have to be fiction, I said, but where's the satisfaction in that. The three men and two women politely listened and then spoke among themselves about things I did not understand. They spoke about Sweden or the Pacific Islands or Southeast Asia, and it seemed the whole world was theirs. They saw no shimmers. They went everywhere it was possible to go, and in every place they found a piece of themselves. Threads from their collective past dangled down everywhere – especially in the city. I told them they should feel lucky to be from England, an actual place, and they laughed and said they understood, and mentioned the weather and the water. I told them that the water was empty, that it was only an edge, that it meant nothing. Oh yes, they said, it was the sand that was best, and the sun. And I suppose I spoke more than I normally would, and much louder too, like an authority, about how everything they knew about the city and the country here was maybe not so true. I told them everything was true about England, that I could detect it in all of their proximities. That they all radiated truths about England. They started to shy away from me. I was escorted off the premises in the morning, Ciara's and my plastic bags shoved into my arms. I don't remember who started the fight.

———

I spent four days in the city looking for Ciara. I followed the streets that fanned outwards from the park by the central train station, though for all I knew she had boarded a plane or swam out to sea. Maybe she had entered one of the buildings and stayed there. I never once thought to look inside of buildings.

Some areas of the city centre were more city-like than others, like the area hidden behind tall buildings on a hill near the sea. People drank there at all hours of the day, and drugs were dealt conspicuously at a street corner near the train station. There were drug addicts here and there, some screaming at passing cars, and muscled men guarded neon-striped nightclubs. They did not really try to block anyone entering, but rather encouraged it, even me in my stained Woolworths uniform. This neighbourhood seemed to demonstrate the most uninhibited essence of people in cities. The men and women wore expressions of tacit aggression: pre-emptive refusals to any contact. They jeered while watching football games on open balconies of drowsy bars, and they sipped their beers deliberately. This region seemed always on the brink of panic, dangerously close to eruption. When the men fought they did so vehemently, like warriors or soldiers, buoyed by witnesses, dulled with the fug of spirits or beer or something else. Only under these circumstances could they reward the impulses the rest of the city condemned. In that region on the hill, men and women entered an arena every day and every evening. The pace and density of the city accelerated their tensions. The strips and the alleys served as a receptacle for everything they usually held too closely. It was little wonder that eventually I found Ciara there, on a bench, calmly monitoring a famous fountain.

I sat beside her and waited for her to speak. She didn't. She was watching the fountain. I placed a single cassette, ruined from the friction in my pocket, into her lap, and she laughed. Then she tossed it into the fountain. She said she was getting too old for the strange keyboard music. That's ridiculous, I said. I told her that the strange keyboard music was not for young people anyway, that it was too sad. Young people listen to dance and techno music, or they just scream. She didn't register my reference. She might have already forgotten.

She said I lived a strange life. I only ever went places and watched people. I didn't live among them, I only witnessed, as if behind a pane of glass. She said that was all she had ever done, too.

We went to the McDonald's and ate Value Meals. Pigeons inside tottered between our feet as we shovelled our chips. It was possible Ciara hadn't slept since I'd last seen her. I had, on the trains on the lines leading far out west and then back. With no book to write anymore, I had nothing to say.

She'd been living in an underground tunnel. You enter near the docks, she said, on a strip of concrete between two traffic thoroughfares. No one ever went there. It was off-limits to foot traffic. There was a rusted metal flap there the size of a man. You lifted it, and there was a ladder. You climbed down for a minute or so and then dropped onto a landing. It was pitch black, which continued until an invisible corner, around which yellow light emanated. Then there was a fairy-lighted stairwell at the end of the passage, leading downwards for a long time, maybe for fifteen minutes. Then there was a large room with many beds and people, and then another stairwell leading further down.

She scrunched her wrappers up and wiped her hands on her pants. She hadn't gone any further than the first stairwell yet. She hadn't needed to.

The people there were unlike any she had met above ground. Some were vagrants, and others were just people fed up with life in the city. Others didn't have any particular reason for being there. There was always music on and someone to talk to, she said. She'd met a man named Rob. He wasn't the same as the old Rob, but also, in some ways, quite similar. He was a normal man who happened to live nearly a kilometre beneath the city's surface.

I said I wanted to live in the underground city too, but Ciara said it was forbidden for her to take me, that I had to find it for myself. That was the only rule. There was no referral program, and if you lead someone there then you got evicted. Ciara had already seen it happen. Someone named Iris had brought back a man when she was drunk. Ben, an underground person who was not the boss but played by the rules, did not even give her a warning. He just chained up the gate leading to the first room, and for many days Iris and her man lingered there. That was okay, Ciara said. Anything before the gate wasn't strictly part of the underground city. But after a while Iris's protests included threats to advertise the location of the entry to more people unless they granted her and her new man amnesty. So Ben beat him senseless and warned Iris that if she ever spilled the beans, the underground city would find her.

There were artists and musicians down there, but they weren't in the majority. There was a band that played sad music with a recorder and two guitars. They played all the time and never stopped. Maybe there were other bands on the other floors—she pointed to her feet—but she didn't know. She was saving her visits to those floors for when she got tired of the top one. If she practiced restraint, and only ever descended when she had become well and truly fed up, then the underground city might hold surprises forever.

I grovelled. Surely it would be okay to tell them that I had found the underground city independently. Surely if Ciara provided the directions I could arrive separately, and we could lie and say that we had never met. She told me that was impossible. It was against the rules.

Sympathetic, she suggested that I might find another trapdoor somewhere else. But I shouldn't look on normal roads. I needed to look in strange places where nobody ever went. The city was so big that she thought my chances were high.

We walked in the direction of the city centre. Ciara was happy, but ambivalent towards me. I think she felt obliged to catch me up on her new life in the underground city. As far as she was concerned I had carried on in our old groove. I wanted to tell her to be quiet about her secret, because wasn't she breaking the rules? If I could not live there too, I didn't want to know anything about it.

She said we could still meet up from time to time. Most people in the underground city slept during the day and lived during the night. They sat around on bean bags and talked about ways to furnish the underground city, and ways to keep it secret. There were some people down there who thought the secret couldn't be kept for much longer.

I struggled to tolerate Ciara's ramblings. She was much younger than I, barely an adult.

She told me that the people down there said that the world was changing. Everything was all going to be the same eventually, and then all the world's secrets would be washed away. There would be no room for unusual feelings, nor any time to reflect. This was because people everywhere were preparing to be annihilated. Cities would be gutted towers, all the better to watch the carnage from. The world was getting hotter, would probably be ruined, and nothing could be done about it. It was because everyone knew deep down that things had gone too far, and that everything in the past was better. And if things couldn't be better they might as well end. The past was a comfort and a source of sadness. From a distance it could demonstrate that we were once something else. But the past also demonstrated what was no longer possible, even if the past wasn't what it seemed.

Others in the underground city said that they shouldn't worry, because by living in an underground city they had found something so new and strange that they needn't think about how old things were different. And when the city above ground did die, they all would survive beneath it. When the city was bombed or drowned, their underground home would remain. They could crawl out once the bombing was finished and start the city afresh, exactly as they imagined it. Or as some of them imagine it, she said. She didn't yet know how she would imagine it. She wasn't sure anyone did.

We had walked into one of the oldest parts of the city. And it looked old, but truthfully it wasn't as old as it looked. The buildings were designedly old, and their grandiosity was laboured, attention-seeking. There was a library here, probably the biggest one in the whole city. I implored Ciara to follow me inside. Maybe we could find some books about the disappeared towns and about her town. Maybe I could feel at peace that I was no longer writing a book of my own. Ciara wanted to wait outside and smoke, but I insisted she join me. I wanted her to learn about her region. It seemed important. She followed me in, maybe because she felt indebted to me.

We passed through the turnstiles into the library. Ciara told me that they had books in the underground city, even though barely anyone read down there. They were all too busy talking. Everyone had a lot to say. Their circumstances were so novel that they never tired of wondering what might lay in their future. Books didn't have much to say about the future. Nothing true. Nothing that could really anticipate life.

As we passed through a huge chamber full of reading desks, Ciara whispered that there was someone down underground who was writing a book about the underground. It would be silly for the writer to try to publish it, she said, but she was going to try to publish it anyway. Ciara thought the writer was only writing it to be certain there was a book about the underground city. There needed to be a book about the underground city.

I found a terminal that you could use to search the library's catalogue. It was necessary because every book ever written in the country was available in the library, and some were even kept in dark rooms to ensure they didn't fade. Shelves lined every wall all the way to the ceiling, and there were dozens of rooms, all tall and wide, lined with smaller shelves of lesser books.

Ciara supposed the book about the underground city wouldn't have anything about all this, and she gestured at the city and all the books. It would be a new type of book, on a topic never addressed by any other. This book would be about them, the underground city inhabitants, and not anyone else. To think, she said, that their history would have a whole hidden layer, that everything above ground would be unwritten.

Imagine people reading it after the world ended. Everything we took for granted now would be cloaked in mystery. Everything around us—and she waved her arms in all directions—would be the ancient history. Ciara said she'd definitely read the book then.

The terminal searched not just books but the indexes of books, and it was only in these indexes that I found small mentions of Meranburn, or Bocobra, or Gumble, or Garra. I searched 'disappeared towns' and found nothing. Many of the names I had found on obscure maps resulted in no search results. And yet there were many hundreds of books about the city, and about other cities in other states. People argued, via books, about specific truths pertaining to their origins. There were books about the feared expanse long past the Central West, and many about the mountain ranges west of the city, where people had laboured under torturous conditions in what seemed to be a truly historical fashion for years at a time.

I searched my name, and found nothing. I searched Ciara's name, and found nothing.

Ciara said that they'd only need one book about the underground city. It was being written as the city grew, and it would never even need to be edited. If the city was bombed or some other catastrophe occurred, there would only be one book left:

theirs. No doubt other books would be written, and no doubt some of these books would try to relate from memory what had been there before, but it'd be obscure information. They'd just be books written for the sake of existing. She flicked a shelf contemptuously.

I suspected she was accusing me. But she seemed oblivious, lost in her thoughts, as I typed into the terminal. And then there it was: I found a book about her disappeared town. A substantial tome of 439 pages. Published fifty years ago, written by someone whose name I didn't recognise. I pointed to the screen. Ciara read the short title out loud, which was simply: *The History of* _____.

I wrote out the details and took it to a librarian. She knew the book was there in the library somewhere and only wanted to find it for me – she did not want to know why I wanted it. We all walked together for ten minutes, out of the main gallery, up narrow stairwells, through escape doors and then back down again, and then up ladders, through trapdoors and attics, and then down into another library, an alternate library, where people sat reading at tables too. Then, from that chamber, we entered a long tunnel lined with nothing at all, until we entered another room lined with books, with a low ceiling and no computer terminal. She pointed at the book and left.

I set it down on a reading table and flicked to the contents page. The first chapter was not about McGee's cattle or the drought, nor was it about the town in particular. Books of such heft often spend many chapters qualifying their substance. I suppose those qualifications were evidence enough that Ciara's town was important, in some buried scheme. Books of that kind need to labour in order to lend credibility to the content inside. How else would someone feel inclined to read about a disappeared town?

The first chapter seemed to align closely with the beginning of the country. What is this book about, Ciara asked. It's about the town, I said. She pulled the book towards herself and flicked through the last pages, to see if she was included. Have a look at the contents page, I said.

The book did not concern itself with Ciara or her contemporaries. It had been written long ago. The contents page itself was two pages long, proof enough that many events had occurred in Ciara's town.

Ciara was amused that the last chapter was about the train station, about its grand opening. I didn't read over her shoulder, because I had long suspected what she would find.

We may have spent days in the library. Ciara read the book from beginning to end, taking great care to study the glossy black-and-white pictures, which featured illustrated flat expanses dotted with gums and figures. They also showed early photos of her town, streets lined with horses and carts. And then, finally, a train parked at the platform, with a lone figure standing in the foreground. A silhouette, but unmistakable.

When she finished the book she did not speak. She exited through a nearby fire escape, into a quiet back alley of the city, and I didn't think it right to follow her. She took the book with her. I don't know if there's another copy.

On the morning I left the city, brown-clothed elderly people marched the main street. Men and women stood on the footpaths, solemnly observant, faces carefully severe. The elderly marched to remember a war. It was impossible to believe there could ever be a war. I suppose I had spent too long in towns.

But there had been a war. Everyone was certain of it, though it had been a long time since. There was a dreadful mood on the main street of the city. A bugle sang forlornly, and it might have been one of Ciara's cassette tapes, the way it wavered in the chill autumn breeze, merging with distant traffic, reverberating off the crystalline faces of impossibly tall buildings and into the central park where many onlookers sat. Children cried. Perhaps it was because they saw some of the adults crying. The adults seemed to have lost something, or gained something. From that eerie melody, more an anthem than anything else, they found a longed-for unanimous sadness. And from that unanimous sorrow grew camaraderie, and then, I don't know. The past they marched in memory of seemed more valuable than now. All those people standing on their picnic mats on that crisp autumn morning in the city. All those people with other people. There was rarely another time that life was more certain.

If there's a town in the countryside where I belong, it might already be hidden by some impenetrable shimmer. How could I ever arrive at it? What if it's an island, or a crawl space, or somewhere in the sky? If I did stumble on it one day I might not even know. I suppose the right vantage point would need to present itself. Maybe it would be obvious. Maybe I would arrive and know—with little to no resistance—that I am of that town. If I was, and if I understood why, I don't suppose even then that I could ever stop the town from disappearing. No town continues to just be a town. No answer remains true to the end.

Acknowledgements

Thank you to Rachel, Edith, Darcy, Elizabeth, Phil, mum and dad. Thank you to Brett Weekes and Rosetta Mills for their work on making the book look good, and thank you to Chad Parkhill for proofreading it. Thank you to the friends who have tolerated me bringing up this book in conversation. Also, my most appreciative thanks to editor Sam Cooney, for not only editing the book so closely but for everything else he did related to the making of the book, and for being such a tireless and passionate advocate for words in this country.

This book is set predominantly on the land of the Wiradjuri people, to whom I pay my deepest respects.